Corporate

Revenge

J.P. Osterman

Corporate Revenge

Copyright © 2013 J.P. Osterman

All rights reserved.

CreateSpace, Charleston SC

Published by J.P. Osterman.com

ISBN-10: 0692220577
ISBN-13: 978-0-692-22057-3
Date of Publication: May 2014
Printed in the United States of America

Cover Photo: Bertrandb | Dreamstime.com

Corporate Revenge

DEDICATION

For my husband, Drew

ACKNOWLEDGMENTS

I thank Drew Osterman for helping me edit *Corporate Revenge*.

Chapter 1 – You're Fired!

"The electric bill, $162.53...groceries $150 a week...and how much should I budget for gas? Wow, these sure are hard times," Rae Anne Westman said, scratching numbers down on her list and writing checks. All the while, she felt her stomach in knots. *If we have an emergency, we'll be in deep trouble! But, if we can just weather this hardship for a few more weeks until Tim gets the commission his boss promised, we'll be in the clear...we'll be safe."* She felt a rush of hope and optimism about her family's future, until she remembered the facts.

She had no job, a toddler, a teenager, a husband Tim who had started a new job three months ago, a dinky apartment, and a house under construction in Carlsbad, California. A few weeks ago, they put down a twenty-five thousand dollar deposit. They were scrimping to live until Tim would have that commission check in his hands. Complicating their lives—tax time. They owe the government five grand!

Pulling the calendar in front of her, she circled a date in red: Wednesday, April 10. We *need* this commission to pay off our bills, the IRS, and put more money down on the house. He better get that commission...it means everything!" She believed it would be like a lottery winning, except Tim's boss owed it to him.

"At least these bills are paid," she exhaled, slapped the check book closed, and began staring out the window. "There has to be something more than paying bills and counting pennies," she said to her little canary chirping in front of the window.

She had left her secure job as an engineer to raise her children after their three-year-old son Joey was born. To make up for lost income, she had resumed her hunt for work, and was hoping to secure an interview. She'd been job hunting for weeks, with no results, and feeling discouraged.

Then she spotted beautiful monarch butterflies outside her patio window...flittering butterflies in groves! For the past two days, a colony of them had been migrating from Mexico to Canada, reshaping the blue sky into a tapestry of orange glitter. Walking out on the small patio overlooking several lush green hills, she smelled the fresh ocean air and felt a wave of gratitude rush through her lungs. Not everyone has a chance to see this rare event, to stand outside and say out loud without giving a care who hears: "God, it's great to be alive!" After spending minutes watching them dance and drone next to her ears, she closed her eyes and prayed, "Please, time, stop, just once, now," and she breathed.

Ring, the Panasonic interrupted...

Racing into the kitchen for fear the sound would wake up Joey, she wondered who could be calling. She had no friends, and hadn't had a friend in years because of all their moving. They had just relocated to Carlsbad, their *seventh* move in *seven* years of marriage. The caller had to be Tim, telling her about his day on the job as he'd done for the past few weeks since starting at Riata Technology, Inc. in San Diego. But Tim wasn't supposed to call until noon, until after Joey woke up from his nap. She felt gnawing anxiety.

Corporate Revenge

"Tim?" It was him...the caller ID confirmed it. "Tim!"
No answer. Something was wrong.

"Hey!"

His heavy exhale was a big scare.

She glanced at the time: 10:03 a.m. She felt tingling in her arms, and then sick. "Tim, what's going on?" Her voice cracked in her dry throat.

"I've been fired," he said.

Fired...fired! She tried to picture his face as everything around her appeared white. Seeing the checkbook, she believed it was a giant weight. "What happened?" *Breathe, breathe.*

"Steve Lerrefeiht fired me for doing my job," Tim replied, "*that's* what happened."

She had always hated that strange name, but now the sound of it made her stomach ache and her eyes burn. She plopped down, missed the kitchen chair, and landed on the floor. "Ouch," she cried, rubbing her head.

"Rae Anne! You all right? What happened?"

She picked up the phone. She was seeing spots, and the chair arm was now a large dangling splinter on the floor. "Yeah, just a second." She grabbed the edge of the table, pulled herself up and began rubbing her aching neck. "That can't be right though, Tim," she said, sitting down. "No one fires someone for doing their job. That's plain crazy!"

"You calling me a liar?" He sounded *real* mad.

"No!" she countered; but firing a person, especially at the level of Tim's expertise sounded so far-fetched. Did he do something wrong and was hiding it, or was there something bad going on at the company? She couldn't gather her thoughts to focus on any other issues other than Tim's horrible situation.

"It wasn't my fault, Rae Anne," he said.

She couldn't hear his words that were stutters over all the confusion going on around her: the checkbook, objects in their small apartment, and scattering bird feed the canary was flicking out of his little white dish. She felt her life energy

J.P. Osterman

heaving out of her chest just like that bird food! Her mouth dried; her shoulders felt like pinching balls. Seven moves, and *four* jobs with *three* layoffs—or firings!—in seven years of marriage.

I can't handle another! Do I keep believing his reasons, or has he been lying about what really happened and blaming all his bosses?

Corporate Revenge

Chapter 2 – Denial

Dashing to the patio, she threw open the door and began heaving in draughts of crisp air. With her eyes closed, she tapped her forehead with the palm of her hand, trying to knock stability back into her confused mind.

"Tim, the bills! Food!" She ran to the refrigerator and flung open the door. "You've only been working there four months, Tim. What the hell happened?" She felt as if she sounded like a broken record. When she spotted a loaf of bread and a full carton of milk, she slammed the door shut and gazed out the kitchen window to the apartment garages and alleys that looked like the grounds of a storage facility.

After a layoff in Los Angeles, Tim took a job as V.P. of Sales and Marketing at Riata Technology, Inc., in San Diego, but everyone just called the corporate conglomerate, RTI.

RTI had become "the star of the New Economy," after the market crash of 2008, emerging as a paragon of THE intellectual capital company with an enviable array of intangible resources, including political connections, a sophisticated organizational structure, a highly skilled workforce of the world's best chip engineers—all gathered under a single roof. RTI also had sophisticated, financial instrument traders, and a secret state-of-the-art semiconductor manufacturing facility that would make Intel jealous. They were all supported by the world's best information system and expert accounting knowledge. In 2011, Fortune magazine knighted RTI: "America's Most Innovative Company," "No.1 in Quality of Management;" and, "No. 1 in Employee Talent." An army of scientists, business people, and academics sat rapt as Fortune hailed Steve Lerrefeiht, "The #1 CEO in the USA." Technology and leadership conferences across the United States and around the globe were continuing to recruit Steve Lerrefeiht. *Everyone* wanted to know the inside information about how RTI was not only embracing innovative technology, but also developing innovative theories of business, all while making billions.

Rae Anne and Tim believed the V.P. position would be permanent, and they'd never have to move again. Permanence, the American Dream! Now nothing.

Again she asked, "Tim, what happened?"

She heard a deep sigh, and then he said, "Remember when I told you that I sold a hundred million dollars of sensor chips?" His voice was at a whisper, obviously trying to hide his conversation.

"Yeah, I remember." The scene flashed through her mind: They went to Chili's restaurant to celebrate—one of the best nights ever. Now she imagined another exhausting move— another roller coaster ride. She braced herself, believing Tim would veer off course from talking about being fired to what this person said and that person did. Excuses! He was a salesman, to her too now, and really had always been a salesman. When she realized that—after having a baby, after giving up a career as a system's analyst to be a stay-at-home mom—her immobilizing depression began again, and by the second, the depression was snowballing into a hollow sinking feeling in her chest and fog in her brain.

"Ya hear that?" he asked.

Corporate Revenge

"Huh?" she replied, gulping down some ice water, trying to sooth her dry sore throat.

Tim's voice changed to a high-speed rant. "Steve said that the company's new line of imaging chips wouldn't be ready even next year, after I'd already booked a hundred million dollars in orders. That means a huge drop in sales this year at RTI. So he wants to cut back, now. He says my orders will put the company in the red."

The boss's logic sounded circular to her. "Then why did the guy hire you in the first place?"

Silence.

She believed Tim was trying to sell her on something. "This doesn't make sense, Tim. Something strange is happening at RTI. That bastard Steve Lerrefeiht and his big shots are covering up some kind of dark secret." Lerrefeiht was French-Canadian, but nationality had nothing to do with his rotten dastardly personality. Everything she'd ever learned about Steve Lerrefeiht was morphing into poison she wished she could load into a syringe and stab him! She clenched the edge of the table, focusing on Tim's every word, and then she said: "This means you probably won't get your commission, right?"

Another deep sigh from Tim.

"Tim, the commission! RTI promised it to you! You earned it! The commission's for us!" She felt like dropping everything, driving right down to San Diego, and confronting Steve Lerrefeiht. She breathed. She had Joey, still asleep. She couldn't conduct a shouting match at a major corporation and risk jail time.

"Steve's been burying the company in debt combined with some very *creative* bookkeeping to make the balance sheet look good." He cleared his throat, the sound make her believe he'd been crying just like her.

"How's he doing that?"

"He's telling investors and shareholders they're making a profit." His words were staccato quick, through the sound of box lids slapping cardboard. He was packing up his office.

"That's fraud!" Believing she had heard a whimper from Joey, she lowered her voice. "Can't you tell someone that the executives are cooking the books?" She began packing up a diaper bad. She imagined herself speeding down the I-5 Freeway, with Joey in his Baby Bjorn, marching into Steve Lerrefeiht's CEO office, and cussing him out!

"Of course what he's doing is illegal," Tim said.

She could hear metal clashing and paper shuffling—Tim shoving everything on his desk into a box.

"But I can't prove it, Rae, and if I'd try, Steve would have security guards on me before I reached the hall if I download anything off the company's laptop." He often called her Rae, her nickname.

She heard the sound of box tape, *stretch screech*, across a box lid, and then a gnashing of the serrated edge, followed by a knock on the door. "Ya almost finished? When do ya think you'll be home?" Maybe later they could both return to RTI and confront "the bosses" together.

"Rae, I have Ginnie Reidel at my door now. She's the Director of System Architecture…hold on. She's bringing someone in from Personnel to debrief me, and watch me," Tim said, his tone of voice perturbed.

Rae Anne cupped her hand over the mouthpiece, trying to hear him through the background noise.

Then he returned to their conversation. "Corporations can fire anyone they want at will. They don't need a reason." He sniffled. He was choking up, and coughing back tears. He never did articulate much emotion, but this time so much of it was bleeding through his every word. "I'll, *uh-uh*, look for a job, *uh-uh-uh*, when I get home. Kiss Joey for me when he wakes up. I, I love you."

She quickly said, "What are we gonna do, Tim? Ask them about the commission!" She felt her mind lifting from her body. She grew dizzy, the room feeling as if it were spinning.

Corporate Revenge

He said nothing.

She could tell he had his hand over the receiver. Obviously, someone was in the office with Tim, someone he didn't want her to know about or their conversation.

"Someone should pound Steve Lerrefeiht's face into the concrete!" she screamed, slapping the kitchen table, glancing around the room. She started crying when she realized they might have to pack up tonight and leave everything behind, once again. Then images from horror movies flickered through her mind. "Someone should cut off Claude Filmer's balls. What a liar! He also promised you that commission a few days ago! Whoever is in the office with ya right now, Tim, ask them for your commission check!"

She recalled what Tim had said about Claude Filmer, the company's V.P. of Contracts: "The Peter Principle is alive and working where that ding bat Claude Filmer is concerned. He definitely rose to his level of total incompetence."

She had to keep Tim focused on getting the money he was due before he'd walk out his office door. Maybe the Research and Development guy was in the office with Tim! "Someone should gut that Kent Smith!" Or maybe the V.P. of Technology, Thornton Manning, was his office! "Cut *his* throat with all his sensor-chip inventions and then leave both bodies bloating on a beach!"

"Rae," he whispered, "hold on a second!"

When a butterfly smacked the sliding glass door and its guts splattered, she stopped, ran her fingers through her hair, and grabbed the edge of the kitchen counter.

"Stop Rae," he finally said, "you're wasting energy on people who don't matter. You're getting depressed again."

She sat down, feeling dizzy, the backs of her eyes heavy and hurting. "No I'm not."

"Did you take your medicine?"

She had shoved the meds to the far back end of bathroom cabinet. "I threw them out weeks ago, after I believed your job was okay this time!" She felt more tears on her stinging cheeks and reached for a Kleenex.

J.P. Osterman

"Find a psychiatrist in the phone book then…or call the last one you had for a referral," he said, concern mounting in his voice.

She felt angrier. "Do we have insurance, Tim? Are we gonna have insurance after today, 'cause there isn't a doctor I know who's gonna see me or *anyone* in our family without getting paid…*paid!*"

"I—"

"Did ya ask for your commission, Tim?" She drank some more water, wishing it were booze, but she knew that would be a wrong direction. Again she stopped everything and dried her eyes.

In the background noise of his office, there was more shuffling of feet and the door closing. "I know all the job searching you've been doing has left you, well, not feeling yourself lately. There's nothing wrong with taking that medicine if ya need it, Rae."

She hated when he used that tactic on her. "Yeah?" she huffed in disgust. "As if pills can cure a human reaction to something bad happening…right!" She waved in frustration.

He lowered his voice. "You need to take those antidepressants, Rae, and if this one doesn't work, you need to call that doctor in L.A. Maybe he'll call in a prescription for you at a local pharmacy." He began issuing her step-by-step orders.

"Stop it!" She sucked in her tears. "Be quiet, Tim! I don't wanna hear what's wrong with *me* right now. I wanna know what's wrong with *you!*"

Ouch! His silence indicated she had dug deep into him. All she could hear over the phone were his groans and cusses as he continued swiping objects off his desk and bookcases.

Watching the butterflies fluttering, but then noticing some clear blood mixed with black body matter on the patio glass, she grabbed the bottle of Windex and the roll of paper towels,

Corporate Revenge

walked outside and began scrubbing the large splotch of slimy goop off the sliding glass door. When she reached the butterfly's body with its wings lightly vibrating. She stopped everything, staring at the butterfly's injured and dying body. That was her, lying there. "Poor thing…just think of the life ya coulda had somewhere else." She knelt beside it, watching the last beats of its wings. She couldn't stop crying. She didn't care if close neighbors heard.

"Ya have to make this worse than I already feel, Rae, huh? Do ya?" he screamed.

She could hear throwing noises—pens and pencils hitting his wall. Then she felt self-loathing for what she had said as she continued staring at the butterfly's remains. Now only the ocean breeze was fanning its orange wings. "I'm sorry, Tim." She began peeling the thin wings off the glass as if she were separating rice paper off candy. "I'll find a new doctor, and schedule an appointment." She was lying, just telling him what he wanted to hear to make him feel better. Gently setting the remains of the butterfly's dead body on a piece of printer paper, she folded it for burial, placed the white mound in an empty half-n-half carton, and then set it in the trash can. As Tim continued to pack and talk, she returned to cleaning the glass door, using all her energy to rub out the butterfly's clear blood stain—all the while, crying, but trying to conceal her flood of tears from Tim.

"Everything'll work out, Rae," he said, his voice raspy. "You'll see."

He's told me that four times before, now this makes five!" Suddenly, she imagined Joey falling down on his little three-wheeler trike, his face in agony, and needing a doctor. "Tim, I know I just brought this up, but what about insurance? Did they leave anything for you to fill out?"

Another sigh. "There's COBRA after this month." He was shuffling papers that someone had left for him to peruse. "But we have to pay for it. So I guess if anyone of us needs to see a doctor for any type of care…like shots—"

"No, Joey has what he needs."

J.P. Osterman

"Or a physical."

"No, we don't need one of those." Then she remembered another potential source of income that might help them. "What about the stock options Steve gave you in your employment contract?" She put elbow grease into another window stain that had the consistency of Super Glue.

"I needed to work at RTI for a year before getting those," he said, his tone of voice now dejected.

She heard another knock on the door coming from Tim's end. "Who's been coming in-an-out of there so often?"

"Wait a sec, Rae."

She could hear mumbling and then he returned. "The HR lady's giving me two minutes to finish packing. I don't have time to talk now. Guards will be here any minute to escort me outta the building."

Rae Anne felt personally insulted by what he'd said, and she threw down the soggy mess in her hand. "Why? You're not some criminal!" She began scraping off splinters on the doorframe with her thumbnail, anything to bring back some feeling into her numb skin.

"It's just policy, Rae. They don't want laid off employees walking away with computer files or confidential material. It's just policy." Tim now sounded beaten.

"Yeah, right," she exclaimed, "I bet security guards will be drawing their guns on you the minute you open your door for that HR lady."

He laughed. "Well, we gotta keep a sense of humor."

She sprayed a strong stream of Windex along the window and began doing squats to clean the entire pane.

"What ya doing there, Rae? Ya sound outta breath!"

"Cleaning…just trying to keep focused so I don't break down and start crying all day…'cause that'll be one bad path to go down and I don't want that."

"Good, just hold on, I've got ya on speaker."

Corporate Revenge

As she waited, another image came to mind that paralyzed her: a concrete foundation on an empty lot. "Oh my gosh!" She dropped the Windex bottle. It smacked the ground, and blue liquid gushing on her bare feet. "We're gonna lose it all!"

J.P. Osterman

Chapter 3 – Losing Everything

"What was that, Rae!? I heard it all the way to the bookcase!"
He was shoving books in boxes and sealing them.

"We have so much money invested in that house, Tim!"
Again she believed she was seeing spots in front of her eyes.
Her stomach felt sick. "We're gonna lose our deposit, twenty-
five thousand dollars!" Seeing the busy street winding around
a hill far below, she watched cars dart in and out of traffic on
El Camino Real. They were oblivious to her, and she to them.
So many bad things are happening so suddenly, and people are so clueless.
She felt as if all her thoughts were stopping, that everything
was moving in slow motion.

"Rae, I have an idea," he said. He had obviously picked up
on her spiraling into a depression and was trying to counter it
with a positive solution.

Ripping off more paper towels, she threw them on the
ground and began stomping up the splattered Windex.
"Remember your *last* idea you had for me?"

"Do you have to put me down constantly?" Tim had fight
in his voice. "Do you—"

Corporate Revenge

"*You* moved us here." She slammed shut the sliding door. "You promised we wouldn't have to move again!" She stomped open the silver garbage can and hurled in the grimy paper towels. "You said we'd build a house." The lid snapped shut. "What's going to happen now?" She wanted to slam the phone down, cut him off, and make him pay for the past. "This is the *fifth* job in seven years. We've moved *seven* times, Tim." Her throat burned; her voice cracked.

"Let *me* talk!" he shouted. "You keep interrupting. That's *your* problem."

A possibility crossed her mind. "Call a lawyer?" She whipped out a phone book and opened it to the yellow pages.

"*Hmmm*, I want to see if I can find another job first," he said. "Steve gave me a two months' severance package."

At that news, she closed her eyes and sighed in relief. "Two months is better than nothing."

"I don't think talking to a lawyer will do us any good though," he said, sounding hopeless.

"Why?" she asked, still hunting for an attorney.

"When Steve hired me, there was an "At Will Termination" clause at the bottom. The HR lady showed me the page minutes ago. I signed it when Steve and the top execs hired me."

She gasped. "You didn't ask Steve *why* he was including a clause like that when he hired you?" The more facts she was learning, it appeared that hiring Tim in the first place was some sort of corporate stunt. She clenched her fist on the table. "What a jerk!"

"Prosecuting Steve Lerrefeiht, or RTI, will be tough, Rae. And suing them won't get me my job back."

Her throat still dry and her tongue still tasting sour, she got a glass of water and again tried quenching her thirst. "Then sue RTI for breach of contract." She believed she had a successful counterattack. "Steve promised *in writing* to pay for the move into our new house, the closing costs on the new house, and for storing our furniture."

Storing our furniture!

J.P. Osterman

Suddenly, everything made sense. The whole employment contract was too good to be true.

Tim took more time than usual to answer. "That contract was just ink on wet paper, Rae." Then there was another knock on the door on his end. "Steve let me go. That's just the fact." Then he called out a muffled, "Just one second."

"You mean, fired you," she said, acid-anger churning in her stomach. "But there has to be more than what you're telling me, Tim." Now she realized she was going to hit a sensitive nerve. "You must have done something." Something had to be *Tim's* fault. "Companies just don't fire someone for doing a good job, do they?"

"You're right, Rae." He sounded beaten. "This was my fault that he fired my ass! I'm crap!"

Beeee... He hung up.

Rubbing the bridge of her nose and sighing deeply, she felt ashamed and helpless. If she had a job instead of being a stay-at-home mom, maybe they wouldn't be feeling so pressured about financial matters. She began blaming herself. *I haven't found work. Do I sounding stupid on interviews?*

Trying to think of solutions, she breathed in and smelled a strange odor like a hot iron sealing sweat into a shirt. Her blouse was sticky on her skin, and she realized she was perspiring, hard. Walking outside, she noticed it was drizzling, and she held her hand into the light rain water, splashing some of its relieving coolness on her face, neck and arms. Then she saw another dangerous game unfolding in this new rain.

In the downpour, butterflies began dropping from the sky, and chattering hungry birds were swooping down on them, picking them out of the air. Some butterflies were managing to survive, gently descending, gliding to refuge among shrubs and trees. Some were heaving against the heavy drops of rain, straining to hold their flight, lifting off like strong 747s, while some monarchs were losing the race to reach safety, their rain-

Corporate Revenge

soaked bodies slapping the ground, their injured wings sulking curls of death. Where ever they'd land, most likely snakes and lizards would feast. The others were surviving the treacherous streams along their delicate journeys by making frantic darts to the tall weeds, branches, and beautiful wild flowers. Those were the ones who would most likely thrive in the game of Survival of the Fittest.

The light rain turned heavy. "So many beautiful butterflies, dead, their futures cut off so unfairly." She slumped down in a chair with her hands over her face, believing she could feel each and every pain. "Nothing's ever really safe and secure." The heavy air settled into her chest like after a long run. "I thought that this time, we were gonna be all right...that this job would be a solid one...that we'd never have to move again." Like the rain coming down heavy, she cried.

She imagined packing up and moving again, but this time penniless. It would be hard on the kids, Carolyn and Joey. "We're gonna lose everything. And I can't do a darn thing to stop it."

She felt hopeless, with no one to call except her parents. She stopped before dialing their number. They had been the brunt of all her complaining in the past, and she didn't want to put them through all the excruciating details of how she had married the wrong man, how she should have never given up a great job for a white-washed promise of love and matrimony, of how she needed money, again. No! They had given her enough. Now, she was on her own. That's what she told herself if ever Tim would be laid off from a job again and if she'd have to leave her home-making lifestyle for another job as an engineer: I can't ask for help anymore. I have to do life on my own.

Then she thought of her fourteen-year-old daughter Carolyn. She'd have to tell her the bad news, soon. She sank into her chair. *I can't...can't do this to her again.* Carolyn had suffered so much by changing so many schools and loosing so many friends and being forced to start over with her life and new teachers.

J.P. Osterman

Carolyn had just started middle school. This was her third school in three years. Now, at her current school at Carlsbad Middle Academy, she was popular; so much so, that she rushed to the car every afternoon to tell Rae Anne about her day. And Joey liked Rainbow Preschool. He had the day off today because of a teacher's in-service meeting, but he normally attended 9 to 3 so Rae Anne could look for work. This was Joey's *second* preschool, but he was thriving, and resilient to the change. Telling them both the bad news, she believed Carolyn might completely fall apart, and it would be worse than when they moved before. She had shouted everything from, "I'm not moving!" to "I hate you...forever!"

Anger...that's all Rae Anne could feel now, and it lodged in her throat, pulsing in her neck, speeding up her heart so she could feel ever beat in her chest if she could focus on it long enough.

"I hate Steve Lerrefeiht!" she said, digging her nails into her kitchen chair. She picked up the roll of paper towels and tossed it into their tiny living room. "I hate RTI! Somehow, I'm gonna get all you sons-a—!"

A vase on top of a bookshelf tumbled down, but the carpet stopped the glass from shattering. She grabbed the broken armchair on the floor and jammed it into the trash can— stopping when she noticed the sharp point would slice open the dead butterfly's burial mound.

"Look what that Steve Lerrefeiht's doing to our lives!" Walking over to the vase, she whisked it up and beat it into a line of self-help books on a shelf as she had once pummeled a couch in her psychiatrist's office with a baton. "It's like— he's—getting—away with—murder—treating people like— dirt beneath his feet!" Crying, and falling down on the carpet butt-first, she felt her arms, like leather, her chest rising and falling. She remembered sessions with the doctor and strained to remember everything he had told her, but the only word she

Corporate Revenge

could conjure up was, "solution." She didn't have one.

She stared at the phone until her eyes burned. Now a full-blown panic was bubbling up inside of her. Rae Anne was an emotional wreck. Tim and her entire family had been profoundly betrayed. She was justifiably angry. All their money was gone, invested in the new home they were building. If they couldn't follow through with the builder's contract, they'd lose everything. She was feeling so far down she didn't even know which direction was up.

She was further outraged that after Lerrefeiht had intentionally bulldozed Tim and her family's life, Lerrefeiht was facing absolutely no consequences. Steve the predator had simply moved on to a new target, leaving her family in a heap of ashes.

Rae Anne wanted her life back, and she wanted that sociopath to pay for the destruction he had caused, and she absolutely wanted to make sure he'd never lie to and betray another human being. As many potential solutions she could conjure up, no one she could think of could help her in her time of need. RTI and its powerful lawyers prevented anyone from penetrating their BIG Company defenses. Indeed, RTIs legal department was a profit center—not a cost center as with most reputable companies. Rae Anne wanted revenge, one way or another. *How?* She began making a mental list of everything she knew about Steve Lerrefeiht:

Along with other executives at RTI, Steve Lerrefeiht is President of the definitely-for-profit corporation. He is out to make as much money as possible and gain as much power as possible, by any means available, regardless of who suffers, even children. He appears perfectly willing to violate business and social ethics, commit crimes ranging from fraudulent accounting and stock market manipulation to the thoughtless destruction of families to meet his goals. He was probably not only lying to prospective employees, but also to investors.

"Those are the people who really need to know," she said, lifting up a self-help book on depression and anxiety, smoothing down a torn corner. "But how on Earth can I

J.P. Osterman

make that happen? A peon, like me?"

Shoving the book back in place, she felt complete defeat as she remembered the word her doctor once drove into her: "solution." But pacing around the living room and doing research in books, she couldn't think of one.

Arms folded, she walked back to the kitchen table, and spotted Tim's RTI employee pin on the center divider. Picking it up, she walked over to the mirror behind the kitchen table, and held the RTI insignia up against her blouse. Circular, with a tiny computer blaring out a signal as if from a radio tower, the pin had a wee green stone on the *enter* key, but to get a good look at it, she'd need a big magnifying glass. She thought maybe she could pawn it, but then realized it was probably worthless. If RTI couldn't pay what it promised employees, the company sure wouldn't put thousands of expensive gems in its employee pins.

Still, with the pin held face forward in the mirror, she imagined her old professional look: nylons, a white blouse, a navy-blue suit and a pair of plain black shoes. That's the way she used to dress as a system's analyst. Reminiscing about the past, she began comparing her old self of over three years ago to now.

"Little crow's feet," she said, tapping the areas around her green eyes. Brushing her brown bangs off her high forehead, she remembered how her mother used to describe her geeky nerdy features: "Beautiful, like the goddess Athena."

She laughed and told her reflection in the mirror, "Not anymore mom…just when I was a kid." Still, she believed she could pass for twenty eight, if she didn't look so teary eyed and red-faced angry, but thirty three was still young, her real age. With a little foundation, some eye makeup, and little lipstick she could have back what Tim had once complimented as a Sissy Spacek look.

"Solution," she said to her reflection, inspecting it, turning

Corporate Revenge

from right to left, lifting skin at the back of her jawline. "Oh gosh, how am I gonna hide this?" When she let go, she saw a *tiny* jowl under her chin. "Maybe that's why I haven't been able to get a job." Another sad wave hit her. She really hadn't been taking care of her appearance. "But how could I?" she blared to the languishing vision that had a look of smothering hopelessness. "I've been so busy packing and moving and unpacking and rearranging that I'm exhausted!"

She wiped more tears off her cheeks, thinking about where all the time had gone, about how much time she had been wasting just on life's details, and how much she had forgotten about herself. Leaning into the mirror, she saw red rings around her eyes that looked like a cosmetician had painted on cherry juice. Patting the areas under her eyes, she saw more gray shadows that looked as if someone had used her skin for a silly putty experiment.

Sighing, she wiped away more tears with the backs of her hands. "I hate you, Tim!" A scowl twisted into puckering lines of murder. "I hate you!" She pounded the framed mirror. "I hate you! I HATE you RTI!"

The mirror smashed against the wall, but didn't break. Steadying the shiny silver frame, she smelled the scent of ionized rainfall; and at the corner of her reflection, she spotted orange wings—a monarch butterfly flittering around the gold kitchen light fixture over the table. Turning around, she noticed the delicate creature light gently on a light bulb, its black body steady, and its wings flapping to the rhythm of stable heartbeats.

"Come here," she said softly, tip toeing over to the lost butterfly.

Its orange wings fanned. The butterfly appeared healthy and unscathed by the rain.

"Stay...stay," she whispered to it, trying to reach it. Slowly climbing on the table, she remembered a time in the past when she had tried capturing butterflies and fireflies in the summer. For seconds, she felt like that child again, trying hard to get a special look at such defenseless and delicate works of nature so

J.P. Osterman

as to remember them forever.

"Come on…I won't hurt ya." Sweeping the butterfly into her cupped hand, she slid open the patio door and unleashed the Monarch into nature.

"Survive! Live!" she shouted, watching the butterfly bob along in the breeze. Seeing the orange wings disappear north, she wondered about its final destination. Would something so fragile have even the slightest chance of making it to Ohio let alone Canada? It was weak and fighting against so many obstacles. She too felt so small.

Then she spotted the dead butterflies on the cement. Some were flowing down stream to gurgling drains at the base of the large hill on El Camino Real. Suddenly, she felt a rush of fight. Her thoughts focused into one purpose as she watched birds feed on dead butterfly bodies on the busy street and parking lot of the Carlsbad shopping mall in the distance. *Black crows are the worst, but at least I can see them. It's the snakes that are the most dangerous…Steve Lerrefeiht, the Snake, and his minion snakes!*

From deep within her came the words, "No, I really hate myself for not doing something about what had happened right after he told me he was fired…not Tim. I don't hate him."

Walking back to the mirror, she paused in front of the oval giant. She watched her rib cage rise and fall. "I'm alive. I'm breathing…and I'm not stupid," she told her reflection. "Now, how am I going to handle all this? What're gonna do, huh? You *can* do something!" Then she felt a sharp prick. "Ouch!"

The RTI pin had pierced her palm, drawing a pin-sized spot of blood. Grabbing a paper towel, she pressed it into her skin and smiled at the mirror. When she noticed years of wear and tear vanish off her face, she smiled again. She saw two selves in her reflection: One, the angry and tired person feeling sorry for herself; the other, a woman all suited up in navy blue and

Corporate Revenge

ready to take action.

"That's it!" Her eyes lit up like a green beacon. "I *could* get a job at RTI!"

Then she spent the next moments arguing with herself: "No way! That's a crazy idea!"

Still, the more she concentrated on the new image of herself, the more she realized that *she could* get a job at RTI. But first, she'd need to discover what had really happened to Tim so she could home in on her targets. Second, she would need to know the department or departments within RTI she would need to gain access to in order to find and nab evidence of Steve Lerrefeiht's corruption. She also realized she couldn't tell Tim *any* of her plans. He would accuse her of having a wild imagination and threaten her with doctors, hospitals, or medication. Her third step? Take action, find corruption at RTI, and find people there who would help her expose Steve Lerrefeiht and his minion snakes.

Now, she finally had some focus and energy, and her depression felt lifted like a cloud breaking up in the sky. Pacing around the kitchen table, she also realized that someone at RTI could throw her in jail. That bad cloud returned. High-tech companies don't like nasty secrets being disclosed by whistleblowers. They can make people disappear! Except Tim hadn't told her of anyone mysteriously disappearing from RTI. Still, she hated the injustice of Steve Lerrefeiht firing Tim in spite of his excellent job performance, at least that's what Tim had told her. Either RTI was at fault for some secret that Tim was getting close to discovering, or Tim had done something unforgiveable on the job that he was ashamed to tell her.

The fact was clear in any case. Steve Lerrefeiht fired Tim, *her husband*, on this day, April 10, exactly three months and ten days to the day after he'd hired Tim. Steve Lerrefeiht had to have been plotting Tim's demise from the start, and he also had to have used Tim for some personal or professional gain. And when Steve Lerrefeiht didn't need Tim anymore, he tossed him away like garbage.

Garbage! She clenched her fists and hit the top of a chair.

J.P. Osterman

The word was like a hardball smacking a bat next to her ears.

Rae Anne needed more information, and a specific plan of attack. Was there some technological glitch in the sensor-chip for which Tim had booked a hundred million dollars in sales and that RTI didn't want customers to know about? If she could get her hands on the engineering specifications, she could make a mad dash out of RTI, go directly to an investor, and expose RTI's corruption.

And what about Lerrefeiht himself? She raced to her computer and began gleaning more facts about him and RTI. She had already done some preliminary investigative research into the man before Tim had a second interview with him. She wasn't "business minded" like Tim, but even after just cursory investigation on Google, she could guess that over the years with the use of accounting loopholes, special purpose entities, and poor financial reporting, Steve Lerrefeiht could be hiding multiple-millions of dollars in debt from failed deals and projects like the one Tim had uncovered. Many of the acclaimed "Big Deals" over those years just didn't make business sense, even to her.

To make matters worse, that would mean that Lerrefeiht's personally appointed ally and friend, RTI's Chief Financial Officer, Susan Gurkle, had not only misled RTI's board of directors and audit committee on high-risk accounting practices, but also pressured their accounting firm Andersen to ignore many of the questionable issues.

If clerks had compiled records of all those transactions, she would need to figure out how to get access the real books and financial statements. With copies of those records, she would expose Steve Lerrefeiht's fraud to investors.

That investigation led her down another rabbit hole: Did the fraud extend beyond RTI to a Ponzi scheme or stock market manipulation? Writing down every question, she folded the paper and stuffed it in her purse. She became

Corporate Revenge

determined to draw out a more definitive plan, but she'd need more information from Tim. *When's he gonna get home?*

Her stomach felt like a ball of churning anxiety. She tried to be quiet while taking out pots for supper, but her anger was transferring to all the stainless steel like percussion instruments on her stove and counter. They had moved to Carlsbad on Steve Lerrefeiht promises of Tim acquiring a high-paying VP job with security and great commissions; but instead, Lerrefeiht's deceptions were going to hurt their family. Grabbing a pack of hamburger out of the frig, she unwrapped the blood-red mess and threw it into a bowl—meat juice hitting the back splash.

She began punching the ground meat. "All our money's gone from the move—*smack*—and all our equity is in our new home—*pound pound*—everything Lerrefeiht promised Tim…no, promised us is gone! *Smack punch.* And with just two words, 'You're fired,' that *thief* stole *everything* that's ours."

She threw a container of minced onion into the meat, shoved in her fingers into the cold slimy mixture, and began churning away at the raw-flesh meat-loaf mixture—onion air drifting into her eyes, stinging them to crying. "I don't know how I'm going to do it yet," she said, wiping her eyes on her sleeves, "but I'm going to get a job at RTI!"

When Rae Anne heard the sound of Tim's engine revving and then winding down, she checked the time: 1:53 p.m. She ran to the door and threw it open. "Tim!" He didn't say anything, but peeked around the trunk at her and waved. He had a look of defeat on his face as if he had just learned of the death of his favorite pet. She imagined the car chock-full of books and boxes of family photos. When he looked at her again and gestured for her to wait at the door, she noticed his appearance. The wind had tossed his blond hair like a surfer just coming in from an ocean run on a wave. The humid afternoon air had crinkled his white shirt. The sweat from the long drive had stained his sides and the areas under his arm.

Rae Anne disobeyed and ran to help him. "I'm sorry for what I said, Tim." She glanced around the trunk, gauging which boxes might be the easiest for her to handle.

"I've got these two," he said, his cheeks blotchy red. Then he kissed her on the cheek and nodded toward the right. "That one's not so heavy." He spoke softly, obviously forgiving her a long time ago. The little garage door was open. They already had it packed to the ceiling, and now they were about to add more.

She felt guilty. "I've got it," she said, lifting out a box with a picture of their wedding setting cockeyed on top.

"Those go inside," he said, gesturing at the door, and then he continued unpacking the car.

Her stomach ached; her head felt like a fog bank. On the walk inside, she couldn't take her eyes off the picture. It was a time when they were both dreamy-eyed and smiling with love and longing in their eyes. Every step up the stairs felt like a ticking time bomb. How many more lay-offs, job hunting, packing, and moving could their marriage handle without shattering? Could any couple keep surviving on this wild-ride type of life they'd been living? If so, she'd give anything to talk to them about it. Anything to not feel so alone and angry. Life had become a constant fight against rain storms, with an upturned umbrella!

Stepping through the door, Tim dropped a box, shed his shoes and plopped his briefcase on the table.

He leaned on the kitchen counter. "How's Joey?"

She thrust the meatloaf bowl into the refrigerator. "He ate lunch an hour ago and fell back to sleep. It seems like he's been napping half the day."

He lifted out a beer, flicked off the cap and glugged down a quarter of a bottle. "He's smart for a three-year-old. Maybe he picked up that something bad...happened."

Wiping her eyes, she grabbed him around the chest, and hugged him as if for the last time. "I'm so sorry this happened to ya again," she said, pulling away and then searched his watery, shell-shocked eyes. She saw a tiny spark of a lost child in his blank stare, as if he'd been wandering through aisles at a grocery store in search of his parents. That insecurity beat right into her, making her whole body tremble. Steve Lerrefeiht, no RTI, had broken him. *They're gonna pay...just wait, they'll pay*! Everything inside her felt like a cracked disk wanting to spill out all its important data—her plan. She couldn't. It was her plan, her plot; and if it wouldn't succeed, people could blame her, not him.

"One day and everything's changed, huh?" he said, beer in hand, and slumping over the kitchen table. Now-and-then he glanced up to stare out the window. He didn't even blink when she touched his shaking hands. The rain had stopped, and the monarchs were back on their path toward Canada. Outside homeostasis; inside silent chaos.

She sat down next to him as Joey darted out of the hallway and into his lap. "Daddy!" he exclaimed happily.

Tim swept him up and held him tightly against his chest. Joey giggled and nuzzled into his neck. "I love you, Joey" he said, kissing Joey's hair that lifted feather-fine against Tim's afternoon stubble. His eyes closed as he smelled Joey's baby-fresh shampooed hair. He was cherishing every second of Time's sudden stop. Then he breathed deeply and kissed Joey again. A tear fell. His face reddened; he cleared his throat like he'd accidentally swallowed salt water.

Walking over and hugging them, Rae Anne tried to think of positive words to tell Tim, but couldn't as she waited for him to redirect Joey's attention to a cartoon on TV.

She could say, "Everything's gonna work out just fine," or "Vengeance is mine sayeth the Lord." The former she had said many times before, the latter she was going to enact herself.

After he inserted a DVD of Thomas the Tank Engine, and Joey began playing along with the show using his own train cars and wooden railroad ties, Tim came back to the table, plopped down in his chair and took another swig of beer. Rae Anne remembered her plan to secure a position at RTI and needed to extract information from Tim in order to home in on targets at the company.

Checking to ensure that Joey was out of range of their conversation, she then said, "Are you going to use any of your former colleagues at RTI as references?"

He glanced beyond her to where the butterflies were caressing the air. "Yeah, a few." He gave out a sigh. "There's that V.P. of Systems Architecture I told you about, Mira Padeson. I worked with her when I needed details about their new chip so I could call on customers."

Rae Anne glanced at a paper and pencil on the counter. She had to mark down all the information Tim was giving her fast. She needed a lot of information and, remembering names wasn't her strong suit. "Just a minute, Hon," she said, dashing toward the pad and pencil. She grabbed them, rushed to Joey's dresser, and wrote down the name Mira Padeson and her job description. She decided that each time Tim gave her a name she'd excuse herself, run to Joey's room, write down information, and then return to cooking supper. She hoped he wouldn't become suspicious.

"Okay, I'm back," she said, "so, go on. What were ya saying?"

"You asked me about colleagues and who I might be able to use for references." Tim was watching TV from the kitchen table. "I've called some former colleagues from other companies too, but connections don't necessarily mean interviews, Rae." Papers from the builder of their new home were underneath a glass vase filled with artificial flowers. Taking the papers from under the vase, he flicked through them, and tears welled in his eyes.

Inhaling, she touched his hand. "It's not over yet, Tim." His head slumped down toward the table mat. "We made the deposit on the house, but if you can find another job, we can make the next deposit. It's due in thirty days."

Corporate Revenge

"Or we lose the house, and the money we've put into it," he said.

Silence, again. She'd get the subject back on track to RTI. "Are there any other contacts at RTI you can think of? Or any executives who might be able to help you?"

Standing, he put his hands on her cheeks and gazed at her with loving eyes. "Rae, come on! They've all been scoundrels!" He laughed a little, but she heard anxiety in his voice and saw fright in his eyes. Tim was definitely afraid for his safety. "I had dual reporting, both to Susan Gurkle, the CFO for all the contracts, and to Thornton Manning, the V.P. of Technology for all the details I needed to take to customers. Aside from Steve Lerrefeiht, I really didn't interface with a lot of employees. I was on the road."

He was right. In the past three months he had made presentations in New York and Washington, D.C. He even had a Secret Security Clearance. Some projects he couldn't even talk about.

Repeating the names, she said, "Hold on, I have to take clothes out of the washer so the colors won't bleed." Darting into Joey's room, she wrote down the names Tim had given her. On the way back, she stopped in the hallway, telling herself: "I can't do this. No way! I can't! This is nuts!" The long road ahead felt like the time she had to wait for her last C-section.

Then she remembered what her psychiatrist had once said: "Negative self-talk won't make you better." Repeating those words, she felt energized as she breathed in the fresh scent of rain-drenched air. This time she didn't leave the paper on top of Joey's dresser, but stuffed it down her blouse to shove into her wallet later. "Yes, I can do this," she told herself. Those words just had to stay at the forefront of everything.

After Tim gulped down the last dregs of his beer, he changed clothes and walked into the living room where Joey was still engrossed in TV. He sat down at his small desk nestled in the far left corner. "I have to get on the computer, email a few contacts, and start looking for work." Rubbing his hands together as if he were eager to jump into the big hunt, he waited for the computer to fire up.

"Go ahead and start, Tim. I'll pick up Carolyn from school," she said, walking over to him and hugging him around his neck. Inhaling his spicy scent, she remembered the time she first saw him. Two friends had put them together for a blind date at a Pasadena restaurant. She felt instant attraction. As their early evening dinner lingered on past eleven, she believed he might be the one she'd be with forever.

Then she remembered the times when she believed she hated him. They had been married seven years. He had taken on the responsibility of being a father to Carolyn, her daughter from a previous relationship. He was a good father, so her negative emotion for him never lasted long, and they had always managed to weather the storms of job layoffs because she realized she had problems too, baggage. Sometimes their relationship was a mix of love and hate mixed with true commitment. She may have thought about a divorce, but she realized that today, she had Tim, Joey and Carolyn. They had to stick together.

"That's what families do during bad times, during hard times," her mother once said. "People stick together. That's how marriage *used* to be; but today, people seem to marry and divorce based on *their feelings*. Well, if everybody'd do that, there wouldn't be marriage! Marriage is commitment, no matter what…and you said, *I do*, to Tim, and he said, *I do*, to you, so there." The last time Tim was laid off, before his L.A. job, her mother told her: "Rae Anne, people make it through life by helping each other in the down times. Leaving Tim and starting over again shouldn't be an option, especially since you have a child together, and Carolyn now has a good and decent father." After her father gave her some money to help them with their rent until Tim could get his next paycheck, her mother told her: "So, you don't like Tim very much right now.

Corporate Revenge

But sometimes commitment trumps love, and some day, you'll need Tim to stand by you!"

After I infiltrate RTI, and hopefully not go to jail in the process, that time might come soon.

J.P. Osterman

Chapter 4 - False ID

Glancing at the time, she grabbed the keys and said, "Tim, it's 2:35...I have to pick up Carolyn."

"Okay, Hon!" he called, his fingers typing fast as if he were a piano player at a rehearsal. He was also scrolling several job-search engines and had three resumes on his desk!

Joey ran up to her and hugging her; and then she lead him back to his train set, turned on a battery powered blue engine that beeped and tooted just like the one on *Thomas and Friends*. "I have Joey busy again," she said, "so at least you can concentrate on your hunt while dinner's baking." She doubted he had heard her. His fingers were speeding along the black keys, and she knew he'd never leave the monitor until after ten. That's when he was always the most tired, the most vulnerable, and also a good time to question him for specific details about RTI.

As she backed the car out of the driveway, she remembered one giant problem. She stopped suddenly, and the brakes squeaked. "Damn!"

Tim raced out. "Ya alright?"

Corporate Revenge

She waved an A-ok signal, but felt like crying again. She realized she couldn't apply for a position at RTI using her name Rae Anne Westman. "This is one giant obstacle!" she said, drying her eyes. "How the hell am I gonna overcome it?" She continued on driving, swerving a few times to miss a low-flying butterfly. Still, that obstacle bloomed into a full-blown depression; and she pulled over to the side of the road, parked, rolled down the window, and inhaled some ocean air deep into her lungs. Cars honked as they passed her, and she turned on the windshield wipers filled with bug juice and grime. She felt her stomach heave, and she threw open the door and threw up.

Regaining her composure, she looked ahead. The busy street was lined with towering eucalyptus trees, their bark shedding like carrot peels, and the sidewalks were bustling with the midafternoon traffic of people walking children home from school. She had a solution! "Call Gene!" Her stomach ached again. "It's the only way around the problem. Gene will know what to do…Gene will be able to help me." Realizing she had just ten minutes before Carolyn would be at the pickup line, she pulled out her cell phone; but before she dialed, she realized Tim would get the bill. He would ask her about the number. She was going to call Carolyn's biological father, Gene Mure. He had worked for the Los Angeles police department and knew people who could help her acquire a fake ID. But the thought of talking to him after a ten-year period of silence made her arms numb and her foot tremble on the accelerator pedal.

Driving into the shopping center just around the corner from Carolyn's middle school, she spotted a public phone, raced out of her car, and dialed the number she thought she had long ago forgotten until adrenaline kicked in, making her remember. Her heart rate felt like 120 beats per minutes, her mouth felt dry as from a hang-over. With each ring, she felt her vision and hearing sharpen as she glanced around the busy markets and shops trying to keep her conversation a secret.

"Hello?" A man asked.

"*Ahem*, Gene, it's me, Rae Anne." She could picture his

J.P. Osterman

face as he talked, a man in his mid-forties who looked like James Bond and acted that way around women.

"Rae Anne, I haven't heard from you in a while," he said. "Is something wrong with Carolyn?" Tim adopted Carolyn after Rae Anne had played a two-year game of court cat-and-mouse with him, even though he had no interest in seeing his daughter. He said he never wanted children, and Carolyn was unplanned, Rae Anne refused to acquiesce to Gene's demand to "not have a baby." Their marriage deteriorated, and Gene moved out when Carolyn was a year old.

"No nothing's wrong with Carolyn, Gene." She gulped hard. Clenching the receiver to her ear, she felt the vibrations of her anxiety clattering on her earring. "I need a favor, Gene. Please. I've never asked you for anything. Not one cent, one dime—"

"Now hold on a minute!" He dragged out the words as if he were being attacked.

She remembered his bushy forking eyebrows on his angry face, but at least she was talking to him over the phone. She had to calm down and couldn't be defensive. Buttering him up and brown nosing were her allies right now. She needed something from him: A new name, and a new identity, and he was the only one who could give them to her. He knew people and had contacts, he always claimed. She remembered he'd managed to always keep a mistress on the side. He had extra income, from somewhere.

"This is the only time I'll ever call you, Gene. I need a fake ID."

He gasped, followed by a great pause.

"What makes you so sure I can do that?" he asked gruffly.

She breathed, and steam hit the receiver. "You have contacts. I remember you talked about people who make fake IDs. Remember? When I was pregnant with Carolyn, you busted up a huge forgery ring in L.A." She hunched her

Corporate Revenge

shoulders to conceal the phone. "You could do this for me, Gene. Please. I'm in trouble."

There was another long pause but she could hear talking on his end as if he were in some type of high-tech cubicle facility. "Trouble, huh?"

"Yeah, Gene." She began crying but stuffed an outburst of sobs down into her throat. "I'd never ask you for anything, Gene. But please, can you help me?" Always playing needy and a stray cat worked on him. He just never believed in commitment.

"What *kind* of trouble?" he asked.

He was being his same-old self, always prying, always controlling. "I'm applying for a job and I can't use my name."

"So the husband's name…what's his name again?" He was being condescending, his voice sarcastic.

"Tim," she said. She wanted to say: *You know his name*, until she realized that Gene was just being a jerk and purposely prolonging her begging.

"This Tim's in some kinda trouble, huh? Or *you*?"

"Well, not IRS or FBI trouble or anything like that." She coughed to clear her throat as she glanced at her watch. "I have to pick up Carolyn in five minutes, Gene. I don't have time to explain everything." She began tapping her fingers on the phone booth's silver frame.

She heard him sighing on the other end as his voice drained down to a whisper. "Give me your address." She could hear a computer mouse move and click on the opposite end as she gave him the address of her storage facility instead of her home address. "You'll just have to take the name I give ya though. I'm working with the Victim Witness program. I can access the equipment I need here."

She remembered she had sent him a picture of herself and Carolyn about seven years ago. "You have that picture I gave you still, right?" She felt the tension of their entire divorce pulsing through her.

"Yeah, right here, somewhere," he said. She could hear a drawer rolling open and the shuffling of papers.

J.P. Osterman

When it comes to relationships with women, Gene Mure was like a ritual serial killer. After progressing through a brief courtship, followed by a brief but intense relationship, he then dumped the poor vulnerable soul who'd worked so hard to keep him. But he always kept souvenirs; and somewhere in his desk, her picture was among them.

"Got that picture," he said.

"Great." She heard the crinkling of a photograph. He was smoothing it out; then the sound of his drawer smacking against steel. "You can use *that* picture, Gene. " Again she glanced at her watch, the dial sweaty on her wrist bone. She still had another big request. "Can you get me a social security card to match?" She knew she was testing his patience, and she cupped her fingers over her mouth as if protecting herself from one of his old outbursts.

"Those are hard, Rae Anne! Jesus Christ and—"

"I know, I know, Gene," she said softly, trying to calm him down. "But you're the only one who can do this for me—*help* me I mean." Glancing down, she spotted a cement crack and began lightly placekicking a weed with the tip of her shoe.

"Hmmm."

"I'm in trouble, just me, not Carolyn. Everything else is okay, really." Waiting, she coughed and held her throat. She knew it had to be beet red, and Carolyn would see it. Pulling her small water bottle out of her purse, she took a quick swig and began dabbing her cheeks and neck with it.

"*Hmmm*, well."

"I need that new ID and social security card. It's for a job, that's all." Inhaling, she felt fog-air in her throat. "I need a whole new identity, Gene." She felt tears stinging in her eyes and coughed to damn them up. Hoping he was the same now as back when she had known him, she remembered one other major personality trait about him—his savior complex that was part of his narcissism: if she could make him believe he was the

Corporate Revenge

only one who had the power, she would secure what she most desperately wanted..

"Huh!" He huffed in a victorious tone of voice, and she could hear his office chair squeak as he rocked. Obviously, he perceived her as being needy and he was gloating. "Okay, Rae Anne." There was a huge pause where he was stalling, waiting for her to beg some more. "But this is it, Rae Anne. You *can't* call me anymore about this." He gave out a gruff laugh. "New identity—by God!"

"Definitely, sure Gene, no more calls." she glanced at the time. "I only have a few more seconds to talk, then I gotta go. I have to pick up Carolyn." She kept saying his name, knowing full-well he was relishing the repetition.

"How is she by the way?" he asked, his tone of voice suddenly up lifting.

Taking in draughts of relief into her lungs, she replied, "Fine." Suddenly he sounded concerned. Uh-oh...she had to nip that in the bud! "She's popular at school, and she gets As and Bs. She's making a lot of friends." Not wanting to say Carolyn's name for fear he might begin to feel a strand of emotion for someone, she also didn't want to keep him too long on the topic of her personal life. Those could ignite guilty feelings; then she realized that in the four years she had known him, he had never shown a single sign of feeling guilty over anything, only the suave ability to circumvent problems and flee responsibilities. "I have to go get her now, Gene. When can you put those IDs in the mail?"

"Not today!" he retorted, in a hostile tone of voice. "It's almost three. I have a few people to call, and then I have to meet someone." His breathing was wild. "For cryin' out loud, Rae Anne." He was lashing out, and mad, but she wasn't taking it personally, but held the phone away from her ear. "You're always so demanding...and you're a train wreck!"

Realizing he'd continue listing her faults like objects on a conveyor belt, she interrupted him. "You're right, Gene."

"Huh? You bet I—"

"I said you're right." Tears stung her eyes. She felt

humiliated, ashamed, and depression sick. She so regretted having ever gotten involved with him. The only thing good that came out of that despicable union was Carolyn, her beautiful beloved daughter, who she'd do anything and everything in her power and might to protect and nurture.

"Fine, *uh-uh*, well, great," he exclaimed, sounding perky, his usual response after having beaten her to an emotional pulp, which he hadn't, but believed he had, so she had really won.

She got what she wanted by playing the loser and failure. Now all she had to do was to act like nothing happened. "How long before you can send those then, Gene? *Pleeease*, I really need this favor."

Another long pause ensued as she heard him click his mouse and tap computer keys. "Okay…I'll process them today. I'm entering your information now. You should receive them FedEx by the earliest, tomorrow afternoon, but at your home address, not the address you gave me. I can see it's a storage facility. We can't send any IDs to that kinda place."

She began calculating the time Tim might need to schedule interviews and the time she might need to search for jobs at RTI. "Four days will be fine, Gene. Thanks. Thanks so much."

"And Rae Anne?" he asked.

She could hear the snap of a book closing. "Yeah?"

"Don't, call me, again."

She remembered his hard and harsh sides. He always treated everyone, men and women, as a means to an end, up until the moment when he'd ditch them, after using 'em up, and zapping 'em of every crumb of energy. They'd be left depleted, and asking his unfading ghost: "Who the hell are you, and how the hell did I ever get involved with you in the first place?" They'd be asking those questions forever!

"Sure Gene. Fine." She purposefully sniffled. He'd like that final touch. *Snake, scum-bag, jerk, walrus*!

Corporate Revenge

She remembered their split. They had bought new wedding rings because he claimed he wanted to renew their vows. He was in between jobs. After a week of wearing his, he acquired his new job. Then he said the gold plate was creating a rash that was spreading up his arm. She believed him, brought him ice packs, and pampered him, until she found a hidden vial of poison oak oil behind the spices. The next day he left, telling everyone, including her parents, that the breakup was her fault.

Click. He hung up. He was gone.

"Thank God! Never again!" She felt her entire body almost collapse in relief.

She slammed the receiver on the hook, ran to her old white convertible Mustang, drove to Carolyn's school, and turned into the procession of cars that had rambunctious middle students darting in and out of pickup lines. She sank behind the steering wheel when she saw her tall, blond happy daughter making high-fives with her circle of surfer girlfriends. She looked vibrant and energetic as her body language and gestures moved in harmony with those of her peers. This new school had healed her from all her prior hurts from all the previous moves. Before they moved from L.A., after Rae Anne told her they had to move again, Carolyn had screamed every day for an entire month: "I hate you," and, "I want to live with my *real* dad!" For days, she took Carolyn shopping, and had makeup artists give her make overs at the mall. That seemed to cure Carolyn from her threat of leaving her for Gene, whose name she'd never revealed to her. Now, all those distractions might not work this time, and she knew she'd be in for another bout of severe tantrums if she were to force Carolyn to move again.

"I just can't tell her," Rae Anne said herself, leaning into the speedometer. She remembered a time when Carolyn had played *Duck Duck Goose* and *Ring Around the Rosie* with her preschool friends. For over seven years Carolyn had been living a life of being ripped away from everyone close to her. "I just can't tell her about her dad losing another job."

Carolyn waved to her, and Rae Anne shot her a hand signal from out of the window. She looked like a blossoming surfer girl, blond haired, thin, and bouncing happy.

Wiping away tears and inhaling deeply to keep from crying, she said, "I *can't* put her through any more packing, or saying good bye to all her friends and leaving another school and neighborhood."

Carolyn began running to the car.

"I can't do it!" She would give Tim a few weeks to secure another job. If he hadn't by then, then they would tell Carolyn about the job loss, together.

On the ride home, Rae Anne smiled as she and Carolyn talked about the new girl in her English class. She held back all the bad news and swallowed down every impulse to blurt out Tim's lay off. All the while, she couldn't wait to get her hands on the new IDs. In the meantime, during alone times at home and the library if she couldn't find enough alone time at home, she would check out available positions at RTI.

That night, after Joey and Carolyn settled into bed, she told Tim she wanted to keep his bad news a secret for a short while, and he agreed. Then she went to the bathroom, flung open the medicine cabinet, grabbed and twisted open her bottle of 0.5 milligram Xanax tablets, and shot a pill into the palm of her hand. Before taking it, she stopped and stared at the hard yellow shot of comfort. Turning the pill between her fingertips, she really didn't want to begin another regimen of anxiety medication just because she was feeling afraid of her future, scared of facing head-on all her out-of-control events, and depressed over her powerless situations. *That's life! Aren't firings, kid problems, bad bosses, and ex-husband encounters what people go through at some time or another in life?*

On the other hand, she couldn't stop shaking. Part of her wanted to schedule an appointment with a psychiatrist she had just discovered in the yellow pages, and part of her just wanted to cope with Tim's being fired, securing a position at RTI, and managing all her tag-a-long emotions. She threw the pill in the

Corporate Revenge

toilet and watched it flush into oblivion. In bed, she breathed while remembering serene locations: their honeymoon in Chicago, and watching the moonlight glisten on the water of Lake Michigan on Lake Shore Drive.

Just before midnight, Tim finally slipped into bed. "I have two interviews scheduled in San Jose, but I should be back next Friday."

"When do you have to leave?"

He yawned. "In the morning."

"Great!" *But San Jose? Oh no! Another move!*

"Great?" he asked sitting up. "You seem happy to see me go."

"No—no way," she coughed. "I'm just happy you found something." Then she sighed, "But San Jose?"

Shhh, he whispered, gesturing at the hall. The kids were sleeping, but sometimes Carolyn would go to bed late after homework.

Even though she felt a speck of relief that he had secured an interview didn't stop her from obsessing about RTI, and that he might be able to secure a job so quickly didn't surprise her. In spite of layoffs and firings, Tim had always been the driven and industrious type, managing to find new positions. He did know a lot of CEOs and V.P.s whom he had help vault to high places in the past. He told her the top job interviews were those few individuals who were helping him procure interviews now. The only devastation in their lives had occurred from their being so constantly uprooted. She remembered a time when she had planted thirty roses on the side of a brand new house they had bought only to watch their blooms through a moving van's side-view mirror. Not wanting Carolyn and Joey to see her cry, she buried the loss at the time, until the next time, when another out-of-control situation occurred, and they were forced to pack up and move again. With every new move, all those farewell images compounded, flooding her brain ten-fold, multiplying in intensity in depression and anxiety. She had layers of losses and grief, with no idea of how to get rid of them except to see yet another new psychiatrist in another new city, and pop down antidepressants and anti-anxiety medications. *Not this time, 'cause I'm doing something about it, something big at RTI!*

She wanted to encourage Tim's job hunting, but dreaded the thought of moving to San Jose, one of the most expensive places in the world to live. Still, his leaving was essential to her plan. She could search for positions at RTI while waiting for her new identity, and she needed time to secure references from people and colleagues whom she had trusted and counted as friends. But first, she needed to know the names of his enemies and if he had any friends at RTI.

He turned to kiss her on the forehead, his blue-green eyes filled with love and support. He brushed back his sandy hair and his fireman-strength muscles rounded like steel as he pulled her close to him. "You think you can handle both kids by yourself for a few days?"

She interpreted the question as an insult to her emotional wellbeing. "Of course I can! Joey has preschool, and I can put him in full-time if I get a job interview."

"So you're gonna continue looking for a systems analyst position?"

"Definitely!"

"Ohhh." He sounded disappointed.

"Why?"

He shrugged and swallowed hard. "I guess we better hope you can get a job this time…that is, if I can't land one in San Jose."

"We might not have to move if I can find something!"

He had told her once that he'd liked her staying home full time, and she had several sewing and ceramics projects she liked working on. Now, that stay-at-home dream had changed. *Maybe he's afraid I'll leave him if I get a job.* She had to reverse the subject, make him feel like the man of the house again.

"Carolyn's within walking distance of school." She kissed

Corporate Revenge

him on the cheek and handed him his glass of ice water which he sipped. "So if I do happen to secure a position, she can hold down the house until I get home, 'cause I'll probably have to work until five-thirty or six at night."

He winced and glanced at her askance. "Carolyn? Boy crazy? And home alone?" He laughed, his eyes showing expressions of fright. He was imagining her having countless parties with her friends.

"She'll be fine," Rae Anne said, "but now I have a few questions." She bit a little piece of skin on her lower lip.

"Fire on!" He rolled on his back and stretched; then he began staring at the ceiling and wiggling his large toes. He was trying hard to stay awake.

She had to focus and link names with images so she could remember them and write them down later. "Tim, who do you think was really behind your getting fired?"

Hazy light from the lamp and humid air caste long shadows over his body. The sheet rippled when a crisp ocean breeze wafted into the bedroom. After he rolled up the thin covers to his chin, she could only see his lips move as he began speaking. "I think Steve's old buddy and former V.P. of Sales and Marketing in San Jose, Kip Tempulous, was in part responsible. Steve and Kip worked together for over ten years at a high-tech company there. They invented a special sensor-chip that they're all hyped up about, and Steve's paranoid that someone'll come along and steal his technology." His chest rose and fell in normal rhythms of relief. He was finally calming down from the day's catastrophic activities.

"You mean Steve doesn't trust that you'll keep his invention a secret even though you signed a nondisclosure?" she asked, rhyming Kip with cat nip in her mind, to remember the name 'Kip Tempulous' after she could secure a job at RTI.

"That's about it;" he replied, "never mind that I made over a hundred million in sales selling his special sensor-chip already. And never mind that Steve gipped me out of a 0.5% commission." He huffed in anger. "That would have been $500,000…enough to pay off the house we're having built."

"Easy!" she added.

His lips moved, repeating the number, magnifying the loss.

"Since you're no longer there, Kip can claim the deal as his own. He'll get the commission next year when Steve cooks the books." She felt burning anger.

"Pretty much so," he said, "and Kent Smith, that V.P. of Engineering guy will get a chunk of it too." Squinting, he then rubbed his tired eyes. "Smith will probably also share *my* commission with Claude Filmer as well since Filmer handles *all* of RTI's contracts."

"That's so unfair!" She hit the head board with her fist. It made her even more determined to expose RTI's corruption.

"Hey, I'm ticked off too, but don't hurt yourself over it!" He chuckled and kissed her stinging fingers.

She kissed him back. "What they're doing, hiring people and then firing 'em before they can pay commissions is exploiting new sales employees though, isn't it?"

"Sure, and—"

"I mean, to hire someone promising them all sorts of perks, and then fire them At Will so they don't have to follow through with a contract is so illegal!"

His eyes filled with glaring anger. "Of course, Rae, but try proving that!" He lay back down, beaten. "Try proving corruption at the top. All the CEOs and CFOs and...well, you name 'em...they make billions, and rob their employees of what's rightfully due them in their contracts, everything from commissions to stock options. Impossible to prove."

"Unfair! If people do the footwork—"

"That's why they call those type of people, marketing and sales people like me, foot soldiers," he interrupted.

"People like you *should* reap the rewards of all their hard-earned work, even if the higher-ups fire them At Will." She wanted to tell Tim right there that she was intending to infiltrate RTI, find proof of fraud and corruption, and then

Corporate Revenge

expose the company to its investors or whoever would listen. She wanted to ruin them as they were ruining her family. But she couldn't tell Tim. She knew he'd label her *crazy*, call someone at the company, and tip them off to her plan. As Tim began telling her about a rumor he had heard that RTI was shipping faulty sensor-chips in the hope of replacing them later, Rae Anne became even more determined to nail the corrupt RTI executives. After all, if executives had lied to Tim, they had to have lied to so many others. If she could expose their fowl business tricks, other victims might stream out of the wood work and support her. She believed she had invisible allies rooting for her.

"So Steve fired you—"

"Actually laid off," Tim corrected, glancing at her askance.

"Okay, laid you off because he didn't want the investors to know how much you were really selling." She turned to get a better look at him, propping herself up on the pillow with the palm of her hand. "I mean, if the word went out that Steve's technology was faulty, the investors would lose more than millions."

"Try billions!" Tim winced, rubbing his eyes and face until his knuckles turned white.

She couldn't keep him awake, and angry, much longer. He had a huge trip ahead of him early in the morning. She then realized she'd have to target RTI's engineering section as well as their research and development area.

Tim pulled the pillow from behind his back and punched it. "Damn corporate honchos, especially Thornton Manning."

"What about him?" she asked, conjuring up a way to imprint his name and position in her memory.

"He's Steve Lerrefeiht's hotshot whiz kid," he replied, sitting up, grabbing his cold water and slugging some down. "Manning's The V.P. of Technology and can do no wrong."

She lowered her voice, suspecting that if Tim were to detect any type of anxiety, or inquire as to why she was asking so many questions, he might realize her plan.

She only had a few more questions. "Who else do you

think is crooked?"

"Oh, definitely that Head of Engineering, Kent Smith." He exhaled as if his lungs hurt from smog.

Kent Smith, bent teeth...she was memorizing his name. "What do you think his part is in all this corruption stuff at RTI?"

He raised his voice. "Smith sent me emails to contact potential customers. Most companies answered, but some didn't."

"So?"

His jaw stiffened. "Well, when I continued to contact those companies, I discovered they weren't active, but fake."

"That's strange." She sat up. "You mean you were selling RTI sensor-chips to fake companies?"

His eyes widened like a cat inspecting a stranger. "Yeah, I couldn't believe it. I searched for proof of their existence, but couldn't find any."

"Did you tell anyone?" She reached for his cold water and then sipping it.

"I went to the execs. No one had an answer." He rubbed his eyes. "I linked from site to site. No company." Clinching the sheets, he unruffled them and pulled them across his chest. "But I did find something."

"What?" She listened so intently her eyeballs hurt.

"All those fake companies merged into one firm. I searched for financial connections and a prospectus on each one, and found none, only a Swiss merger."

She was a systems analyst, didn't know much about business, but knew enough to realize a prospectus was a necessity and paramount for investors. "That's definitely not right."

"But as a Swiss Trading company, the foreign ties are obvious." He stared into the distance, obviously perplexed by the puzzle. "So, the firm appears solid."

"What's the web address?" Finding what Tim had missed

could help her achieve her goal.

"Easy. The web address is www.HermesTrading&Cie.ch." His head shot in her direction. "Why?" He began scanning her.

"Why what?" she asked, picking up on his suspicion. She straightened her sheets. The rustling noise might distract him from asking more questions.

"Why do you want to know all this stuff?" He leaned into her.

"I don't know." Fluffing her pillow, she turned around and tucked herself under the covers to her chin. "Just ticked off I guess, like you."

He laughed and shook his head. "Rae, I know the companies are fake in that Swiss Trading company." He punched his pillow and then fluffed it with his hands. "What I don't know is whether or not this fake company had something to do with why Steve let me go. I was told it was a production thing."

Stringing together her words softly so as not to alarm him she asked, "Did you *like* anyone at RTI?"

Tim began telling her about the V.P. of Systems Architecture, Mira Padeson, who was at least ten years older than Tim. "She's the V.P. of System Architecture, the one responsible for smoothing over all the problems between RTI and its customers. She's great! But I never did trust that Ginnie Reidel, the one right under her."

"Who's she?"

"Technical Director and Chip Architect." His expression was gritty, and then he smiled, obviously having a fond memory of someone else. "Maybe I can call Mira Padeson and ask her for a solid reference, if I need her…not that I'd give anyone at that company any kinda of information about me. Never know who could get their stinking hands on it." As he expounded on Mira Padeson's good qualities, he had an excitement in his voice, portraying her as a wise magician, an underpaid scholar, and a miracle worker all rolled up into one. "Mira can jostle phone calls, come up with impromptu excuses, and keep a customer occupied while tracking schedules and telling jokes at the same time!" He sighed in obvious memory of her. "Now that's a lady I'm gonna miss!" Then he chuckled as if she was in the room with them and they were laughing at a good story.

His voice sounded so light and uplifting, and Rae Anne found hope. *Perhaps Mira Padeson was sad to see Tim leave. If so, that means that she has a kind heart. I can befriend her.*

But before she turned out the light on her nightstand, Tim sat up and began stroking his forehead. He was giving off gestures of puzzlement; then he turned and looked her in the eye. "There's also something much deeper going on at RTI, Rae. It's bothering me." He was ghost white as he bit his lower lip and gazed at the crack of their open bedroom door.

She hated seeing him so hurt, dejected, and scared. "What? Tell me...after all, like, who am I ever gonna be able to talk to about it even though it's so secret?" She wanted to lead him on a false trail. "I'm applying for work around Carlsbad. I'm not going *anywhere* near San Diego. It's too far with the kids going to school here. You can trust me."

Nodding, he then drank more cold water. "All these top execs are doing way too much sneaking around. They're hiding everything from someone high up in the chain."

"What?" She touched his arm. "Where could they be hiding such big developments in technology and vital research?" She remembered seeing the seven-story facility that looked like a huge hospital with a medical center attached to the side. Research had to be conducted under strict conditions and be open to inspection, supervision, and evaluation.

"There's a top floor no one's allowed on. Only the V.P.s and execs. I only saw it once, but then Mira scooted me out." He twisted his body toward her. "She told me I hadn't worked at RTI long enough to enter the place." He coughed, choking on the mystery. "She even told me she had saved me from

Corporate Revenge

being fired." His eyes turned sparkle-watery, and Rae Anne believed she saw guilt. "Mira pointed out the sign above the elevator panel. I should have seen it. I shouldn't have accessed that part of the building." He slapped the side of his cheek lightly in a show of self-punishment.

The mystery puzzled Rae Anne too as she saw self-blame rise in Tim's each and every breath. "That was just a mistake, Tim. Anyone can miss seeing a sign." She watched him shake his head as he lifted his gaze to the ceiling. Feeling helpless to console him, she added: "Maybe that's where RTI's assembling a prototype. Or maybe Steve stores all his closely guarded specifications there."

He gave out a deep sigh of defeat. "There's more though." He pushed his back against the headboard. "Just before Mira shoved me into the elevator, I saw a name, a name I'd never ever heard of before."

"Yeah, what?" She grabbed a pillow and held it tightly against her chest.

"Justin Phillips."

Rae Anne repeated the name. "Did you do a search on Justin Phillips on your computer at work?" *Anything* could have got him fired.

Tim exhaled in frustrated. "Yeah, but nothing. It's as if Justin Phillips exists in RTI's high-tech world, but according to Google and LinkedIn, Justin Phillips doesn't exist."

She laughed. "Maybe Justin Phillips is a financial donor." She thought of her ex. "RTI's just using some billionaire for money." She thought of money laundering!

"Or he could be some high-level board member to whom Steve Lerrefeiht has to report." Tim shrugged and then lay back down. "Whoever this Justin Phillips is, I don't think he has a clue as to what's going on a RTI. This person appears to be completely off the grid."

"Did you see a picture of him anywhere?" she asked.

"Nope, just a huge plaque right above that elevator door. That's it." He yawned. "But I sure would have liked to have met Justin Phillips." He nuzzled his cheek into his pillow. "If

J.P. Osterman

I had the nerve, I would have told him everything that was going on."

Trying to make sense of all the facts from the morning's phone call until now, she said: "This RTI sounds like it's a cesspool of corruption. Those executives do everything from committing fraud against their employees, to funneling government funds into bogus companies." Rubbing her neck, she huffed out air into her bangs. "They're also lying about the accuracy and origination of their inventions to fleecing the investors. This is crazy! *I* see what they're doing, and I've never worked there!"

He reached up and turned off the light. "I worked there, but I can't prove it."

After she heard his light snores, she tiptoed through the dark corridor, pulled out the pad and paper from her wallet, and jotted down all the names Tim had given her, particularly Justin Phillips. If she'd ever make it into RTI, she was determined to hunt for the reclusive billionaire who obviously had the status of a living Howard Hughes. Even if she were caught, she could head *right* to that person. That was plan A: to take evidence that she could find of RTI's corruption to Justin Phillips. Plan B would be: if someone were to catch her, enlist the help of Mira Padeson.

The next morning, Tim left early for the airport. Carolyn wept. It was obvious he wasn't leaving for a business trip because he was dressed in the formal suit-and-tie he usually wore for interviews. When Rae Anne told her that he was on the way to San Jose to look for another job but that he hadn't been laid off or fired, Carolyn folded arms, stomped and proclaimed: "I'm not moving!"

"I'm not asking you to," Rae Anne said, her eyes tearing. Sitting down next to her, she continued: "I'm looking for a job here…around Carlsbad, and I know I'll find one 'cause I was good at my job before, and I'll make anyone who'll listen to me

Corporate Revenge

believe that I'll be a great systems analyst for them as well. So don't worry. I'll find something great, right here!"

From his booster chair, Joey watched Carolyn's blond hair toss through another tantrum. He had mashed his scrambled eggs and was flinging the spongy mess at the walls until the surface resembled speckled paper.

"Mom, I'm just gonna walk to school today!" Carolyn whipped her backpack over her shoulders and began packing a lunch.

"Carolyn, here's a key!" Throwing it, she watched Carolyn catch it in midair. "I may have a job interview, so I might not be home after you get out of school."

"Okay, Mom."

Then Rae Anne turned to Joey who had egg plastered in his eyebrows. He was laughing and mashing toast between his fingers. "Oh my gosh, you need a bath little guy," she said, thinking about the time and how she didn't want him late for preschool.

Her surfer skirt well above her knees, Carolyn flicked her hair behind her shoulders as if telling Rae Anne she could care less about *her* life. "I get it mom." She had one hand on her hip and was giving her the evil eye.

"Get what?" Rae Anne asked softly.

"*You* just get a job." Then she pointed her forefinger over her heart: "*I'm* not moving! I'm staying!" She appeared about ready to run away.

Before Rae Anne could retrieve and throw her a jacket, Carolyn had already disappeared behind a row of apartment garages. Still, the butterflies were everywhere, but less in number than yesterday.

After giving Joey a quick dunk in the tub and dropping him off at Rainbow Preschool, Rae Anne came back to the apartment, fired up the computer, and found jobs posted on RTI's website. She had worked as a systems analyst, but never an engineer. No one would hire her as a secretary. She stopped when she saw Assistant to the Director of System Architecture. She fit all the job qualifications.

J.P. Osterman

Believing she had a chance, but not yet having a new identity, she flipped through her address book, looking for the phone numbers of old colleagues. It took her hours to muster up the courage to dial them. What would she say for small talk? What info would she give her about her life should they ask her in-depth question? Especially concerning her past? When she finally balled up enough nerve to dial one number, she ached. She hadn't spoken to some of them in years: Lyle Reyner, Tina Moreland, and Henrietta Stockington. She felt like a failure compared to what they had done and accomplished. They were all high-level employees, people in front of whose names she'd put rows of stars. She felt ashamed to tell them how her life had been progressing since she had last seen them. She didn't want to lie, but to achieve her goal; she'd have to tell a few white ones.

"I had to move to Carlsbad to get away from an abusive husband who was in the Mafia," she told them, clenching the phone, her voice fast paced. "I'm in the process of getting a divorce. The guy was so secretive about his past that I have to go into Witness Protection and testify against him. So can I count on you to be a reference for a prospective employer when I call you back with my new name? Of course, you'll have to swear to secrecy!"

After trying to pry deeper into her life, unanimously they agreed, and Rae Anne gave them details on how she needed them to respond to anyone who might call them from RTI. Then the hard part of all her conversations with them began. They told her she was smart for leaving Tim. They had tried to talk her out of marrying him in the first place because his job history appeared wishy-washy. She remembered their advice, but ignored them.

When she finally hung up after being on the phone for over a half-an-hour with each person, and in between tasks of tending to the kids, housework, and getting them off to school,

Corporate Revenge

an entire day had passed! It was Friday, April 12!

The next day, at the same time, after she finished her last conversation, she walked to the corner bar at 1 o'clock in the afternoon, sat down on a stool, and ordered a beer. Now, she was ready to do a little bit of celebrating. She had survived step two of her plan for action. To actually begin step three, she'd have to wait for the mail, for her new identity cards to arrive from Gene.

Chapter 5 – Step 2 of My Plan

The bartender was a thin woman in her mid-fifties, but athletic and muscular, robust and fiery. From her wrinkled weathered face and tattoos on her upper arms and neck, Rae Anne surmised the spiked red-haired woman had survived some pretty wild trials in life, much worse than herself. Glancing around, she noticed the bar almost empty, and a soccer game playing on a wall-mounted screen on silent-mode. At the back of the bar and huddling in a corner booth, a couple was having drinks, now-and-then laughing. Their red high-backed booth was situated next to a huge juke box that set next to a dingy corridor leading to the bathroom. The linoleum floor throughout the bar was bubbling in spots, and scuff marked, like someone had dragged black licorice over it. Bouncers must have had a heavy fight last night while forcing drunken patrons out the door. The air was curling smoky, even though a non-smoking sign had been posted above the long mirror. The base of the mirror was lined with various sizes and shapes of mottled liquor bottle, giving the entire bar an antique atmosphere.

Corporate Revenge

"Having a tough day, hon?" the woman asked in a gruff voice.

Startled, Rae Anne coughed. "Not really." Having been alone with no friends for quite some time, she felt compelled to trust her and added, "Well, sort of a tough day."

"What'll ya have then, hon?" she asked, showing her a shot glass and a beer mug.

"Beer...a Miller draft please," Rae Anne replied.

The woman grabbed a wet grey rag and began putting some muscle into the counter. A man staggered in, the bartender pointed forcefully at the door, and the man lumbered outside. She laughed and nodded at Rae Anne. "We don't get many of your type in here this time o'day." She picked up her smoldering cigarette and took a drag, her eyes squinting through a plume of smoke, her lips puckering and wrinkling like a prune.

After taking a quick sip of her beer, Rae Anne glanced at the smudgy door. Part of her wanted to make a quick exit, but the lonely part of her wanted to talk. "I just have to do something risky. I don't know how I'm ever going to pull it off."

The lady gave out a big huff. "Whataya thinking about doing? Robbing a bank or something?"

Rae Anne laughed. "No! No way!"

The bartender leaned on her elbow and placed her other hand on her hip. "Well, when ya said *risky*, I thought you meant like breaking the law or something." She glared at her, but the look wasn't mean, just pressing. She was inviting Rae Anne to open up some more to her.

Rae Anne felt uncomfortably shy. "I've just been staying home with my kids...raising them...taking some time off work, but now I need a job." *What a hell of a job I need!*

"What's your name?" she asked, picking up two bottles of liquor and aligning them among other colorful bottles on her shelf. She was exacting, her attention to detail obsessive. Her precision to order, and her exotic appearance, would be a perfect fit in a shop selling Depression Era glassware and discontinued china.

Rae Anne was feeling uncomfortable, and her sweating beer was shaking in her hands. "Rae Anne." The lady was getting a bit too close for comfort.

"I'm Betty," the bartender began, "pleased to meetchya." She offered Rae Anne's her hand; and as she shook it, Rae Anne felt her uneasiness melt right out of her. Still, she hoped Betty might move on to another one of her chores.

"What's *risky* mean to ya?" Betty poured two ounces of scotch into a glass over three ice cubes. The expression on her face contained a voyeuristic intrigue. "Whataya have planned, Rae Anne?" She chugged down her drink.

Rae Anne watched her amazement. "Betty, if I'da drank what you just did, I'd be out on the floor." They laughed as Rae Anne gazed into her light brown bottle of scotch, now half-full. "I've just been out of work for so long, and I want to try something different, that's all."

Betty's eyebrows lifted and her green eyes rounded. "Oh yeah, what?"

Rae Anne glanced at the open door. The arched entrance leading out to the sidewalk felt so near and she felt guilty for sitting there celebrating while Tim was on an airplane to San Jose and most likely discouraged and downhearted. Yet Betty was so real, so authentic, and her personality so inviting that Rae Anne felt compelled to stay a little while longer. Maybe Betty might have some practical advice, some wisdom. "I'm looking at getting a job at a really big corporation. But I've never worked in a big facility before. And this place might be one of those dog-eat-dog businesses. I need a job there and I want a job there, but I'm afraid of being there. That's all."

"Wow! That's heavy!" she exclaimed. Then Betty pointed outside to the speeding cars on the street. "Ya just go and get that job." Her buff arms were firm with fortitude. "Ya put one foot in front of the other, and ya move forward one step

Corporate Revenge

at a time." She slammed down her empty glass and doused her cigarette with serious drive. "Forget about the past," she grimaced, waving at the restrooms as if they had dirty seats and barf rings. "Move forward with your life. Apply for that job. They're no better than you! Then hit that interview. You can do it! You got drive, girl. Just do it." She whipped up her long grey rag and slung it over her shoulder. "Just remember this."

"What?" Rae Anne felt an energy she hadn't experienced in such a long time.

Betty snapped her fingers. "In a blink-of-an-eye, life's all over, Girl."

"You seem to know what you're talking about," Rae Anne said, taking another drink of her beer.

"You bet I do!" Betty then leaned into her, slowly. "I was given a second chance, Rae Anne. I almost died once—" She picked up her stain-soaked rag and stared at it, obviously a symbol of mistakes and failures. "But I didn't. The jerk who hurt me is in jail, and I'm alive. No knife's gonna kill me!" She slapped that stinking rag into the small sink next to her and began washing it with soap and water. She had an inner strength, and fire. She began wringing out all the dirty parts, hating the filthy spinning down the sink.

The longer Rae Anne watched her, the more of Betty's determination and drive transferring onto her. "Well, you survived, so I suppose I can too, Betty."

She propped her head on the palms of her hands. "Ya know how I make it?"

"How?"

She gently unwound the rag. It was almost white. Obviously she had bleach in that soap she was using! "This place came along. It was an opportunity. I'd been living in a homeless shelter for battered women. And when this job opening came up, even though I lived in Riverside, I grabbed it. I coulda stayed in my old bad cycle...coulda stayed with that scoundrel..." She opened a small dishwasher and inserted her empty shot glass on the top rack. "But I didn't. I took a risk. I came here, and started from scratch. Just do it. Go apply for that job ya want."

Rae Anne set down her half-full mug of beer that thudded on the bar's shiny varnished wood. "Okay, I will!" She felt uplifted, half-believing she could really pull off her entire plan, and then she stood up to leave. "Nice meeting you, Betty." She glanced at her watch. From just that little amount of beer, she was feeling slightly tipsy.

"You too," Betty said, waving her clean rag.

Rae Anne walked back to her empty apartment.

She spent the rest of the day recuperating and watching spy movies and detective shows. She had to glean how best to infiltrate a target and extract information without getting caught by security. As a girl, she had watched re-runs of *Mission Impossible* and *Mannix*. In between calling her old colleagues, she had stopped at Redbox and rented *Haywire*; at home, she found a whistleblower movie, *The Insider*, on Netflix. Spies, detectives, and whistleblowers had many common characteristics and tools of the trade: fancy weapons, confidential informants, gadgets, distractions, callousness, knowledge of their major targets, and building plans and information on other surrounding structures.

One obstacle she'd encounter would be RTI security! She remembered what Tim had told her about RTI being a ten-story conglomerate containing levels of cubicle mazes with cameras in every corner. RTI also employed a team of highly-trained guards. Pacing around Joey's train set, she realized she needed a get-a-way plan as well as an entry plan. She noticed in several of the shows, that all spies and operatives have one thing in common: disguises. She would need one in case she might find herself trapped, needing to alter her appearance, and outwit RTI's hidden cameras and vigilant guards.

Searching through the phone book, she found a thrift shop on Roosevelt Street. Noticing she had time before Joey's

Corporate Revenge

preschool ended, she drove to the shop and began flipping through racks of dresses. She'd need a thin one so she could roll it without wrinkling it into a large handbag. She sorted through clothes like a speed reader scanning pages, so much so that an attendant began eying her just as she was donning sunglasses and a black wig.

"Ma'am, can I help you?" the sales woman asked, her aged arms extended as if pleading for Rae Anne to hand her over some dresses she had draped over her shoulders.

"No thanks," she told the elderly woman, "I'm just in a bit of a hurry. I have two kids...and a job."

The woman was stepping with her in a gentle gait. "You just look like this is your lunch time, or you're running late for a business meeting." The woman had kind eyes. "I was just trying to help. You professional women have so much pressure on you these days." She shone an expression of awe on her face. "I couldn't do it...no way...I just couldn't do it!" Then she scurried away, shaking her head. Obviously, she had once walked in corporate shoes, had had it with the cold business world, and left her old impersonal chaotic job for this easier one so she could help people and engage with people on a much deeper and personal level.

Watching her offer help to another patron, Rae Anne realized she'd have to put on an entire fake persona to last even one day at RTI. She'd have to change not only her name and social security number, but also her personality, the way she walked, and her body language. To fit in, she'd have to become impervious to criticism, unaffected by back stabbing, and resistant to those wanting to climb *through* her on their way to the top—brownnosers. People climb the corporate ladder in so many ways that she wouldn't fit in with them naturally. She'd have to become unnatural. From what Tim had told her, Mira Padeson seemed to be the only executive there who managed to have a heart and keep her job. Rae Anne wondered how.

After she thanked the elderly saleslady again when she rushed back to offer her another wig, she dashed into the dressing room and sat down on a bench. Suddenly, the word *professional* came into her mind. She had called her that, but Rae Anne never saw herself as looking very business-like and professional in years. Again there was another mirror, and she peered into her reflection. She began whispering, talking to herself: "Wow! Maybe I've been completely wrong. Maybe I've been looking at myself totally wrong!" She was seeing someone entirely different from what the attendant saw in her. She had been telling herself she was a flop, a failure, a loser. She rubbed her hands across her face, trying to wash off all those dirty tags she'd been wearing. "I've been my own worst enemy!"

After paying for the beige silk dress, wig, sunglasses and soft soled shoes, Rae Anne smiling at the attendant at the register. "Thanks so much. You really helped me here, a lot."

On her way out, the bell jingled at the top of the door, and the attendant called, "Have a good rest of the day."

When Rae Anne returned home, she ran to the mailbox. While there, the FedEx truck pulled up. Gene's letter! She signed for it, and raced into the house. Nearly breathless, she tore it open and spilled the contents on the counter. There, and without any note, were her new ID cards: A driver's license, a social security card, a passport, and a secondary California ID card all with a new address, plus a blank website she could log into and recreate herself. Then two more cards slipped out. Visa cards! Was Gene being overly generous? Feeling guilty for being the jerk he was and leaving her…she saw the amount on each Visa card: $2,500.00. Maybe Gene had a standard package from Witness Protection and she was now a beneficiary!

"Hurrah!" she cried, kissing them, throwing them in the air and watching them rain down on her. Picking them up, she read the name: *Mary Elizabeth Hershel.* She closed her eyes, repeating the name and burning it into consciousness: "Mary

Corporate Revenge

Elizabeth Hershel."

Suddenly, another idea occurred to her. She imagined herself standing in front of the Eifel Tower, or kissing the Blarney stone in Ireland, or climbing one of the Egyptian pyramids. She could go anywhere, disappear, and completely become this new person, Mary Elizabeth Hershel. One of the cards showed her profession as Systems Analyst. The back sticker had a bar code. Any agency anywhere in the world could automatically access her clean record and have proof of her education. She could have a complete do-over, anywhere in the world—leave everyone and everything, right now. These new IDs and their perks were like a magic wand; and she could wave them right now, and create a new road in her new life!

Then she spotted Joey's picture, Carolyn's school picture, and the picture of Tim and her on top of their entertainment credenza. No way. She'd be lost and a mess for the rest of her life if she'd even spend a month away from them. A day, yes; a week, okay; but more than that, no way. She walked over and kissed their pictures. "I love you...love you too much!"

Dumping out her purse, she took out all her old IDs and inserted the new ones. Guilt wafted through her, and she felt sick. "How could I even *think* of picking up and leaving?" She choked back tears. "How could I even *think* to do such a thing to my kids...leaving them without a mother? What the heck am I becoming here? Insane? Cold? Callous? Those are the types people I want to expose!" Not wanting to become like the executives at RTI, but also needing to become like them so she could get close to them, she set out her thrift-shop clothes and began hanging them up in the closet next to the front door. "I'm not some lone-wolf CIA operative or indifferent FBI agent...I have to remember that!" She spoke so loudly, she thought the neighbor must have heard, and she turned up the volume on one of her TV detective shows.

Plopping down on the couch she began watching a DVD of *Mission Impossible*. It may not have been FBI or CIA training in covert operations, but she believed she could get some ideas from the spy movie writers on what to do once she actually secured a job at RTI, if that was even a possibility. She hadn't even applied there for a job yet! Settling in with a handful of popcorn, she began talking to herself: "At least spies know who they are, glean all the information they can about their targets, and delve into the many ways they intend to retrieve information. They make plan A, a plan B, and even a plan C." Then she flicked off the TV. "Most times, they improvise, and that's when they put their lives on the line. I could put my life in danger as well…real life, not just a screenwriter's imaginary life." Part of her believed that everything she had been planning was just a bunch of nonsense while the fight side of her believed she could really pull off infiltrating RTI and exposing at least a little bit of their corruption.

Noticing the clock, she realized she didn't have much time before Carolyn would be home. And it had been a day since Tim had left for his interview in San Jose. He'd be home in another three days or so, and she hadn't even applied yet for that System Engineering position at RTI. With her left palm holding up her chin and her right hand mouse-clicking, she retrieved her email. Clicking on Tim's in-box she noticed a message from a software company in Los Angeles, Ready Tech. The HR representative at the company was responding to a friend of Tim's who had referred Tim to the position. The HT rep was writing Tim, asking him to confirm an interview time for Monday. It was Thursday already! Quickly, she called Tim and relayed the message.

"It looks like when I finish up with this interview here in San Jose, I'll give Ready Tech a call and schedule an interview for Monday," he said, happily. He sounded confident. "Looks like I'll be spending the weekend away from all of you though. I hate that!"

"Me too, Tim." [*Hurry up. I gotta hang up.*]

"But the time away is worth an L.A. job as opposed to a job in San Jose. I still have another day here, then another

Corporate Revenge

interview in a suburb, and then I'll fly down to L.A."

"Uh, yeah, great, uh-huh." [*Hurry, I gotta go!*]

"You don't sound happy 'bout that Rae. Is something wrong on your end? Something come up? Don't worry about money for all this 'cause the companies are paying."

The name, Ready Tech, suddenly flashed in her mind like the shark in *Jaws*, scaring her. Still, she said, "No—everything's fine! So you'll be gone another four days?"

"Looks that way."

"That's fine." After she told him the kids were all right and the apartment still standing, they said their goodbyes. Relief filtering through her muscles, she hung up the phone. "Thank God! I have another four days!"

Then, that Ready Tech name flashed in her mind like a red light. "Ready Tech, Ready Tech…where've I seen that?" Somewhere, she'd seen it; and the mere repetition of it make her stomach churn. She began rifling through her address book. "Nothing! But I know I've seen it…" Slapping the flowered book shut, she spotted the FedEx envelope from Gene on the table.

Her hands hit her chest. "No!" She lifted up the envelope. "No way!" There in the corner was the stamped return address of Ready Tech. Flinging it on the table, she believed everything was turning from bad to worse. "What if Tim bumps into Gene?" She gasped. Then she realized that Tim had absolutely no idea that Gene even lived in Los Angeles, and Gene hadn't ever met Tim. The only way they'd meet is if someone were to introduce them to each other. Still, she knew her husband disposition. If Tim were to find out she had contacted Gene, and why, there'd be a fight between them that the cops would have to break up.

Pacing the floor she wondered what she had gotten herself into. She began conjuring up possible scenarios of how Tim might run into Gene, finally concluding that Gene was in Records, and Tim was Sales and Marketing. "No way could they ever possibly come together at that big company." She was just imagining the two of them clashing when in fact the two departments were totally separate. "I'm safe. I just know I am." However, she knew this added stressor would continue to prick at her insides until Tim had finished interviewing for the position at Ready Tech. Finally setting the subject at rest, she walked over to the computer and pulled up RTI's job website. She began scanning job openings at RTI.

As she scrolled down the list of openings, she saw the position: *Assistant to the Director System Architecture*. After taking her new IDs out of her wallet, she began filling out each and every block of information in the on-line application. Focusing on the words on her bright monitor, she felt like she were scuba diving twenty feet under water, straining to see colorful coral, but also mindful not to touch black sea urchins with hurtful stickers. One wrong move filling out the detailed application could get her into serious trouble. Every nuance of her new identity had to be perfect.

As her address, she wrote in the place of her storage facility; as her phone number, she typed in her cell number. She had already created a new Gmail address on the new website Gene had provided for her, and her old friends would be solid references. As she drummed her fingers on the desk trying to think of what she'd do if RTI Personnel should question her about her degrees, she contrived reasons to stall them should they want more proof other than what Gene had provided on that special card. "I just need a week there, only a week to target my marks and extract the necessary documents to prove fraud.

Her shoulder muscles ached from the tension. Her fingertips were sweating on the keys. The ocean air swept through the apartment, whipping the curtained while a gray fog began to move in, increasing the humidity. When she finally finished rechecking all the information on two necessary forms, she stopped before pushing the icon marked 'send.'

She was close to the point of no return, and began

Corporate Revenge

wondering at what point exactly could she quit her entire retaliation fantasy and just abandon this crazy pursuit of justice. Her stomach aching, and staring at the picture of Tim and her, she answered her own question: "Anywhere between now and accepting an offer. I can stop anywhere in between those two points without counting everything I've already done as a waste of time and energy." She clicked *send*. Her application to RTI was now in play. Now she was in a game of wait and see. The day was Friday, but RTI had labeled the position *critical*, and emboldened it. *They have to call me…they just have to*! Every time she glanced at the clock, every *tick* sounded like an explosion of the second hand! Waiting felt intense, and heart pounding! She had to keep busy to keep her mind off the time…and she had an entire weekend, unless RTI Personnel would call her late on Friday.

Before picking up Carolyn from school, she dropped off her navy suit at the cleaners for one-day service and stopped at the office store on the corner of State Street and 3rd to pick up a pack of writeable DVDs and a few flash drives. She wanted the maximum storage capability possible to hold whatever information she might glean from computers she intended to access at RTI. The last place she patronized was a quaint shop on antique alley. She had seen a really big handbag, very high quality and handmade in Italy, but a quarter of the price she'd pay at a Louis Vuitton store. She bought it!

From the time she arrived home with the children until after she bathed Joey and tucked them in at night she checked her email on the half hour to see if RTI had responded to her job application. At 4:45 p.m., she opened her email. Good news! A Ms. Ginnie Reidel had received her application and was writing to schedule an interview for 10:30 a.m. on Monday.

She remembered her name from Tim's past, the woman who kept interrupting him when he was packing up his office to leave. Ginnie Reidel was one of RTI's executives—right under the V.P. of System Architecture, Mira Padeson. Tim had liked her, but was wary of Ginnie Reidel. She read Reidel's job description in the company's list of V.P.s because most likely she'd be reporting to Ginnie Reidel before interviewing with Mira Padeson. Reidel was responsible for overseeing the company's chip design and architecture, from circuit design to chip layout, from chip simulation to Built-In Self-Test (BIST). Rae Anne decided to sell her abilities as chip simulation. Since that fake foreign company was the seat of operations for assembly, RTI first would have to have assembled the chip they were purchasing. That's one of the areas she'd need to home in on and specifically infiltrate. Sitting on the edge of her chair while reading Reidel's email, Rae Anne was clenching the arm of her chair, attending to her every written word:

Dear Ms. Hershel: Your three years of experience with Moinahin Securities as a System's Analyst and your B.A. in Communications should be a perfect fit for what we're looking for as an Assistant to our Director of System Architecture. Please contact us as early as possible to confirm the above 10:30 a.m. interview on Monday, April 15 as we need to fill this vacancy ASAP.

Sincerely,
Ms. Ginnie Reidel
Director of System Architecture.

She quickly responded, confirming the 10:30 appointment.
Suddenly, she realized that she'd need a place to hide her writeable discs and flash drive. After picking up her suit from the cleaners that night, she sewed in pocket liners into her blaze. She also sewed two liners at the inside of her right cuff, the most convenient place to hide a flash drive, and the place from where she could slyly extract it at the spur of the moment. She also make a quick stop at their storage unit and tore open half of Tim's office boxes to find his miniature

Corporate Revenge

digital camera. Her iPhone wouldn't do because of the inadequate resolution. If she were going to take pictures of illegal documents, she knew she would need one of the best cameras on the market.

Then she went to the pet store, bought a canary, and a bottle of wine for supper. She thought a pretty song bird might soften the news to Carolyn, because now that she might have a job, Carolyn would have to walk to and home from school. She wasn't used to that. She also made a list of chores for Carolyn to accomplish until she'd arrive home at nights, along with a chart of rewards. She wanted to keep her busy instead of her turning the apartment into a party zone.

She uncorked the bottle of wine at supper. Now I can begin Step 3 in my plan and infiltrate RTI!

J.P. Osterman

Chapter 6 – The Interview

After staying wildly busy with the children over the weekend, she popped wide awake on Monday, shuffled the Joey off to preschool, sat down with a pencil, pen, notebook paper and coffee and called Ginnie Reidel at 8:50 a.m. Carolyn was up and dressing. Her school started later that morning at 9:30 because of testing. Tim had said that Ginnie and several other workers in that department were always at their desks by 8:45. As the phone rang on their end and the operator put her on hold, she made a firm decision. From now on, she would have a double life and begin inventing another entire persona—that of Mary Elizabeth Hershel. Until her plan was over, at any other place other than home, she would refer to herself as Mary E. Hershel.

During the confirmation of her appointment, the only trouble she encountered was when Ginnie Reidel asked her for her address.

"Just a moment, Ms. Reidel," Rae Anne told her, shuffling through papers on the kitchen counter for the address to her storage facility. She hadn't memorized it, a mistake.

Corporate Revenge

"*Ahem*, you don't know your own address, Ms. Hershel?" Ginnie asked, in a suspicious tone of voice.

"Yes, uh, please wait a second Ms. Reidel," she chuckled innocently. The pause was long as Rae Anne hunted for her wallet, but quickly retrieved her information from her email address book. She read off the address of her storage facility, but with a suite number, and nearly dropped her cell phone. "Sorry about that, I just moved here to Carlsbad. "I've been assembling all my documents for our interview. I'm great at juggling tasks, but better with software and writing code."

Ginnie Reidel chuckled in acceptance. "That's understandable. So I'll meet you at the reception desk at 10:30 a.m."

"I'll be there," Rae Anne said, picking up the RTI pin on the countertop. Tim had thrown it into the trash, but she fished it out from all the spaghetti sauce.

"And Ms. Hershel, our interviews usually last about four hours. You *could* be meeting and also interviewing with some of RTI's other employees in various departments," she added, her voice sounding upbeat and positive.

The longer Ginnie Reidel spoke, the greater the chance Rae Anne believed she could land the job. "Does this mean that if I interview well with you, that I could also interview with other high-level executives?"

"Most certainly, Ms. Hershel!" she said. "You should meet most of them, including my boss, Mira Padeson, she's V.P. of System Architecture, and most certainly you'll meet the CEO of RTI himself, Mr. Steve Lerrefeiht."

"Great!" Rae Anne felt her chest tighten and her shoulder muscles pinch. "I'm so looking forward to meeting you at 10:30 a.m., Ms. Reidel."

"That's an hour-an-a-half away, so yes, Ms. Hershel, see you then!" She hung up.

The interview was set in stone. The drive to San Diego at that time of day was forty-five minutes. She had forty-five minutes to finish dressing and make it at RTI by 9:45. She couldn't find her wallet! The most important thing containing all her fake IDs. *Where the hell did I put 'em?! Crazy to loose 'em now! Who does that?!*

She felt as if she might have a heart attack, she was that nervous, no, anxious. Over the weekend, she had cleaned the house from top to bottom—scrubbing the floors, twice, cleaning out the refrigerator, scouring the toilets and sinks, wiping down all the appliances, and vacuuming the carpet and baseboards. Then, she found her wallet! Under the couch. The corner of it was wet. Joey must have accidentally spilled his Sippy-cup juice on it and shoved it under there so as to not get into trouble. Her adrenaline stopped pumping, leaving her feeling relieved as she gently set her precious wallet into her new large shoulder bag.

Straightening her blazer, and trying to apply a last touch of make-up to her eyes in the mirror, she saw Carolyn walk into the dining room.

"Mom! Wow!" She nearly dropped her books.

"What?" With a swab bobbing at her lower eyelids as she tried to remove an eyeliner mistake, Rae Anne turned to her, her hands shaking. "What's wrong?" Behind Carolyn, sunlight was streaming in from cracks in the blind. Outside, the butterflies were gone. All the rare events of nature were being replaced by calm ordinary days. She knew differently. Today would be one of those rare days for her—the risk of a lifetime—if she could get inside RTI.

Carolyn grabbed her lunch off the counter. "Nothing. It's just, well, you look good, Mom." She walked up to her and put her cheek against Rae Anne's shoulder. "I'm so happy you have a job interview here, Mom."

"Me too, honey." Rae Anne kissed her on the top of her head, her blond hair scented of ginger and lemon.

"We might not have to move if ya get it." Shoving her books in her flowered backpack, she lifted her smiling face to the ceiling as if sending a silent prayer of thanks to Heaven.

Corporate Revenge

Rae Anne shrugged and said, "I'm doing my best to keep us here." Her make up as good as she could get it, she snapped the mascara lid into place and hugged Carolyn again. "I love you. I really do." Then she began another lecture on safety measures, including the big one: "Don't let anyone inside when I'm gone, and don't answer the door."

She laughed and shifted her feet. "'Kay, Mom." Then she stopped with a sad expression on her face. "What about Dad? What if he gets a job up there somewhere?"

Rae Anne bit the bitter taste of uncertainty from her maroon lipstick. "We just have to hope that the one I get can hold us all up until your Dad finds something around here I guess." She gave her money for lunch. "Everything'll be okay. You just wait and see."

After Carolyn left, Rae Anne packed her wig and thin dress inside her handbag, way at the bottom, in case guards might search her at RTI. She had no idea what to expect at the gate or security. Tim had told her there were security booths and kiosks in front of the corridors leading into the main building, along with cameras and monitors at the receptionist's desk. She put little reminder cards into an inside pouch of her handbag. Yesterday she had forgotten the address at the storage facility; today, she didn't want to make any mistakes and generate suspicion.

J.P. Osterman

Chapter 7 - No turning back

Rae Anne glanced at the time when she stopped at Starbuck's: 9:40 a.m. Her appointment was at 10:30. She didn't have much time to grab a latte. The drive would take about forty-five minutes, the dregs of rush hour traffic; and the longer she sat gridlocked on the I-5, the more she knew her anxiety level would rise.

As she walked inside the coffee shop, she realized she could still quit her plan at any point along the drive. Continuing her drive and sipping her coffee, she spotted the next exit, five miles south on the I-5. She could get off the freeway at Encinitas Boulevard and make a U-turn back to the apartment. *But what do I really have back there? Nothing, except to wallow over Tim being fired and ruminate about what RTI did to us.* She remembered another option. She could job hunt around Carlsbad, but she hadn't noticed a job that would fit her resume at all in yesterday's paper. All other options other than infiltrating RTI looked bleaker than just doing what that bartender Betty had suggested: "Put the past behind you, take your greatest risk, and do something totally new."

Still, she was afraid of what those risks might entail. She had told Betty only a half-truth, not her plan. She would meet

Corporate Revenge

people at RTI. People in very high places would ask questions, questions about her employment history, her family, her husband. The barcode on the back of a Witness Protection card was great, but might not be enough. What if someone had seen her picture on Tim's desk? How would she redirect a conversation? She always believed herself to be an honest person. What if she were to slip up and say the wrong thing? So much could go wrong, and her stomach ached from all the coffee acid churned by her nerves. She realized she was walking into greatest lie ever: Splitting her life in half and being two people at the same time.

Before pulling into RTI's parking lot, she stopped in front of an industrial mall and shot her hands against her forehead. "Crazy! This is all so crazy," she shouted at her reflection in the rear view mirror, remembering plots in those spy shows and real-life whistleblower scenarios. Never had she heard of one instance where someone had maintained two identities for very long. Such a person was eventually caught, killed, tortured, jailed, or living out his or her life in a self-imposed exile in another country. "But what harm is there in me spending just one day at RTI? Two days as Mary Hershel at RTI?" She gave herself a week to boomerang in and out of the giant corporation.

Arriving at RTI's smooth blacktop parking lot just before a giant wrought-iron guard gate, she gasped in amazement. The ten-story glass facility was so secured it could have passed a Pentagon inspection, except for the blue-suited guards wearing large blue-brimmed hats pacing inside the perimeter. The guard at the gate waved her down as she approached the tall hut separating two-way traffic. She noticed each camera and the directions in which they were pointed. She felt like a hunter searching for open pathways through a dense forest. She might have to make a fast get-a-way.

The black guard said, "Your name please?" He had a microphone attached to his outside pocket connected to a black spiral cord around his neck.

Pulling out her new ID, she replied, "Mary Hershel. I have

an appointment at 10 a.m. with Ms. Ginnie Reidel, the Technical Director of Chip Architecture. I'm applying for the position of Assistant to the Director of System Architecture. I'll be working with Ms. Reidel, I believe."

As he called Engineering, Rae Anne kept repeating in her mind: *have calm hands, don't shake! Use smooth movements*, and *breathe in and out…nice and steady.*

Then she saw a tiny weakness in RTI's security: A small corner window on the south side without camera protection on the first floor. It didn't look like much as she pictured herself squirming out of it and toppling to the ground; however, many small weaknesses could add up to a great escape opportunity should she need to make a wild dash out of RTI.

The guard turned around and glanced up at an opaque window on the second floor. "There's Engineering, but ask the guards for Ms. Reidel when ya get inside, Ms. Hershel. She's expecting you." Then he pointed at another small aisle in the parking lot. "Go straight and make a right at the T. Drive along the entire front of the building until you reach another gate where a guard will direct you to park in Visitor parking."

Saying her farewell, Rae Anne felt her arms tingle and her pulse beat in her diaphragm. She hadn't expected so many obstacles before even reaching the building! Complicating matters, Tim called. He told her he had just pulled into Ready Tech Industry. He was calling to see how her day was progressing. Glancing at glass opaque windows, Rae Anne surmised that RTI could have such advanced spy ware that it could intercept phone calls. "I can't talk now, Tim. Joey's a mess here in the high chair! I'll call ya back later. Love ya!" Realizing she would be in trouble later, she still hung up on him.

Around the building, another guard motioned her through a steel tunnel where a woman phoned in her appointment information and then directed her to park in front of RTI's administration building. She thought it odd that RTI's main point of entrance was at the back of its huge facility. When

Corporate Revenge

she looked at her odometer, she realized she had traveled an entire mile from the opposite side of the building. Perhaps that was RTI's intention, she speculated, to confuse people, to keep people off balance, off guard. That was one of the company's protective security strategies. In its entirety, the RTI was a maze of security systems. "The technology it harbors must be state-of-the-art and Top-Secret!" she whispered, looking up and inspecting RTI's sleek-glass-shiny façade.

Pulling into the visitor's section, she saw an open spot behind a truck. She parked there, hoping to keep her license plate hidden. Sitting in her car and leaning over the dashboard, again, she rolled her eyes up into each long line of windows in the ten-story facility. They were those tall hurdles she had tried and tried to jump over again and again in high school PE but couldn't. She'd come to a sudden stop right in front of them. She felt like a failure. She just couldn't surmount her fear and jump over those blasted hurdles! They were so high and terrifying. She believed her PE teacher labeled her a failure too. "Not this time, not now! I'll prove it!" She had to push on; and as she patted her cuff under which the flash drives set tight within the concealed lining, she exited her mustang and whipped her handbag over her arm. Inhaling and exhaling— she felt her feet, heavy as if she were plowing through sand on a beach. She kept tapping her fingertips in an effort to shed all her anxiety as she put one foot in front of the other. Finally, she reaches the opaque door. *I can still turn back...I can still go home.* She pushed the buzzer over the Visitor's sign. *Nope, I can't go back...not anymore.* She was at the point of no return.

A guard let her in. "I'm Mary Hershel. I'm interviewing for a position. Ms. Reidel is expecting me for a preliminary interview."

She was now in the main building. *I made it inside!*

Glancing at the corners of the ceiling, she noticed cameras tracking her as another guard approached her, greeted her, and began escorting her towards a set of interlocking hallways. The tile was shiny, mother-of-peal colored, the walls white and blinding. All she could hear were the sounds of her shoes tapping and shuffling across the checker-board patterned floor. The air was cool and lemon scented, the polish smell lingering on a long line of black picture frames—a photo gallery of RTI's top executives and board members. She looked for Kip Tempulous' name. He was the man Tim had said would replace him. But she only saw a blank name plate with the inscribed words: "Incoming." That meant that Kip Tempulous hadn't yet arrived at RTI. She saw lower-ups transition to high-ups, with Steve Lerrefeiht's name and CEO position almost at the tail end.

When she arrived at the end of the Hall of Employees, she noticed a name plaque at the base of an empty frame: Justin Phillips. She wanted to read more writing beneath the mysterious name, but the guard was whisking her away to an unspecified destination through another set of double doors. She didn't even have a chance to home in on the tiny inscriptions that looked like ancient hieroglyphs from a distance.

Once inside another corridor and heading directly to her interview room, she saw scurrying employees dressed in blue and black suits and carrying briefcases and folders. They seemed more like submarine sailors rushing to their posts at the captain's call, "dive, dive, dive!" Joining the throng, she began to feel claustrophobic, until vents flushed in fresh air, and she gulped down clean oxygen, taking in deep and heavy breaths.

I'm in! I'm really here, and in!

Then she spotted an arrow on the ground, and the stoic guard guided her down another long hall. For a moment, she believed she was on death row, the one she had seen on the news over the weekend. The office doors on both sides had opaque, yellow-netted glass windows, and this corridor was much narrower. The builder must have constructed the company to be escape proof. In the distance, she saw a dwarf man holding a big platter containing name plates. He looked like a waiter carrying a giant serving tray. With hunching

Corporate Revenge

shoulders, he was adding and removing employee names so quickly. He seemed afraid of someone. Glancing up, she noticed the ceilings contained holes for recessed lighting, excepted they lacked bulbs. They might be sockets for emitting electrical shocks to stop intruders—or employees— they suspected of stealing technology.

Her throat dried. Now, employees were everywhere. The scene was akin to a mall on Christmas Eve. People were passing her by, never smiling; and some individuals appeared sweat-worn, a few totally gray-eyed and fatigued. The latter were the ones she believed had to be overwork and working overtime for fear of losing their jobs. Unable to smell the scent of coffee, or food being microwaved for lunch, she felt trapped—suspended in some sort of anti-gravitational drum— or experimental labyrinth. Glancing over her shoulder, she almost turned around to make a run-for-her-life and dash out of RTI. Working more than a week in this place she believed would give her a heart attack!

Finally, the guard approached a brown-haired receptionist with a Bluetooth phone on her ear. "This is the place, Ms. Hershel." Then he left.

Sitting at an aluminum desk with a laptop in front of her and a long florescent light above her, the receptionist asked, "Are you Ms. Hershel?" Her smile appeared over-rehearsed, and her over-the-ear microphone appeared part of her hair as if she might never take it off.

Rae Anne speculated, *perhaps she's wondering why anyone on Earth would want a job at RTI.* "Yes, I'm Mary Hershel. I have a job interview at 10:30 with Ms. Reidel." She noticed the woman's name tag. It wasn't Ginnie Reidel or any name Tim had given her.

"Hi, I'm Barbara Winston, please follow me," she said, standing and turning as a robot in human skin. Rae Anne thought the place might be a facility that had manufactured the woman on *The Stepford Wives.* Barbara escorted Rae Anne into a cold conference room with white accordion partitions lining the walls. The room was cafeteria size, containing white shiny tables and white chairs with tie cushions. Obviously, this interview room was purposely furnished for RTI to make a best first impression on perspective employees. "Please, take a seat, Miss—"

"Mary," Rae Anne interrupted, "please call me, Mary."

Shrugging shyly, Barbara Winston blushed. "I'm so sorry…Mary." She cleared her throat in a perfectionistic gloating manner.

Rae Anne felt sized up, a part of some unspoken competition with someone at RTI.

"Ms. Reidel will be in here to meet with you shortly. Please take a seat." Then Barbara turned around and scampered away, her legs moving like a chipmunk rushing at a tree.

Anxious, but also keenly aware of each and every inch of her surroundings, Rae Anne rubbed her shoulders and glanced at the time: 10:20 a.m. *Wow, I musta flown down the I-5 to get here so early!* She must have walked into the building right after 10, so all the walking and escorting and meandering through corridors had taken ten minutes. Her shoulders hurt; her neck ached like pins in her muscles. Whipping off her handbag and setting it on the table closest to the door, she let it drop and she rolled her shoulders. *Ahhh, relief!* The thudding sound echoed off the acoustic white walls. Then she sat down, noticed two cameras pointing at her, wiggled in her seat, folded her arms and began waiting…waiting.

At 10:22, two tall men walked into the conference room and stood stoically by the door. Nodding at her, they had the muscular physiques of professional wrestlers. Right behind them appeared a short woman in her early thirties with a bouffant hairstyle and white cat-eye glasses. She had a tip-toe gait, the stride and grace of a professional dancer. Her blue eyes magnifying into little marbles through her prescription lenses, she smiled at Rae Anne.

Rae Anne noticed her right eye, bright blue with a brown section. She recalled her mother's heterochromia eyes. The woman had to be Ginnie Reidel. Tim had talked about her wild 1960s hairdo and her 1950 retro-style dresses.

Corporate Revenge

"Hi, are you Mary Herschel?" Ginnie's soft voice was distinguishing, likewise her eyes, pools of blue with a splash of brown paint, the first feature anyone had to notice upon approaching her, very rare. Her voice was as light and airy sounding in person as it had been over the phone. She motioned for Rae Anne to wait for a second as she searched for a pen and pencil in her black Chanel handbag. Ginnie exuded a calm and collected disposition, holding herself tall in irreplaceable and indispensable posture. When she found her sleek pen and firmly clicked it on, she had stern eyes. Rae Anne sensed a hard side of her—an inspective, intense, and get even side. She'd never want to piss off Ginnie Reidel! Tim was also suspicious of her, especially since Ginnie was there on the day he left. He hadn't said as much, but Rae Anne believed Ginnie was monitoring his every move while gently pushing him out the door.

Rae Anne stood up, a show of respect. "Yes, hi, I'm Mary Hershel."

Turning around, Ginnie waved at the two giant security guards who didn't return a friendly gesture; however, they nodded at her, and then walked over to a long table at the opposite side of the room where they plopped down in two chairs.

"Please take a seat, Ms. Hershel. I'm Ginnie Reidel."

Shaking her hand, Rae Anne saw its smooth delicate features and felt her solid grip, strong and self-confident. "I'm Technical Director and Chip Architect." She extracted a list out of her open briefcase, and then sat down opposite Rae Anne. "You'll be working under me, Ms. Hershel, so let me get your job description."

Ginnie had a smooth complexion and wispy bangs that parted at the side. Her stiff, tall hairdo looked held in place by thick shots of hair spray. When she peered over her wide-rimmed glasses, her brows were barely discernible, stubbles. Had she burned them off on purpose?

She broke the silence through her thin bright red lips. "I worked as a librarian back in 2001, after the dot-com bubble burst, and engineering jobs were impossible to find." She smiled, her shoulders rising and falling like sparkling Champagne effervescence. "So I can really relate to someone beginning a different kind of career after a few years of experimenting with the job market."

"Experimenting?"

"Yes...well, that's what's on your resume, Ms. Hershel, the one Personnel printed out from that Confidential website you sent us."

"Oh, yes, right!" Rae Anne then noticed Ginnie's 1950 retro dress that made her appear odd next to all the other blue-suited employees she had seen at RTI. However, the little black bow in the center of her blond bouffant put Ginnie over the tipping point of professionalism. How could RTI let *her* dress so out-of-the-box? Then she remembered bartender Betty. Betty probably would love to sit and chat with Ginnie Reidel. Then she retracted that when she realized that Betty was eccentric but authentic while Ginnie didn't appear to have an honest bone in her body. When Rae Anne pictured the two of them together, she coughed back a laugh because she'd rather be at the bar with Betty than at RTI.

"Are you okay?" Ginnie asked her, blinking, then ordered one of the guards to bring her a glass of water.

"Yes, I'm fine, sorry...just something in my throat, and thanks for the water."

Reidel then asked Rae Anne to delve into her employment history, and Rae Anne handed Reidel a list of her references.

Peering over the rim of her white cat-eye glasses—she had an overly exaggerated habit of doing that—Reidel said, "You'll be working for me, which is a good thing, because System Engineering has access to almost all the departments on all ten floors." She continued to discuss Rae Anne's duties as Assistant Director of System Architecture. "You'll also be collaborating with our patent department and upper management."

Rae Anne had her shoulders back and kept cleared her throat in between sips of water. She kept nodding at each job

Corporate Revenge

task Ginnie was unfolding. "Yes, I have Layer 2 and Layer 3 Ethernet technologies. I have a strong mathematical background in developing algorithms, and I know C++." She maintained strong eye contact, not her usual manner, but worked hard to change that part of her shy personality. Since her last job was so distant in the past, and since she hadn't had friends for such a long time because of all her packing up and moving, she was pausing through her words and phrases some times. Still, she remained calm and forced herself to slow down in speech and body language, especially her hand gestures. "I understand those job descriptions and I can perform them to your satisfaction, Ms. Reidel. I know I can. I will be an asset to RTI."

She blurted out a gentle chuckle. "Ginnie," she said, "please call me, Ginnie."

"Okay, Ginnie, thank you," Rae Anne said, and then peered up to find the burly guards who had left Ginnie to stand statue-like at the door.

Ginnie wiggled in her seat and bounced a little as she fluffed out her ruffled skirt. She must have had underneath it an uncomfortable slip! She had an energetic manner and quickness about her, revealing a delicate side and bright intelligence. In a company where *perception means everything*, and one wrong judgment can tank a person's career, Ginnie had obviously managed to juggle several roles, survive, and rise up in RTI's competitive environment.

"Your statistics background is the thing that *really* interests me." She was scanning one specific area in Rae Anne's application.

"Thanks," Rae Anne said, "I've written a few research proposals and conducted a few studies on how outliers contribute to threats in validity as they pertain to drug studies."

Her jaw dropped. "Impressive, uh-huh!" She slid her cat-eye glasses down the bridge of her nose and peered again at Rae Anne over the white rims, at least her fourth inspection. "I've really been on the lookout for someone who has a Systems Analyst background and Communications degree."

J.P. Osterman

"I have those," Rae Anne said, pointing to one of her references who could verify her experience.

"Great," Ginnie said, pushing up her glasses. "I haven't been able to find anybody, at least until I found you." She then gave Rae Anne a shocked expression. She was skeptical of Rae Anne who saw thorns in Ginnie's rosy disposition. "I'd be very excited to have you here, especially after I contact your references." She appeared to be enjoying her wielding of power. Then she leaned in, smiled, and winked at Rae Anne. "I bet you're a bit of a computer hacker too, huh?" she asked her in a whisper, giggling.

Rae Anne felt a hot blush on her cheeks as she shrugged and searched the room quickly to make sure the burly guards weren't eavesdropping. "I guess, yeah, I can do some of that."

She remembered some of the code language she had used on her previous job to look—hack—into illegal accounting practices so as to expose a potential thief. One of her former colleagues she had listed as a reference had told her she had a real talent for hacking. That person must have already informed Ginnie. *That means RTI is serious about hiring me*!

"I definitely can write and clean up software," Rae Anne said, smiling, peering over her shoulder to where the guards were standing way back against the wall. They were glancing at each other, communicating with their eyes, brows, and body language. *Spy tools…or secret ways they assess potential employees before hiring 'em.*

Then Noticing Ginnie so animated at her repertoire of skills and abilities, Rae Anne felt her self-confidence surge. If she could gain access to Ginnie's computer, she could hack into RTI's records and discover exactly why RTI laid off Tim.

"You definitely pass *this* stage of the interview," Ginnie said, picking up Rae Anne's paperwork, tapping the stack on the table, aligning all the corners. "If you can wait just another minute, I want to pick up some more forms for you to fill out and then move you onto the next stage of our interviewing process." She inserted the applications packet into a large manila envelope; then sealed it as if its contents were Top

Corporate Revenge

Secret.

After Ginnie stood to leave, Rae Anne asked, "Does this mean that I *could* have a position with RTI?" She peered up at her and then at the two guards towering next to her with their hands behind their backs. They appeared ready to haul her out of the building should Ginnie give them the signal!

"Definitely," Ginnie said, bouncing lightly on the balls of her feet. She was bubbling over with enthusiasm. The guards fell back. "And you'll really be pleased working for RTI, Mary. I've been here five years. I've made several important acquaintances, especially Mira Padeson."

Eager to see Mira because Tim believed she was his ally, Rae Anne craned her neck over Ginnie's grand bouffant hairdo. "I believe I saw Mira's name when I first entered the doors of RTI." She nodded toward the east, but then the west. Now she needed a compass to try to find her way out. "Ms. Padeson is RTI's V.P. of Systems Architecture, right?" She knew the answer...she just wanted to keep her talking—a real spy distraction tool.

"Correct," Ginnie replied, folding her hands, her red-painted fingernails glittering beyond her snow-white skin. "Mira's been my mentor here at RTI since I first started. I'm sure she'll take you under her wing too."

She sounded as if she owed *everything* to Mira, including her upward movement in RTI's corporate ladder. She waved at the guards to follow her. "Come on, Gentlemen, I want you to get up to the seventh floor and ask Mr. Lerrefeiht to come down here and meet Ms. Hershel ASAP."

The hulking men left quickly, and Ginnie faced Rae Anne and said as her nose crinkled in an expression of enthusiasm: "You're going to find our CEO fascinating! He's, well—" She gasped, enamored of him. "He's so brilliant...and a *real* charismatic leader!"

"Oh wonderful," Rae Anne said. *But I know he's a pea-brained dim wit!*"

"Even though he holds the title of CEO of RTI, he has a PhD in Electrical Engineering from Stanford University. Over the course of the past five years, Dr. Steve Lerrefeiht has worked with our R&D department to develop five sensors that have revolutionized the imaging industry." She began walking to the door, slowly. "And our hardware department has probably developed some components *you* have at home in your PC." Ginnie continued to puff up Steve Lerrefeiht, and magnify the importance of all his high-tech inventions as if he were better than Bill Gates and Warren Buffet.

All the while, Rae Anne felt her heart sink. She knew the pain and agony Tim was facing now because of Lerrefeiht— thief Lerrefeiht! *You have no idea of the kind of tyrant the man really is! But before I'm done here, you will.* Then she glanced down at the mother-of-pearl tile-colored floor and for a split second she believed she saw black prison bars. *Or I'll be in jail.*

"Come with me," Ginnie said, turning away and walking in front of her. Her flowing, navy-blue flowered skirt swayed when she stepped, and her buffy-white blouse tucked under her black-belt revealed her ultra-slim waist and ample breasts. As they began walking across the conference room, Rae Anne knew if she could secure Steve Lerrefeiht's seal of approval, Ginnie would certainly be her boss. She felt pumped up with excitement, although somewhat surprised she had actually been able to come this far in her plot against RTI.

Then, Rae Anne spotted a camera in the corner. The light was blinking a steady red. That's when she realized that some camera lights were flashing while others weren't. Perhaps those that weren't flashing really weren't working. Perhaps the entire corporation only appeared secure when in actually it wasn't. Perhaps someone had placed many of the internal cameras as a scare tactic, like so many 7-11s often do. She'd have to experiment further, test the nuances of the security system, before she could come to a conclusion as to which cameras were active and which ones were props.

"I look forward to meeting with Mr. Lerrefeiht," Rae Anne said, "and Mira Padeson. I hope it won't be too long of a wait though."

Ginnie checked her watch. Suddenly, she stopped in the

middle of their sprint down the crowded hall. "Oh, do you have children?" She sounded so negative, as if she might reconsider hiring her.

"Oh no, no," Rae Anne replied, giving her a feigned grin. She felt blood rush to her cheeks as she saw Ginnie's chest rise and fall in a show of relief.

"It's just that we sometimes have periods where we have to work overtime," she said, flippantly. "You know how that goes." She reached up to her white collar and adjusted it as if she were feeling uncomfortable but concealing her lies.

Rae Anne then wanted to know how easy or hard it would be for her to access RTI's computers. "What kind of security clearance does the position you're giving me require, Ms. Reidel? I mean, should you decide to hire me." She swallowed hard to try to keep her mouth from drying and her words from sticking in her throat.

Tilting her head back and glancing at Rae Anne, she replied, "As far as a security clearance is concerned, we issue you a standard Confidential clearance upon your being hired." Then she waved Rae Anne out another door, jiggling the handle after it closed so as to ensure that no one else could enter. "After six months of employment with us, we'll have you complete a more in-depth security questionnaire provided by DCSS to apply for your Secret Security Clearance. DCSS will do an initial background check, and then issue a preliminary Secret Clearance, with some restrictions, while they complete an in-depth background check. Finally, in about a year, you should receive your formal Secret clearance."

"Wow…that's some deep inspection someone's gonna make on me," Rae Anne chuckled. She gestured as if her comment were a complete joke, but they worried her. She calmed down when she realized she'd be gone from RTI way before them. Actually, she just needed a few hours, or a few days at the max to expose criminal activity and vindicate Tim.

Then Ginnie escorted her to the receptionist's desk to fill out more paperwork before heading back to her office to input all of Rae Anne's information into her computer. Her stiff bouffant hairdo appeared frozen on top of her head. "I'll see you later, Mary." She turned down another corridor and disappeared.

Saliva drying on her tongue, Rae Anne filled out paper work which included lines of almost illegible printer ink. In the distance, she noticed a man in his late forties approaching her. He had on his lapel a giant RTI emblem of a computer that looked like a giant Boy Scout badge he had earned for something great he had accomplished. From what Tim had told her, the man had to be a top executive at RTI, for they were the only ones who wore such emblems. Tim said they had ordered one for him because he was the V.P. of sales and marketing.

The first thing she noticed was the man's head. It looked like a fake scalp with a few bristles of gray hairs that someone would wear on Halloween. He had jutting ears, thin sideburns down to his jaw bones, and crooked teeth. A dentist had probably tried to bleach his teeth at one time because when he smiled, she could see a clear dividing line from white to filmy yellow. Dressed in a blue suit with an orange shirt, he had the look of a chauffeur, not a head honcho. His walk was firm, his stride heavy, and each and every employee who passed him straightened up tall, smiled, and gave a quick and snappy, "Good morning, Sir!" Then they glanced immediately downward, their expressions frightening.

The man stopped when he reached Rae Anne.

She noticed the name tag above his emblem: Steve Lerrefeiht, CEO.

When he extended his hand to greet her, she felt her arm numb. Those fingers were poison, but she had to shake his hand.

"I'm Steve Lerrefeiht, CEO of Riata Technology." The words came deep in his throat. He was enunciating with precision for everyone to hear and remember.

"Glad to meet you, Sir, I'm Mary Hershel."

Through the yellow plaque on his teeth he grinned and said, "From what Ginnie Reidel just reiterated to me, you're hired,

Corporate Revenge

Ms. Hershel, that's *if* you like the package we've put together for you." It had to be a standard package 'because no one could compile the complicated folder so hurriedly.

"Oh, wow, great!" she replied, shocked. She felt like a startled animal blinded by a headlight.

"Follow me to the reception desk," he said, waving her on with his bending forefinger. "We keep all the paper work there."

He had a hard walk, a tough strut, the sounds thundering off the long white walls. He carried himself like he owned a yacht, an airplane, and a ten thousand square foot mansion. "Parking is a big concern here at RTI," he said.

"Uh-huh, I understand, Sir." She had no idea what he meant. "I hope I parked in the right place." She remembered parking behind a truck. She couldn't tell him where. No way did she want him to discover it.

"Executives park in front of the security hut," he said. "You'll notice the long, large bright-blue line right when you come in."

"Bright line?" she asked. "I don't remember seeing any sort of line, Mr. Lerrefeiht."

He gave her an insulting glance. "My red Corvette's the first one in it!" he said, his shoulders slightly swirling, his bushy gray eyebrows bobbing at her as if saying: "I'm in my early twenties and ready for a party!" He was over fifty.

"Well, I'll definitely make a point of looking for your—your Corvette then," she said. "I wouldn't want to hit it accidentally," she laughed.

"My please don't," he reeled.

"Just joking, Sir."

"Oh," he coughed, "I'm telling you about the special line so you know about our towing policy." His lips contorting, he added, "A towing fee can be expensive here."

"Um, oh, okay," she said. "I definitely don't want that to happen to me, so I'll just play it safe and park way out back."

He shrugged. "That's your best bet. Some execs do that anyway even though they qualify for the special parking spaces." He appeared terrified that someone might be purposely trying to scratch his car. He began sizing her up as to whether she might be capable of such a thing. "We have a form for you to fill out for your vehicle."

That's when she realized he was also a bit paranoid, but trying to cover up his anxiety. She then grew angry. He had wasted time talking about a car, when what she really needed to know was what he expected her to on the job. After another five minutes of walking down another white corridor and passing nervous employees, they finally arrived at the receptionist's desk, where he attracted Barbara Winston's immediate attention by pointing at her. "Get the *formal* contract together for me will you please. I have this temporary one that'll do for the next few days until we vet Ms. Hershel completely."

"Yes, Sir," Barbara said, her eyes appearing to assess Rae Anne.

"Ms. Hershel is joining our company." He had an overly eager manner as he handed Rae Anne the folder containing the temporary contract.

"Yes, Mr. Lerrefeiht. Welcome to Riata Technology, Ms. Hershel." She began opening and closing drawers, whipping out and stacking papers.

Rae Anne's stomach twitched as Lerrefeiht reached behind the desk, pulled out a temporary employee badge and thrust it into Rae Anne's hand. "This is just a visitor's pass. I'll bring you an official RTI pin later."

Opening the folder, he then told her about RTI's great benefit package. "Ginnie Reidel will soon be joining us to offer you an exceptional salary." Rae Anne wondered how long that "exceptional salary" would last.

When he quickly looked her over from head-to-toe, she felt a rush of anger, especially after what he had done to Tim. Now, he was scrutinizing her like bait, and she was an amoeba under his microscope. She almost careened away from him when his arm accidentally touched her shoulder. Luckily, she didn't notice her quick defensive move, or he might have

Corporate Revenge

changed his mind and not hired her. *Yuck, yuck…*she couldn't stop thinking those words, the taste in her mouth sickening. This was the same man who had once shook Tim's hand over several promises, but then fired him. She couldn't wait to expose Lerrefeiht's fraud.

When Ginnie returned from Human Resources (HR) with more paper work, they guided Rae Anne down a corridor where Lerrefeiht stopped employees and introduced them to her. After arriving at Personnel, and with Lerrefeiht standing right next to her, Ginnie went over the details of the employment contract with her, and Rae Anne found herself signing her new name for the first time: *Mary Elizabeth Hershel.*

Lerrefeiht pointed at a line marked in red. "Do you have a problem with this salary?" His tone was condescending, his posture towering. Should she object, he might lift her up and throw her out of the building.

"How much again, Sir?" Rae Anne asked, squinting, wanting to force him into make a public declaration of his commitment, but also preparing him for the time when he'd have to confess all his corruption. Now, there would be witnesses.

Another man entered the HR conference room and stepped forward. It was Claude Filmer, RTI's V.P. of Contracts. Much shorter than the Steve Lerrefeiht, Claude Filmer was plump and bald, with a thick band of salt-and-pepper hair above his ears that curled into a duck tail at the nap of his neck. He looked more like a drunk on a barstool than an executive in charge of setting up and maintaining RTI's financial books and contracts. He had folds of dark wrinkles under his gray-blue eyes, and a hunching posture. A cancer patient who had just finished chemotherapy looked healthier. Whenever he concluded a sentence, he straightened his lips and dropped his shoulders. Actually, he didn't have much skin for lips at all. A plastic surgeon could do well for Filmer by transplanting some of his pot-belly tissue where the two red lines meet to form lips. He reminded Rae Anne of President Nixon just before he flashed his V-fingered peace sign to the public, only much older, cadaverously older.

Claude Filmer took the folder from Steve Lerrefeiht and shoved it into Rey Anne's hand. "Ms. Hershel, we're offering you Step-5 and a Level-4 salary." His red-lined lips parted into a straight grin, and the image of Herman Munster's thin red lips from the TV show, *The Munsters*, came to mind. She almost laughed, but instead looked at the floor and coughed; and when she glanced up, she saw Lerrefeiht's eyes glower. Obviously, he had perceived her dissatisfaction with their offer.

"That's $8,725.00 a month, Ms. Hershel," Claude Filmer said, snappily. "We're also offering you full medical benefits and a 401K with company matching contributions – up to six percent of your salary." His fingers were like nail spikes, successively tapping the written figures on the page. "That folder contains all the information you need. Read it. Then sign it, if it suits you. Or don't sign it if you don't want the job." His nose flared in condescension, he lifted his head into the air, and then he disappeared among a throng of employees down the corridor.

"Well, what do you think, Ms. Hershel?" Lerrefeiht asked, shoving his hands in his pockets, bouncing on the balls of his shoes.

Rae Anne grinned, pulled her handbag under arm, and glanced around the bustling office. "All this is definitely something to think about, *ahem.*"

"Does RTI sound like the place for you?" Leaning into her, he gave her a coy glance. A magician asking for assistance from the audience couldn't have presented a more enticing attitude.

Exhaling while watching people dart in and dash out everywhere as if they were hearing gun fire, she said, "RTI is *definitely* a dynamic corporation, Sir!" Everyone appeared miserable.

Noticing at all the numbers on the contract, Rae Anne believed this entire hiring process was moving along way too quickly, progressing way too suddenly for her to take her time

Corporate Revenge

studying it. The few lines she could discern on the temporary contract were almost illegible without a magnifying glass. The deal was too good to be true, too forced to be legitimate. The same fast-paced and pressured sequence of events had happened to Tim as well. Then she realized that Steve's ability to corner her so intensely could be a weakness. At the right time, she would rush *him* instead of him—and his minions—rushing her, and bring Steve Lerrefeiht down.

Steve puffed out his chest like a peacock to Ginnie Reidel. "I'd like you to take Ms. Hershel to the third floor to meet your boss, Mira Padeson since both of you report her."

"She's the V.P. of Systems Architecture I told you about," she whispered to Rae Anne. With several more folders under one arm, and carrying her Chanel handbag with her other hand, she nodded at Steve. "Right away, Mr. Lerrefeiht."

"Mira will take you to our IT center, where you can pick up your company computer, provide you with software, and issue you your company codes," he said. Before he walked away, he raised his arm into her line of sight and rolled back his cuff. He tapped the face of his TAG Heuer Grand Carrera watch. "I'll see you bright and early tomorrow morning at 8:15 a.m., Ms. Hershel. I have a high-powered meeting scheduled for nine, and Ginnie will be preparing you for the rest of today on the information I need you to add for my presentation. It concerns our clients, and simulation tools they need for chip architecture."

"Yes, Mr. Lerrefeiht," Rae Anne said, marveling at the Swiss-made piece of expensive art. "What a beautiful chronograph, Mr. Lerrefeiht."

He looked taken aback. "I assure you, Ms. Hershel, that RTI was founded on the principles of American technology!"

"Sorry, Sir, I was just—"

She had lost him as he gestured for her to wait while he checked for an exact time on his watch.

She felt hit. She had made a nice comment about his classy possession, money that could have been used to build a well or clinic in a Third World country. He had totally misunderstood

J.P. Osterman

her. Trying to save herself, she said: "American technology which is everywhere around us, Sir, I understand. I'm completely committed to doing everything I can to increase chip productivity."

Obviously gleaning the misunderstanding, Ginnie quickly intervened. "So you want Ms. Hershel to work for the rest of the day, Mr. Lerrefeiht?" She had a puzzled expression as she adjusted her cat-eye glasses.

Glowering, he huffed. Someone had just imposed their time upon him. Perhaps Ginnie had questioned his authority way too often.

"Of course," he retorted, waving her off with the back of his hands—a master ordering his cat to scat. He hadn't even asked Rae Anne whether or not she could stay. If she hadn't have wanted the job so badly, needed it so desperately, she would have told him where he could shove "his job."

Then he zigzagged around the corner and disappeared so quickly, as if he were in a race to win a drill.

She saw a flush of red hit Ginnie's cheeks as they headed toward the elevator. All her prior energetic movements appeared almost leaden. She had become instantly depressed. "You'll want to make sure you're on time, Ms. Hershel," she whispered as they walked to the elevator. She looked up and around, obviously trying to conceal her words from a camera. "Steve stands out in the parking lot at 8:45 a.m. with a pencil and paper and writes down the names of everyone who's late. That's everyone who enters the building after 8:45 sharp, even though work hours begin at nine sharp."

"Okay, I will," Rae Anne said. The gloomy silence made Rae Anne suspect that those were the employees who lose their jobs immediately.

"Mira Padeson's office is on the third floor," she said quickly, stopping at the elevator and then stepping back.

Rae Anne sensed from her sad and tense expressions that Ginnie was trying to decide whether to accompany her to Mira's office. She appeared concerned about her job. Obviously she needed to get something done for Steve even

Corporate Revenge

though he had ordered Ginnie to accompany her to Mira's office. Trouble could be brewing for Ginnie. "You don't look too well, Ginnie," she said, half under her breath. Ginnie had the same expression she had seen on Tim's face had when he was unpacking his office things out of the trunk of his car.

With her lips parted, Ginnie was staring into space as if Lerrefeiht had just slapped her for making an innocent mistake. She straightened up tall like a shield of protection. "I'm fine. Perfect!" Massaging her neck with shaking fingers, she added, "Everything's fine—peachy really!" She puffed up her hair with the palms of her hands. She looked frazzled, caught off guard—no, deeply troubled. Then she shook her head and smiled as if gesturing that all her fears were complete phantoms in her mind.

After the elevator stopped and a throng of employees disembarked, Ginnie paused in brief indecision but then walked into the elevator. Once inside, two other employees began congregating and talking as Ginnie lowered her voice to a dull testing cough and then pushed the button to the third floor. "Of course, when Mira issues you your PC, you can't take it home with you," she whispered up into Rae Anne's ear. Then she glanced up at a red flashing camera light. "Don't take *anything* out of this building. Don't ever! Not even a pencil."

After the elevator stopped and the door opened, Rae Anne stepped out, turned around to wait for her, but instead saw white fear in Ginnie's terrified expression. Ginnie wasn't going with her to Mira Padeson's office. Holding the elevator at the third floor, Ginnie then stuck her head out of the parting steel doors and peered up and down the half-empty corridor. A few employees were at this part of the building, Mira Padeson's entire System Architecture section. Ginnie looked completely paranoid as if her secure job had suddenly morphed into a vacant position. "Well, we're here." She rubbed her arms. Stepping back, Rae Anne could see thick goose bumps on her arms and gray paste on her checks.

"Okay, but where do I go?" Rae Anne asked softly, almost

wanting to reach back into the elevator and hug Ginnie to comfort her.

Ginnie thrust her hands in between the closing doors and then peeked out of them as the doors reopened. "Go down that hall and make a right." Then she stepped back and planted her back against the mirrored wall. The steel doors began shutting, and she had a spooked look on her face as she glanced upward. She seemed to believe that the elevator might launch out of the ceiling. "Go! Hurry! Mira's waiting!"

Rae Anne took a few quick steps, trying to insert her folder into the closing doors. "Okay, I'll—"

The elevator door hissed shut, a strange vacuum noise that made her cringe. As she walked to Mira Padeson's office, she had her head low, her handbag tight around her hip, and her Kleenex patting the corners of her eyes. She doubted she'd ever see Ginnie Reidel again. If her hunch proved right, she'd be even angrier at Steve and his executive snakes!

Corporate Revenge

.

Chapter 8 – Mira Padeson, Good or Bad?

Stepping into Mira Padeson's office, she noticed its homey
appeal. The warm inviting room had French doors opening up
into a massive reception area, beige plush carpet, and beach
pictures on the walls. Then she realized that the executives
she'd met thus far were expert illusionists. This laid-back look
was most likely deceptive. Still, she stood stunned faced.
Every other location at RTI had been sterile and impersonal,
but Mira's office had a welcoming feeling, making Rae Anne
want to kick off her shoes, bounce onto a couch, grab a
magazine and relax for the rest of day. How did she ever get
Lerrefeiht to agree to this decorative scheme? Walking up to
the front desk centered with a vase of fresh flowers, she heard
an automatic *ring...ring*.

A woman in her mid-fifties stepped into the room. She had
shoulder-length gray hair pulled back into a ponytail, bangs
swept from her forehead, and skin that looked nectarine
smooth. She reminded Rae Anne of Linda Evans from the TV
show *Dynasty*. Dressed in an elegant burnt-orange suit and
white frilly blouse, she had the rare RTI emblem pinned on her
front pocket. She was obviously one of the top-level
executives. She had to be Mira Padeson. She was moving

around methodically through her organized office, and she appeared self-directed and well-focused, like an engineer.

"Hi, I'm Mary Hershel," Rae Anne said. The comfortable atmosphere gave her an easy feeling, and she began to forget about Ginnie scary predicament.

"I'm Mira Padeson," she said, smiling and then shaking Rae Anne's hand. Her face was flawless beauty; her teeth white and straight. She could have once been a *Vogue* model. After glancing at her Timex, her eyes filled with concern. "Have you eaten yet, Mary? It's 11:34, time for lunch. Is it alright if I call you Mary?"

"Mary is fine, Ms. Padeson."

"Call me Mira, please," she gestured warmly, her mannerism open and genuine, her tone of voice optimistic.

Mira Padeson could be the person I can trust! Then Rae Anne realized she couldn't let down one iota of defense. She had to test Mira before she could ever risk putting her trust and confidence in her. "No, Ms. Padeson, I haven't eaten yet, and I'm definitely getting hungry!"

"Well, let's quickly go and get you your computer and other important software from IT on the seventh floor, and then I'll show you to the cafeteria," Mira said.

As they made their way onto the elevator, she proceeded to tell Rae Anne about the delicious food, the specialty cooks, the cheap prices, and even company picnics. "But we haven't had a picnic or Christmas party for the past two years." She gestured in disappointment. "Corporate wants to conserve funds." Then she gave her details of all the places where Rae Anne could pick up office supplies, more software, company clients, and chip samples.

Mira was talking so quickly and walking so fast, Rae Anne couldn't take out scratch paper let alone her pen to write down all those details. And she didn't want to risk sifting through the contents of her handbag for fear any of her disguises might toss out. This new rambling side of Mira's was new, perhaps her attempt to conceal some type of uncomfortable event that had just happened, or an act for the cameras that appeared to

Corporate Revenge

be either working and flashing, or blaring red in malfunction mode. Whatever was transpiring outside her office, Mira was nervous. Obviously, she had a double side to her! Would Mira continue talking so rapidly and moving so quickly while they were eating in the cafeteria? Rae Anne decided to take special notice of the times and places Mira appeared stable, and the times and locations where she changed in personality. Security could be extra intense at those times and places, or she could be afraid of someone or a situation.

As they reached RTI's IT department on the seventh floor, Mira was still booming with complimentary facts about RTI; but so much so, that Rae Anne couldn't even get in two words let alone ask her questions. She felt a pang of sadness, and overwhelming suspicion. *Maybe she recognizes me*?! She discounted that notion when she looked Mira dead in the eye and smiled as she had done for one of Tim's pictures that he had displayed of her in his office. Mira seemed to read right past her expression. If she had recognized her, she certainly would have given her some type of indication. Feeling more at ease with her, she was still hoping Mira might be a good-hearted person, not like Steve Lerrefeiht and his band of frauds. Walking alongside her and nodding in agreement to everything was telling her, even though most times she knew she wouldn't remember any of it, she decided not to judge Mira as a bad person just yet. Somehow, she'd have to put out bad vibes without Mira perceiving her as being mean, and test Mira's sense of justice.

"You did fill out the formal application, correctly?" Mira asked, suddenly stopping in the middle of a long white corridor, holding her back from walking any further.

Wanting to put her at ease, Rae Anne replied: "If you contact Ginnie Reidel, she has the temporary paperwork I filled out. Personnel still has to vet me, but I'll finish the permanent forms Mr. Lerrefeiht gave me in the next few days. I hope I get all the blanks filled in correctly…wouldn't want to show any dishonesty…ya know."

Mira's gaze sank to the floor as if she had just lost her best friend. "Dishonesty no…because I always believe, Mary, that what goes around comes around…at least I *used* to believe that."

"Oh, yes of course, me too." Mira appeared disturbed, and then Rae Anne recalled Ginnie's sudden change in personality from bubbly to terrified, to depressed. She remembered how close Ginnie was to Mira. Rae Anne then surmised that something horrible must have happened to Ginnie, and Mira couldn't talk about it. Mira, Ginnie's mentor, was obviously taking the bad news hard.

Suddenly, Mira recovered with a smile, but then let out a choking coughed. "I'll have Ginnie—I mean, someone in Personnel email your signed temporary contract to me." She ushered Rae Anne down another long corridor. "After lunch, I need to get you situated in your new office with your new software." She began describing RTI's simulation tools they use for chip design.

When Mira checked her Timex, Rae Anne noticed a frown on her lips, and then she exhaled in disappointment. But before Rae Anne could ask her if something bad had happened, Mira said: "Since you'll be working in System Architecture, I've made you responsible temporarily for picking up and delivering engineering documents throughout the company. That way, you'll get to meet most of the technical team you'll be working with."

"Okay," Rae Anne said.

Mira picked up the pace as they walked inside a special chip production facility. They were now walking in between Plexiglas windows through which Rae Anne could see an entire assembly line full of machine arms bobbing and whirring. Automated, precision die pickers were sucking individual computer chips from large disc-shaped wafers and placing them into the cavities of their individual packages. Moments later, the assembly line shot the newly-packaged imaging chips into ovens for vacuum-sealing their optical lids.

After two lab techs dressed in white passed them, Mira came to a complete stop. Rae Anne almost bumped in her.

Corporate Revenge

Turning to Rae Anne, Mira bent down and coughed, like an actor playing the part of a sick person. Then she lifted up her sleeve quickly and flashed Rae Anne a message she had written in blue ink on her forearm: *Do not look into the cameras.*

Afraid of looking up, Rae Anne nearly slipped on the sterile tile as she set her gaze to the floor. Now, she had no idea where she was going, except to follow Mira's tapping black heels. Was Mira protecting her from some type of trouble? Or was the writing on her arm simply standard policy Mira forgot to communicate? *But who the hell writes on their arm?* Now, Rae Anne felt more confused than ever, and she was getting a pounding headache. She was trying to cram an entire day's worth of spy work into the limited hours she had left on the job. Again, she remembered her mission. It might help her not be so hard on herself: *Get in. Nab proof. Get out.* Those words were pills, easing her headache.

Mira suddenly stopped again after walking down five more corridors. Now, they had to be approaching IT; and soon Rae Anne would have a laptop, phone, and a portable device, most likely, the most advanced iPad available to do her special jobs. Mira said: "After I issue you your hardware, I'll give you a tour around RTI and introduce you to the people I manage, people with whom you'll be collaborating closely." Then she began leading her around more employees who had obviously just left IT.

Rae Anne wondered where that message of warning had originated…at Mira's office or when they were in the elevator? Did she write the message right after she had introduced herself, or did she always have it as an imprint on her forearm? Maybe, Mira was protecting her, helping her; but that didn't make sense because Mira didn't even know her! Still, for the first time since arriving at RTI, Rae Anne felt some small amount of control and imbibed the confidence. As she had done with Ginnie, Mira might be taking Rae Anne under her wing. And if not for Mira's secret warning, guards might have rushed in and escorted her out the building even though she would have been clueless as to what bad thing she had done.

J.P. Osterman

Looking at a camera could get me fired? This place is nuts! If cameras and guards at that particular location are homing in on every person's gesture, that must mean that corruption and deceit are abounding inside that location. The target area must be the place that Mira and she had just entered and scrambled to leave like bats outta hell. That sterile chip-fab lab must contain proof of an illegal design!

The hallway still smelled electrically charged; a sudden influx of a chemical scent stung her sinuses until vents rushed on and flooded the seventh floor with fresh oxygen. Their shoes sounded like squeaky rubber on the sterile tile. Glancing around like a frightened Red Riding Hood afraid of the wolf, Rae Anne knew corporate eyes were watching them as they approached the double doors to the IT center.

They walked inside a dim room filled with laptops, cell phones, and other portable devices stacked on shelves against the wall. Mira turned on a few more lights and lifted a laptop off a shelf. She stuffed it at her side. "I need to use the restroom for a moment," she said, pushing away a few strands of her hair off her shiny forehead. She quickly tapped out a message on her cell phone and then said, "Over there are all the cords and software." She pointed to a table in the center. More techs were walking in and exiting the facility, and several excused themselves as they accidentally brushed up against her. At the opposite end of the facility was a check-out area where the facilitator was stationed and scanning devices. The man had several busy people working for him, stacking boxes, and off-loading software and other equipment. Mira now appeared drained, opposite from her previous energetic self. "Along the opposite side of the wall are cartons of blank CDs. You'll need those for Mr. Lerrefeiht's presentation tomorrow. He wants you familiar with his *PowerPoint*. Make sure you pick some up or have them delivered to your office." She launched an app on her cell phone. "I want to make sure you're on Its roster as an employee now…yes, they are expecting you."

"Great!" Rae Anne said, noticing several computers next to the facilitator. Now, her name was among them.

Corporate Revenge

"IT also has everything in stock you'll need for system architecture...so I'm inputting in those software packages for you to pick up."

Hearing the facilitator's computer *dink* with incoming email, Rae Anne made sure her handbag was high on her shoulder so her hands could be free to carry as many things as possible. "Will do, Mira."

"This afternoon, I'll walk you through the presentation format that Mr. Lerrefeiht insists we use. While I'm gone for a brief time—" She checked her watch and grimaced. "You can just go through some of these portable devices and find what you need!"

"Any of them?" Rae Anne asked, seeing the long line.

"Any...you're on the facilitator's list...and I saw that your Clearance transferred from the company you previously worked at...so please proceed to search through any of these and choose what you want. I gotta go! But I'll be back in a few minutes!"

"Okay, thanks, Mira."

Mira dashed out the door with that laptop plastered to her side. She was up to something, and it wasn't happening in any bathroom!

Now, Rae Anne was alone with RTI's valuable computers. Looking up, she saw one camera in the corner, but the red light wasn't on. Another wall camera was working and beaming red, but directed at the facilitator and his crew. The nonfunctioning camera had to be off, disabled, or never initiated in the first place. It was just a deterrent against crime. Feeling at easy, she kept her back to the camera anyway, and began inspecting the condition of a few laptops and other portable devices. On some, she noticed wear and tear. Those had obviously been used. And since she had just been hired, she surmised that the computers, phones, and portable tablets were those of previous employees.

Tim's computer must be somewhere among them!

Hopefully, someone hadn't wiped it clean yet. Most likely, anything he returned will be close to the facilitator and his team who are wiping all the hard drives or preparing to wipe them clean!

She saw several tagged ones feet away from the facilitator who was now busy logging in a new employee's portable devices. They were deep in conversation, and she waved to one of his employees after she asked her if she needed anything. "No, I'm fine!" she told her. "I was just in here with Mira Padeson. She logged me into your system!" The women waved her on in a friendly manner after she checked Rae Anne's story. Her heart beating fast, Rae Anne dashed over to the tagged laptops. Lifting each one as if she were in a mad rush to escape from a smoking building, she noticed the tags were alphabetized. She began hunting for Tim's.

Tennington, Usher…please be here…Vediwelt, Ventnor, Westman…Tim Westman. She found it! No one had wiped it clean yet!

Grabbing Tim's old laptop, she tucked it under her arm, whipped off his tag, and walked calmly over to the section containing the newer portable devices. Putting Tim's tag around a shiny new laptop, she snatched it, scurried back to the older laptops, and stashed the shiny computer next to the older ones. At her new office, she would fire up Tim's computer, examine the contents, and email whatever could help her cause to her home computer, that's if someone hadn't already wiped clean the hard drive. Just as she was searching for a cord, Mira walked back into IT. Rae Anne felt her heart skip. She looked for an indication in Mira's eyes that perhaps Mira had seen *the exchange* from some remote security screen.

"Are you finished here, Mary?" Mira asked, calmness exuding on her smooth-cream face. She was blinking, as if adjusting her contact lenses, and her irises were bright blue rings against watery white-pink sadness. Definitely, something was wrong. She looked as if she had balling her eyes out and had a meltdown in a bathroom stall.

Rae Anne wanted to touch her, ask her what had happened; but instead she motioned at a box containing packs of neatly stacked software. "Is this the software I need for this afternoon? I haven't checked it out, but I was about to."

"That's it," Mira said, sniffling, folding her arms. In spite of her sad emotions, she had to have the strong tough disposition of a marathon runner.

Rae Anne began sifting through a long box of packages.

Mira walked up beside her, picked up three disks, and handed them to her. "This is the Office Suite with the *PowerPoint* software," she said. "This one's a presentation graphics program." She handed her an 8.5 by-11 box. The backs of her hands looked blotchy! She was definitely holding something back, and the damning up of her emotions was intense, at times making the paragon of strength emit a spontaneous shake. *No one can go through what she's experiencing without cracking at some point…at least showing some of her pent up emotions*! She continued: "And with this program we can create custom graphics. You'll love it!" Rae Anne then saw a tearful pleading in her eyes. Mira was afraid, for her life! Rae Anne realized she had to know some type of deep dark secret about something or someone at RTI. "You're in for one heck of a *looong* afternoon, Mary," she said, lightly chuckling. Mira was putting all her energy into maintaining her professional mask.

All the way back to the first floor, Mira walked statue-like and quiet as Rae Anne noticed her peering up into the corner elevator cameras and ceiling cameras throughout the corridors. Each time she looked at them, she smiled as if bowing to a king. She had her arms tight at her sides, and the muscles in her throat and cheeks were bulging and red. The skin on her arms had blotchy circles as if she had plugged up the sink and had yelled into an ice-cold bowl of water. When they reached the Systems Engineering department on the third floor, Mira opened the door and walked with Rae Anne into her new office. It was a corner room with two giant windows. There was an empty desk setting kitty corner to the windows, three file cabinets under one window and bookcases next to the other window facing the sun.

Is this room *my* office?" Rae Anne asked, gazing out the opaque windows with a view of the distant freeway and Pacific

J.P. Osterman

Ocean. "Wow!" She pulled back her office chair and ran her fingers over the brown wrinkled leather. "Wow again!"

"This place is all yours," Mira said, with a smile that looked like the plastic one Barbara Winston gave her when she first entered RTI.

Rae Anne believed that perhaps someone had caught Mira warning her in the Plexiglas chip-fab lab, but she didn't want to bring up that event just yet. Then she noticed Mira's pink and glassy eyes. Obviously, she had been crying on their entire walk to her new office but concealing her tears whenever she turned away. As Mira showed her some systems textbooks, she retrieved her cell phone out of her pocket, and Ginnie Reidel's name tag fell out. "Oh, sorry!" She managed to swoop down on it before Rae Anne could pick it up; but still, Rae Anne saw it...and Mira *knew* she had seen it. A thick pause ensued as they both dove for Ginnie's name tag. Without a doubt, something bad had happened to Ginnie Reidel. Furthermore, Rae Anne hadn't seen a glimpse of Ginnie anywhere, even though she would be her immediate boss, and she was feeling at the boiling point to ask Mira, but then Mira said, "Take a lunch break after you set up."

"Where's the cafeteria?" Rae Anne asked, setting Tim's computer on top of the newly polished and shiny lemon-scented desk. She remembered that Mira had said she would show her to the cafeteria.

Mira's full lips pulled back into a smile, revealing dimpled cheeks. "Straight down the corridor to your left. But I'll take you there in a half hour."

Rae Anne didn't know whether to be happy, or sad, or asked her more questions. Instead she said, "I'll meet you here then." Mira left.

Rae Anne sighed in relief! She had a break, finally, and she began looking around at everything in her new office. However, every time she started perusing one of the books or checking out the automatic light switches, she found herself distracted by the beautiful view. Never before had she had such a spectacular view! Ocean view! At all her previous jobs,

Corporate Revenge

she had either an office exposed to the public so that she could interact with customers, or a little 6'-by-6' hovel that looked like a giant ice cube.

Alone, she sighed, *finally alone, and wow*! She noticed her shiny desk, mirroring the sky from her large picture window. *Look at this place*! *Look at everything*! The IT crew had delivered her supplies and stacked them in two boxes in front of a bookcase. One was labeled *software*; the other *supplies*. She felt tears in her eyes. *My credentials got me this job…I got this job*!

Then she remembered the cameras she had seen from the time she had entered the facility. She couldn't believe that any RTI executives would leave any employee unsupervised even for just a moment. Even that IT facility had to have someone watching her when she switched out a new computer for Tim's old one. She didn't think so, and she believed she had hidden herself from it. But there was something else amiss. While walking down all the corridors to her new office, she couldn't remember seeing one opaque security turret in *any* of the recessed light fixtures. Down other corridors, especially on the first floor, a turret security monitor was situated in the ceiling every six feet! Duplicity is everywhere at RTI! Why?

Opening desk drawers, she saw how clean and unmarked they were. Someone had taken a vacuum to them and washed their insides with Windex. Dropping her purse in between her office chair and the desk leg, she set up her computer, and then stacked the software packages and CD cartons neatly in the drawers. In the bottom drawer she saw pens, pencils and pads of notebook paper, the looking as if it belonged to the previous tenant but which someone—perhaps the quick cleaner—had ripped off and shredded. Taking out a handful of pencils, she accidentally let a few slip, and they fell to the carpet. Bending down and reaching to retrieve them, she noticed writing on the outside wood of the inside drawer, as if a tagger had scrawled them there on purpose.

"Spider bites everywhere! G. R."

Rae Anne glanced around the window frames, looking for spider webs and creepy crawly critters. None. After she reinserted all the pencils, again she glanced at the initials: G. R. The office she was now occupying, and the desk at which she was now seated at, were Ginnie Reidel's. Someone had fired Ginnie Reidel, just like that.

Someone had completely tried to eliminate all evidence of her, probably just minutes before Rae Anne had entered the room. Furthermore, Mira must have known about Ginnie being fired. She had escorted her down several hallways and shepherded her around a small parking lot on their way to the office. Someone had ordered Mira to kill time, until the guards could marshal Ginnie out of the building. All the time she had spent with Mira was perhaps Mira stalling for time. Was Mira part of Ginnie's sudden demise, or was she despondent by what had happened to her? She had to test Mira further, and that time was coming soon.

She then remembered that Mira had checked her watch obsessively when they were together. Was that planned to keep Rae Anne from finding out about Ginnie's sudden dismissal? Rae Anne couldn't believe that Mira could be so cold and calculating! Then again, another scenario could be in play: Mira probably didn't even have the chance to say goodbye to Ginnie. Being friends with someone and then having them ripped suddenly away must have been devastating for Mira, and Ginnie, especially considering that Mira had mentored her. They had to have been friends! Then, she laughed at herself while glancing out the window at her beautiful view—most likely someone's manipulative measure to keep her temporarily happy. No one high-up in business has a compassionate bone in their body!

But why give me Ginnie's office?

Staring at the ocean from one window and then at a bucolic scene of a hillside from another window, she realized that no one would ever dole out such a prime spot to an ordinary assistant. *Something's really wrong.*

Snuggling into her comfortable chair, rocking back and forth, and listening to the light creaking noises, she hadn't a clue. The only thing she could surmise is that Steve Lerrefeiht,

Corporate Revenge

or one of his high-level execs, needed her skills…no, was desperate for her skills; and that task must pertain to his big corporate presentation tomorrow morning. She wondered what was going through Lerrefeiht's mind when he issued her the plush executive room. She surmised: *Give Rae Anne the great room one day; the next day, or few days, or week thereafter, then fire her.* That's what RTI did to Tim, and without paying him his well-earned commission. She felt more than angry; she felt seething, and needing revenge.

The computer flashed on as she peeked out into the hallway. A few people walked by, and she introduced herself. They quickly dashed away from her. They had to be either afraid of her, or afraid of getting to know her. Then she realized something else as she meandered down the long HR hall, inspecting all the name plaques. They were all easily removable, and Ginnie's name was nowhere in sight even though Steve had hired her to work for her. Going back to her office, she saw her name on a gold plate, at eye level. It wasn't there previously when she had opened her office door with Mira. Now it appeared in black engraving as if by magic! Could she even trust her sense of sight?

Sitting down, pulling out the drawer, and rubbing her finger over the words Ginnie had tagged into the wood, she wondered what Ginnie meant by "spider bites everywhere." She conjured words that rhymed with spider, but nothing came to mind except for the corporation, Riata. Like the ink-blot test, she imaged claws, big eyes, fangs, and poison. Those associations didn't make sense, except as attributes of Steve Lerrefeiht and his cronies.

Spider, insect, larva, bug, caterpillar…wait, bug!

Her office was bugged, somewhere, and "spider bites everywhere" was Ginnie's way of warning the next occupant to watch out for what they were saying and doing. Writing that little inscription was Ginnie's little way of getting even with RTI.

Peeling her flash drive out of the cuff of her sleeve, she quickly inserted it into the USB port and began dragging files from Tim's old laptop. With her back to the window, she opened Tim's email, hoping RTI hadn't yet deleted them. Then she heard a knock at the door.

"Just a moment," she called. She didn't have much time. She saw several emails and gave out a muffled, "I'm coming...I'm in the middle of saving a file! Wait a second!" In two minutes, she managed to save the last three days' worth of emails. Running her hands through her hair and straightening out her skirt, she ran to the door and opened it.

"If you'd like, Mary," Mira began, peering around inquisitively, "I can take you to the cafeteria now."

"Okay," Rae Anne said, "but let me first get my handbag."

Mira was waiting outside as Rae Anne initiated a full-systems *trash dump* on her laptop; then she closed the drawer to her desk. She whipped out the flash drive from the USB port and left with Mira for the cafeteria. Along the way, she slyly reinserted her flash drive back into the lining under her cuff. At least now she knew that somewhere around her office, there were bugs of the eavesdropping kind.

While in line at the cafeteria, Steve Lerrefeiht thrust his body in between Mira and Rae Anne. "I present every new employee with one of these." He lifted an RTI pin into a LED ceiling light as if it were a gift from God. "You can take off that visitor's badge now, Ms. Hershel, and put this one on." He gestured at the visitor's badge in disgust. "Wear this RTI pin *every* day." He grabbed her hand and put the pin right into her palm. "See you tomorrow morning, sharp!"

Wiping the back of her hand on her skirt, as if sloughing dirt while watching him strut away, Rae Anne felt stunned and small. She had never seen someone so bold and brazen, entitled to interrupt conversations. Every part of her yearned to give Lerrefeiht a piece of her mind but she couldn't. She kept repeating her goal in her mind, and couldn't afford to be fired just yet. She was giving herself a week. That's what she kept telling herself: just a week to put up with being treated like pawn with no respect. A week to get even! Glancing around the sterile cafeteria and watching employees eat with their

Corporate Revenge

heads bent low and their eyes on their food, she believed the place looked more like a waiting room at a phlebotomist's office, not a place of rest and recuperation from the busy work day.

Slapping the sticky RTI badge on her lapel, she called to him, "Thank you, Sir!" A dull ache nipped at her stomach as she paid for her food and then sat down.

When Lerrefeiht reached the steel exit door, he stopped, turned and called out to them, "Mira, make sure you take Ms. Hershel around the company at some point this week." Rae Anne squirmed in her chair as his eyes continue to size her up. Pointing he said, "Yes, you'll do well on the executive team, Miss Herschel." Then he left the cafeteria with his head held high. Employees in his way parted, creating a pathway for him.

"Wow, I'm an executive now?" she asked Mira.

She shrugged as if confused. "Whatever Mr. Lerrefeiht says goes." Mira's throat turned blotchy red as she put down her ham and cheese sandwich. "We have a lot to do, Mary." She said those words as if preparing to cram for a test.

And for a split second, after she heard the name, *Mary*, Rae Anne looked from side-to-side, thinking that Mira was talking to someone else until she realized that *Mary* was her fake and temporary name. She wasn't used to anyone addressing her as such. She also wanted to ask Mira about the words of warning she had written on her arm that had helped her on their walk through the Plexiglas corridor on the fourth floor technology center. If Mira hadn't done that, Rae Anne might not be sitting with her now. She also realized that maybe she could trust her. But could she trust her enough to tell her about what Ginnie Reidel had scribbled on the inside of her desk drawer? No, Rae Anne had to wait a little bit longer to make sure she could *completely* trust Mira. Then, she had an idea.

After taking a sip of water, she picked up her napkin and set it down on the table. She wanted to see if Mira would open up to her about Ginnie, and Tim. "Mira, it seems that RTI's short on help." The cafeteria was the size of a very large doctor's office but only five employees were sitting by the windowless room, eating.

Mira swallowed her food as if it tasted like chalk and then said, "Well, RTI did have a few employees who left today." She pushed back her shoulders and looked askance, obviously afraid of being overheard.

Rae Anne sniffled, sneezed, and covered her lips with her napkin, hoping the face behind all the cameras would pick up a conversation on allergies, not become suspicious and begin some type of Dragon lip-reading program. "How many people left RTI lately?" she whispered, sipping her ice water.

Through the clanking of her cup on the saucer Mira said, "Fifteen, this week alone." She took a mouse-bite out of her sandwich, chewing behind her napkin. "Two a today, including Ginnie Reidel. The woman you interviewed with, the woman who was supposed to be your boss, but now I'm fulfilling that role." She began swirling the water in her glass as if she were about to take a stiff drink after having an extraordinarily tough day.

Strands of her salt-and-pepper hair had come lose around her temples; and after shoving a napkin under her paper plate, she brushed back her hair with her French-manicured nails and glared into a ceiling camera. She had a powerful poise about her—a spirited toughness. Rae Anne believed that if those burly bouncers whom she had met earlier in the day would have approached them now with intimidation, Mira would put them in place by staring them down.

Rae Anne wanted to tell her about the so called "bug" problem in her office, but then thoughts of Tim stopped her. Getting more information about *him* might help her decide whether she could really trust Mira. He was part of Sales and Markets, so asking Mira about that department would be a good lead in to knowing the truth about Tim. "How are sales at RTI lately?"

Mira's eyes ignited with enthusiasm. "Real good. We had a V.P. here about a week ago who did a fantastic job." She took another small bite of her sandwich, with a bitter expression on her face. Either her appetite had changed, or something was

Corporate Revenge

making her food look and taste awful.

Rae Anne perked up after swallowing a spoonful of her chicken soup. "RTI has an exceptional salesforce then, huh?"

"Fantastic," Mira said, "and we had a real go-getter, until someone from high up said RTI couldn't afford him anymore."

That's not what Tim had told Rae Anne; and after she sipped her coffee, she said: "I know some pretty good sales reps from Los Angeles. What's this person's name? Maybe I've heard of him."

Mira looked up at two employees who had just walked into the cafeteria. After they had passed her to get in the food line, she said: "Tim Westman. But I think he came from Denver, not L.A. Ever hear of him?" Her voice sounded eager, as if desiring to talk more of him.

Every part of Rae Anne wanted to burst out with: *He's my husband. We moved from Denver to Los Angeles to Carlsbad.* Instead she pushed the desire down into the pit of her stomach. "Nope, I never heard of him." Then she patted the corner of her eyes with her napkin to hide her excitement.

"You all right? You look suddenly pale!" Mira asked.

"Allergies," she whispered to Mira. "But you liked this Tim Westman though, huh?"

Mira shrugged and had a lost gleam in her eyes. "He sure worked hard. One of the best V.P. of Sales and Marketing we ever had." Then she leaned into Rae Anne as if embarking on a roller-coaster ride. "The guy brought in a hundred million in sales in less than four months! Can you believe that? A hundred million dollars! I don't think we could ship chips as fast as he was selling them!"

"Wow, really?" Rae Anne said, astounded at the accomplishment she already knew about but was struggling to keep secret. "He must have one great list of clients whom I could call concerning software then!"

"Oh yeah for sure...I'll try and get you the list he left for Ginnie." She paused with an expression of urgency showing on her face. She had spoken without thinking, and then she began hurriedly wrapping up her sandwich. "That office you're in now?"

"Yeah?" Rae Anne was sitting on the edge of her seat.

"His! It used to be *his* office…then Ginnie moved in there a few days ago." Mira sealed her sandwich. She glanced around the cafeteria as if someone had spilled something.

Rae Anne sat up straight. "What's wrong?" Fearing that her new identity might be exposed, she swept up her large purse from off the chair next to her and held it to her chest.

"Nothing, nothing," Mira gestured in embarrassment. "I just thought I saw someone I knew, but I was mistaken." She appeared to be haunted by a ghost! Then she settled back and smoothed out a few wrinkles on the sleeve of her blouse. Perhaps she hadn't washed off the black ink on her arm and was having an allergic reaction. Suddenly, she had tears in her eyes. "Ginnie left about an hour after you interviewed with her." She inhaled and began drinking her soda.

"Oh no," Rae Anne said, her throat stinging. "Why? What happened?" Glancing at a corner camera, she saw it direct at them. Mira suddenly stood up and put her sandwich in her purse. She had spotted the same red flashing camera, and she turned away from it, and shoved her chair into the table. People at the next table stopped everything, smiled at her, and then returned to their lunch. Rae Anne began following her around another table, toward the exit.

"Look, Mary," Mira began, walking shoulder-to-shoulder with her, "I really like you." She sniffled and appeared to have been crying and in hiding for hours.

"Thanks, I like you too, Mira." She felt relief! *A friend and ally at RTI!*

Mira cleared her throat, fanned her face with her hand, and peered suspiciously around the cafeteria. "I read about your background, the jobs you've had, and all your experience. I'll do my best to help you, Mary." Glancing down at the white floor, she whispered, "I don't want to see what happened to Ginnie happen to you."

Rae Anne felt a dark sadness overtake her. Mira was

Corporate Revenge

reaching out to her, trying to mentor her as she had supported Ginnie. Maybe not being able to say goodbye to Ginnie was like the death of a child to Mira, and Mira was stuck in the belief that she had done something wrong and was now trying to make up for her perceived mistake by confiding in her.

She remembered the moment she had helped Tim unpack the car after Steve Lerrefeiht had fired him. She remembered seeing all the boxes, stacked family photos, and the expressions of utter failure on his face. It was anguish to her. She couldn't even imagine what Ginnie was experiencing after having worked five years for RTI and then suddenly fired. She had to be in a pretty dark dismal place, and there was nothing anyone could do to help her.

Once someone's gone, they're gone...that's it. Those are the hard facts of life in the business world.

Coming to that conclusion, she hated having to stuff down her feelings of anger and resentment for RTI. She wished she could blurt them out right then and there! She hated having to be so inauthentic, so plastic, so fake, so impersonal. She also realized that she had to be those things in order to survive at RTI. She even had to keep up her fake persona around Mira, even now.

Communicating with her eyes directed at the camera, Mira said loudly with her arms waving as if she were a game show host introducing contestants: "We have so many *PowerPoint* slides to cover, and graphic presentation programs to install."

"What?!" They were right in the middle of having a friendly conversation and the topic changed so abruptly!

Giving Rae Anne a quick glance, Mira mouthed the word, "later," looked back into the camera, and said loudly, "The big corporate meeting is tomorrow and Mr. Lerrefeiht will be asking you to show all his ideas. We'll work on those after I meet you back at your office."

Rae Anne felt her blood pressure rise in her cheeks. She wanted to know more about what happened to Tim rather than compete with cameras for Mira's attention. Furthermore, she needed more time to scout around RTI, familiarize herself with the ten-story facility, and take a snap shot of its several directories. Doing actual work, time consuming code writing, would detract from her reconnaissance mission.

As they set their trays on top of the trash can along the wall, Rae Anne said: "You know…a spider bit me in my office earlier. I don't see any marks, but the bite sure stings!" She rubbed her arm, but she was really testing Mira to see what she might have to say about RTI's eavesdropping problem, and technology.

"I've encountered one of those bites myself," Mira whispered and winked; "but unlike *some* people, I know how to exterminate them before anyone notices they're gone." As her spoon clinked on the tray, she added, "Check under the desk." Then she thrust her napkin into the trash can as if pushing down her anger into the place where no one would notice. "There, I've helped you a little bit." She began walking with pride out of the cafeteria, embracing a little bit of the power that some high-level executive had stolen from her.

Returning to her office, Rae Anne looked under her desk. Way underneath the top drawer she spotted what looked like a small dime-sized spider. She poked it, and it emitted a *zzzztt* sound. It was indeed mechanical! The newest high-tech drone! Someone was spying on her. For the camera, she would pretend to search for something she had dropped. "Oh, here's that pencil I was looking for," she said. Trying to decide how best to quash the drone, she quickly grabbed a wad of Kleenex from on top of her desk and then snatched up the bug. "There you are! I gotchya before you could bite me!" She let it go on her desk. The moment she poked the tiny creature, it began to move—its tiny claws trying to burrow into the wood work. If she didn't something fast, the bug's creator, or the person monitoring her, would surely conclude that Rae Anne had discovered the technology. She would be in danger of losing her mission.

Taking off her shoe, she smashed the black body with her heal. Clear sticky goo, like butterfly blood, coalesced into a tiny pool on the shellacked surface of her desk. When she looked closely, she saw a green dot the size of small diamond. It looked so familiar. Picking the small stone up gently, she remembered the RTI pin Steve Lerrefeiht had given her in the cafeteria. Taking the pin off her lapel, she held it into the dull sunlight shining through her window. At the center of it, where the logo of a miniature computer was beaming radio rays, set the same tiny stone akin to the one she had discovered in the drone. The employee pins weren't just an RTI insignia and standard issue. They were spy gadgets!

She felt a wave of panic hit her. *Tim has one, and it's at the house! Isn't it?* Questions rushed through her brain: How far could their frequencies reach? From where were its creators monitoring employees? Was Tim's pin still active? She had fished it out nights ago from the spaghetti sauce. Perhaps slime had damaged its internal nano-structure. She felt an incoming heart attack as she tried to decide what to do while inhaling and exhaling and staring out the window. She had hours left of work...so many things to do for Lerrefeiht and her mission to take him down.

Now, she didn't know what to do with *her* pin. She had to wear it, so she put it back on her lapel; but she also grew furiously seething. RTI was spying on its employees even after hours, perhaps through some mobile system. Tonight, mostly likely, they'd be listening in on her and her children.

Another wave of panic hit her, and she began rummaging through her handbag. *Tim's pin...* In a little pocket, she felt it. She hadn't left it at home! Could Tim's pin still be active, and someone at RTI homing in on its signal? She wiped up the goopy eavesdropping drone and threw it into the trash can. She set the drone's shiny spy stone on the window sill. Picking up Tim's old RTI pin, she stepped on it, hoping to crush it, grinding the pin into the carpet. Lifting up her foot, she noticed no change in the steely edges of the small round pin.

This thing's almost indestructible! But I'll show it!

Putting Tim's pin next to the drone's spy stone on the window sill and wanting to blast the spy gadget to smithereens, she hammered away at it with her heel. When she saw shards of crystal slivers, she picked up a notebook. Using its edge as a broom, she brushed the shards into the waste basket and then covered them with more paper and Kleenex.

Mira began knocking on the door.

"Just a minute," Rae Anne called, dousing the papers with bottled water to ensure all the crystal flecks were covered. "Come in!"

When Mira bolted in, Rae Anne stood straight and tall. She smiled as she pushed her hair behind her ears. "I'm ready to get started on Steve's project," she said, taking in a deep breath, but also suspecting that other spy drones might crawl in on them from under the door or through the vent or in between the hinges.

"I brought some of Steve's slides so we can use them for tomorrow's presentation." Mira was looking around the office and set several flash drives next to Rae Anne's laptop.

The rest of the afternoon she spent working with Mira. She took two fifteen-minute breaks, during which she concealed herself out of the line of cameras while taking snap shots of several corridors, elevators, and directories. *Tonight, I'll memorize some names. Tomorrow, I'll search for proof of criminal activities.* When the clock struck 5:00 p.m., Rae Anne said goodnight to Mira who would spend another hour working with Steve on his presentation. Then she dashed out of the building, leaving her RTI pin spinning on her desk.

Corporate Revenge

Chapter 9 – Back Home

That night, after she put the children to bed, Tim called. "Rae Anne, you'll never believe who I ran into today up here at Ready Tech. And for God's sake, of all places, at an interview!" He was red-hot angry.

She felt as if a fish bone had lodged in her throat. That same old bodily numbness wafted through her. "Who did you run into?"

"Gene Mure. Gene Mure, Rae Anne!" Each word was like a dart hitting a bull's eye. "What they hell's going on down there in Carlsbad? You wouldn't believe what the guy told me!"

She had to answer him, had to tell him the truth, but it had to be at a low whisper and out of ear-shot of Carolyn who liked to sneak out of her room for snacks. "Just hold on, Tim. I can explain."

He cut her off. "You wouldn't believe the stuff that Gene character told me. Everything from you changing your identity to starting a new life! What the heck are you doing? Leaving me?" From then on, he hardly let her get in a word edgewise.

"Wait—Hold on, Tim—just a second—I can explain—"

"You're nuts, Rae Anne! You need a shrink, fast!" He coughed, choking on the air, and obviously disgusted at running into Gene Turner. "What kinda crazy scheme ya got going on down there? I don't even know you...maybe never really knew you! Who the hell are you anyway? And I'm leavin' ya with the kids! I—"

"Tim," she interrupted, "I went down to RTI. I have a job there."

"What?!" His breath seemed to blast through the receiver.

His anger was almost debilitating as she began pleading her case with him. "I needed Gene. He has contacts. He does some work with Witness Protection and he used to lead sting operations and bust up fraud rings." She had to align all the facts just right to make him see her perspective. "I had him create a new identity for me so I could get into RTI without anyone knowing I am your wife. It's the only way I can get into the company without being noticed so I can figure out what kind of fraud Steve Lerrefeiht is committing."

"Fraud?" He wasn't cursing at least now.

She continued: "From what little I've been able to glean today, on my first day on the job, Steve's criminal activity could be any number of schemes, from Cross-Border, to Advance Fee, to Investment Fraud, to a Ponzi scheme."

"Hmmm."

"Well? Tim? Do you understand what I'm doing now?"

He laughed. "What you're doing is sheer nonsense, Rae!"

Her heart sank. She was going to correct him, strong and to the contrary. "Actually, it's not stupid nonsense, *Tim*." She pulled out her flash drive and inserted it into their computer.

"How isn't it?"

"I got a hold of your old computer in the IT lab." Through his gasps, she continued: "I'm downloading all your email now onto *our* computer. I'll even create a link so you can access the information."

"What good will doing all that that accomplish, Rae?" he asked. "Just cut out all your monkey business, now. Don't go in tomorrow. I'll call Ginnie Reidel and try to smooth things over with her."

"She's not there anymore, Tim."

Corporate Revenge

"What?"

Rae Anne remembered that she was saying that same word all day long. "Yeah, Ginnie's not there. She's gone. Like what happened to you, someone fired her shortly after she moved into your office." Then she unleashed the entire day's events onto him, from the moment she walked into RTI to the second she merged on the I-5 toward home. "Now I have your old desk. And while taking a few snap shots of the directories, two burly men who look like mercenary soldiers began following me, until I showed them my Confidential Security Clearance."

"God—I know them! They could make ya disappear before ya walk out the door, Rae!"

"Then there was a new high-tech drones I discovered under your desk, Tim." She told him how she had smashed its spyware stone into bits on the window sill.

"What? They were watching my every move?!" He was infuriated.

"Yeah, the pin you brought home had nano-spyware in it too. The company is spying on, and monitoring, its employees after hours, Tim. I don't know how intensely they're keeping track of people or what information they're wanting by eavesdropping on people, but that in itself is completely illegal."

"Yeah, I know, Rae, but—"

"Don'tchya get it?" she argued. "This is serious bad stuff! And I'm gonna expose it to the authorities." She could have taken those two spy-stones to the FBI, but that wouldn't have been proof enough to dethrone such a corporate conglomerate. She needed plans, and designs, and more evidence: tangible proof of RTI's fake Swiss company. She was prepared to let Tim in on all her plans if necessary.

Tim responded, "Uh-huh, I get it, but I don't know about your methods of exposing Steve and his team though."

She could hear car sounds on his end of the phone. He was calling her from a restaurant. At least he had calmed down, and she had his attention. "RTI owes you, no us, a big commission, Tim. If we can prove that Steve, or someone from RTI is committing fraud, we can expose them, get a lawyer, and sue for your commission."

"Huh!" he said. "What you're talking about is revenge. I only have one thing to say about that, or I should say the Chinese philosopher Confucius had one thing to say: *Before you embark on a journey of revenge, dig two graves.* Try to remember that when you are digging around RTI, Rae. Just know, I don't agree with this...I'm really scared for you."

Again she heard "crazy" in the tone of his voice. Tim was probably right. Steve Lerrefeiht the sociopath, of course, would continue a life of destruction. Eventually, he would target the wrong person or seriously break the law. He'd get caught, in the future. Then, someone would certainly contact Tim to find out what he knows about the disordered individual. Tim could then describe his experience and provide evidence to show Steve's bad patterns of behavior. In the future, he could see justice served: whether that satisfaction would come from seeing Steve prosecuted, exposed in the media, or just ruining his or her efforts with yet another potential victim.

Rae Anne wanted justice now. "This isn't stupid, Tim, and I'm not nuts." The computer download had finished, and she clicked open one of Steve's his emails to Tim. "Here's one email exchange between you and Steve. It talks about that suspicious Hermes Trading & Cie you discussed."

"Rae Anne, RTI is known for their impossible to crack and tamper proof security system," Tim cautioned; "however, most security experts will agree that the ease of defeating a security device or system is proportional to how confident and arrogant the company is about it, and how often they use words like *impossible* or *tamper-proof* to describe it. There may be some backdoor or flaw in the RTI system, but you're an amateur, Rae, you'll get caught for sure."

She felt the chill of the night air roll through her curtains as she yawned and lay down for bed. Soon she'd have to hang up. She needed sleep, lots of it! Tomorrow would be one of

Corporate Revenge

the most important days of her life. "Tim, look it's late—"

"That Hermes Trading & Cie company just doesn't make any sense," he said, the tone of his voice inquisitive. He wanted to know more. She had him intrigued! "But RTI is shipping all their products through them. It's a Swiss Investment and trading company, protected by all the Swiss privacy laws."

Getting out of bed, she dashed to her computer and clicked on the icon of all his downloaded email from RTI. She discovered an email dated two days ago, *after* Steve had fired him. "Listen to this, Tim. I found a letter from a company called Lord Howe Manufacturing, Inc., requesting the shipment of Steve's new sensors that you sold to them."

"Yeah," he said, "I remember that deal I put together about two months ago. I booked $2,000,000 in sales with Lord Howe."

"But here's the problem." She grabbed the paper after it printed out and began reading the details. "Giles Magnant, a receiving clerk at Lord Howe, says he opened one of the boxes and discovered faulty non-working sensor chips."

"Faulty packages?" Tim sounded dumbfounded. "No one would do something like that, not even RTI!" He was on the verge of having a conniption fit. "MiniScribe tried a stunt similar to that 1989. It shipped bricks to a holding company instead of finished product in order to close a deal. They intended to recall the bricks after they finished manufacturing, and to replace them with a finished product, but they got caught."

"This is the proof of fraud at RTI then, right?" she asked, extending Tim's email under the lamp shade, the paper rustling as she tried to read all the fine details.

Again he gave out a deep sigh. "Actually, not Rae Anne. You need proof. No one knows where the U.S. offices of Hermes Trading & Cie are located. It's like a back door that leads to a million other doors on the internet, all cloaked in secrecy. The company sounds like one horrible feedback loop. The only way to blow RTI clear out of the water is to have a box of faulty sensor packages in hand with the Hermes Trading & Cie address stamped on top."

"In hand? To deliver to the police then?" she asked, sitting back at the computer and looking for more emails that could expose fraud.

"I'm telling you Rae Anne, what you're trying to do—although I understand—is pretty far-fetched and dangerous. If Steve Lerrefeiht, or whoever is behind this whole scam finds out, your life could be in jeopardy."

"Come on, Tim—"

"I mean it, Rae Anne!" Concern was abounding in his words. "People disappear over these kinds of whistleblowing issues. Their bodies are discovered in landfills and at the bottom of oceans." He was whispering in fast-paced urgency. "Back out of your plan *now*, Rae Anne."

"But I just need one more day, Tim," she said, typing quickly and moving the computer mouse. She opened up several images of the photos she had taken. "I saw the chip-assembly line on the fourth floor. I know I can get my hands on one of those faulty sensor chip packages." She gulped back tears. This was everything she wanted to do for her life, a monumental moment that would give her purpose. He didn't understand her calling. "Just one more day—"

"I know your one day deals, Rae Anne. They turn into two, three—"

"All right maybe two days." Before he could argue more she said: "Just think of Ginnie Reidel, and some of the other people Mira told me about who have been fired. And all the illegal bugging RTI's doing. The law suits we could file could help maybe fifty or more fired employees and their families." She felt out of breath, the situation more than urgent. "Children are being hurt by RTI, and we need to find out who exactly is responsible for families who are suffering."

"Gee, Rae Anne, I don't know," he said.

She could picture his usual gesture when he was saying such things: rubbing his neck while turning his head to the side. The deep consequences of corruption were pinching his nerves

Corporate Revenge

and he was working hard to stop the onslaught.

"Two days, Rae Anne. That's it," he told her.

She gasped in relief: "You won't be sorry, Tim. I promise!"

"*Two*, Rae Anne. No more. Then I forbid you to do any more spy stuff," his said.

That word *forbid* made her lungs flare. "What did you just say? You can't—"

"You contacted your ex, Rae." His resentment was boiling. "Him, not me about our problems."

"I tried to—"

"You went to *him*, Rae. The guy's a complete jerk, who abused you." She heard him sniffle. She had hurt him. "I'm beginning to think we might be over, Rae."

"Tim, don't say that!" Everything around her faded to white as she plopped down in her chair, staring at her new website that Gene had issued to her to reinvent herself.

"I have to think that there's some reason for you to call this—this *jerk* instead of confiding in me." Another long pause ensued as she tried to think of reasons why Tim should change his mind. "Just think about what you did, Rae Anne, 'cause I'm sure as heck pissed off about you even talking to this—this Gene creep." She could hear chattering as if people were calling him to dinner. "Two days Rae. I'll call you then."

She clutched the phone in desperation: "I love you, Tim!"

He hung up.

Pinching the bridge of her nose, she sank low in her chair, feeling like the person in Rodin's *Thinking Man* sculpture. She believed to be on the verge of losing everything that mattered, and feeling too small to stop it. "Now what am I gonna do?" Half the night she popped awake, repeating the same thing over and over until 6:30 a.m., when she woke up and told her reflection in the mirror: "We go in again today! We find secrets and nab what we need today!"

J.P. Osterman

Chapter 10 – Day 2

After hugging Carolyn goodbye and dropping Joey off at preschool, she returned to RTI. As a precautionary measure, she did one thing different from yesterday: She rented a car so she wouldn't have to worry about parking lot surveillance.

On her walk down the long corridor to the bank of elevators at the opposite end of the building, a tall blond woman who looked like a loan officer at a bank approached her before she could take the elevator to her office. "Ms. Hershel, Ms. Padeson would like to see you in her office ASAP!" The woman seemed hurried and frantic. An important event was about to happen, but Rae Anne knew she wasn't late. "I'm Maggie Woodrow. Mira told me to be on the look-out for you." She gestured for Rae Anne to move faster.

Rae Anne believed she might be fired. "Is something wrong, Ms. Woodrow?"

"My Heaven's no," she said, then telling Rae Anne to call her Maggie. "A few of the top execs want to meet with you in Ms. Padeson's office before Mr. Lerrefeiht's big corporate presentation." Onto the elevator they walked, where Rae Anne noticed a sign next to the top button. Tim had ignored the sign that he believed had gotten him into trouble, and lead to

Corporate Revenge

Steve Lerrefeiht firing him.

The sign read: 7th Floor – Limited Access: Special Clearance Required.

Turning to Rae Anne and batting her long black eyelashes, Maggie had an envious expression on her face. Perhaps she had vied for Rae Anne's position but had lost it. "It looks like you'll be working with Steve, Thornton Manning, Claude Filmer and Kent Smith this morning, Mary." The closing elevator door created a vacuum that burst a shot of air into their faces.

Feeling trapped, Rae Anne wanted to choke on Maggie's gardenia scented perfume as the elevator *hummed* up to the third floor. She realized she'd have to face each one of those men whom Maggie just named at some point during her brief stint at RTI, and she balked at having to work for all three of them at the same time, and at the spur of the moment, when yesterday she believed she would only be working for one of them. She was so confused.

Glancing at her watch, she noticed the time: 8:32 a.m. Yesterday, before she left after work, Mira told her that the big corporate meeting would be at 10, but she didn't tell Rae Anne the location of the meeting. Rae Anne was hoping it would be on the fourth floor. From there, she could find quick and unmonitored route out of that area, take the elevator to the 7th floor, infiltrate the Plexiglas chip-fab lab, and nab a package of fake computer chips. That's all she needed, just a little proof of fraud to bring Steve Lerrefeiht down.

After entering Mira's plush and comfortable office, Maggie left like a whirlwind after a storm. Mira came out of a hallway leading to her office, and stood beneath the door frame. "Plans have change, Mary."

"What?" Rae Anne felt stymied.

You'll be working for Kent Smith for the next hour." Her chest rose high and her eyes grew wide. "Watch out for him," she whispered. An employee passed by, and Mira greeted her with a feigned smile.

"What should I watch out for?" Rae Anne whispered back.

J.P. Osterman

"I told you I was going to help you, right?" Her breath appeared heated on her lips.

Rae Anne feared that her spy-cover was blown. She felt a flush of panic hit her arms that began shaking. She concealed her hands behind her back. "Yes, right, Mira, you did tell me you were going to help me," she whispered. Then, she remembered yesterday. Mira was upset that Steve had fired Ginnie. Perhaps last night, Mira had talked to Ginnie. Perhaps she had gleaned from her some of the mistakes that Ginnie had made and was now trying to help Rae Anne avert them and keep her job. She had to remain focused, unwavering in emotion, and steadfast in her new stoic personality.

Mira looked as if she had spent the entire morning on assignment incognito. Yesterday, she had her graying long hair pulled back without one straggling strand. She was model perfect. Today she appeared a big ragged, as if she had tried on a dozen outfits, and her wrinkled suit looked like it had just come out of a suitcase. Facing the front door—and cameras— she smoothed down her hair and her suit; and when she turned around and faced Rae Anne, Rae Anne believed a miracle had been performed. Mira looked perfectly groomed and ready for corporate action. Compared to her, she felt inferior and incapable.

Leaning into Rae Anne, Mira said, "Watch everything you do, what you say, and who you talk to." She twirled around and whipped off her blazer, holding it high in the air as if she were showing a flag to a crowd. Anyone monitoring the scene would have surmised that she was taking off her blazer because she was hot. Rae Anne knew she was buying time to talk to her in secret.

"Why should I watch everything and everyone?" Rae Anne asked. "What's going on? Tell me."

Mira was panting. Close up, the ashen circles under her eyes and the pasty hue on her cheeks made her appear worn out and defeated. "I'm trying to get Ginnie reinstated. That's what I'm working on." Wiggling as if she were trying to fit into a tight pair of jeans, she had her arms stuffed half way inside her blazer. "I'm working to find out exactly who fired her and why."

When Mira finally managed to put on her blazer, she lifted her hair over her collar and smoothed it back with her fingers. "I have a few people pulling some information from accounting on the sixth floor. Ginnie noticed some discrepancies on the seventh floor."

"The chip-fab lab we walked through yesterday," Rae Anne said.

"Yes, she talked to a few people in Accounting. She spotted some discrepancies over numbers and orders. She talked to Accounting over the landline, from inside *your* new office."

"Did she tell you about those discrepancies *before* she left RTI?" Rae Anne asked. *Tim could have been involved then as well. Tim might be able to help.*

"No, she told me last night when I called her." Mira smoothed down her sleeves. "But she did tell Steve something that really made him angry."

"What?" Rae Anne recalled the pompous attitude he had given Ginnie yesterday. That cold shoulder was his way of detaching from his employees before firing them. He had been the opposite with her, treating her so cordially and fawningly after hiring her. He was the master of facial language rather than verbal expression. If an employee couldn't read him right, or discern his thoughts, that employee was gone. He was expecting the impossible—the sociopath's modus operandi.

"I guess Ginnie misunderstood what Steve had told her to do," Mira began, "but that can happen to anyone though, right?" She breathed out a sigh of fear. She appeared terrified of making the same mistake even though she had survived at RTI for years. Obviously, Steve needed her...and had been using her as one of his pawns for a while. Only now was she growing suspicious of him.

Rae Anne hated the confusion. "Well, of course

misperceptions happen all the time! I mean, people aren't mind readers. I can't know what you're thinking and feeling unless you tell me." She pulled the straps of her handbag up to her neck and then folded her arms. "Or, maybe Ginnie accidentally came across some information that she wasn't supposed to." Now she was getting close to blowing her cover. She didn't want that, but she *did* need Mira's protection to continue on her whistleblowing mission. "That Accounting section might hold the key for you to help Ginnie, or perhaps the answer to her getting fired is in Ginnie's old computer that most likely at IT."

Mira's eyes rounded in revelation. "That's it! That's where I'll look. Thanks!" A perturbed expression appeared in her eyes. "I didn't think of Ginnie's iPad and laptop, darn it!"

Peeking around the door and glancing around Mira's plush office, Rae Anne scanned for items that could contain more spider-ware drones. She didn't want to risk any more of their conversation being overhead. Every object enlarged in her line of sight: from pencil sharpeners to a computer mouse; from metal paper holders to the corners of file cabinets. Nothing was safe. At that point, she opened her mouth to tell Mira that she was an ally, and she could count on her to keep secrets, but she stopped short of speaking. She couldn't tell Mira her true identity yet. Too much was at stake to compromise her mission. *Take him down, down, down and get even.*

But she could do one thing to help Mira, and Ginnie. After they walked over to Mira's desk and began discussing the graphic portion of the Steve upcoming meeting, she slipped behind Mira's desk, took a post-it note from its dispenser, and jotted down the website Tim had given her. After folding the paper containing the name, *Hermes Trading & Cie*, she slid it in the top drawer and then walked out of the office with Mira. Then she acted as if nothing had happened. "Where are we heading?"

As they entered the elevator, Mira nodded upward. "The top floor."

"Top floor? The tenth floor?" Rae Anne wanted to shove

Corporate Revenge

open the door and dash out.

Mira laughed and gently grabbed her arm. Rae Anne surmised she was reassuring her that she wouldn't be alone. She felt goose bumps on her arms as she pointed at the sign. "Mira, the signs says I need a special RTI clearance. I don't have any such clearance like that yet." Tim said he'd been fired because of that mistake in accessing that tenth floor, as well as other reasons. At least he was right about giving her *this* reason for being fired; and from now on, she couldn't consider him a liar.

"Steve's already transitioned you to the RTI Clearance because you're part of System Architecture and I need your input," she replied in a whisper. She reached around the line of sight to the camera. She touched the lens with her forefinger. Obviously, her finger had a special blocking agent. Now, they were alone on the elevator, and so early for the presentation. Other employees were incoming at the parking lot or still discussing their duties on the first floor.

Rae Anne rubbed her arms and then touched the flash drive she had tucked inside her cuff. She had plans for the flash drive later on. "I know I had a clearance from my old job, and Steve mentioned that it transferred, but this new RTI clearance is so confusing. I wonder what Research and Development is doing that they can't even inform the government."

"He needs you to have the clearance, that's it. Steve told me this morning that you're good-to-go and that R and D cleared you," she replied tartly.

Her tone wasn't negative, just angry, and a little spiteful. It told her what she had already known about him. Steve Lerrefeiht was extremely charming and charismatic. He always got what he wanted. His personality was described as magnetic; and as such, he generated a lot of attention and praise from others, the proof of his charisma was the Fortune magazine article about him. While Steve liked the attention, he was incapable of experiencing guilt or shame for his actions. Unaware of the emotional, physical, and financial repercussions he was wreaking on the lives of others—without any forethought of his actions—he would routinely betray, threaten, or fire the people who dared to disagree with him, or by whom he felt threatened, without remorse.

Rae Anne knew this *special clearance* would grant her entry into Steve Lerrefeiht's private fiefdom.

Mira had a sly look in her eyes, took out her iPhone, and opened an application. "I know we were talking about accessing the Accounting department, but while you were at my desk, doing a little writing, I received a message from corporate."

That puzzled Rae Anne. She saw their current location in the elevator: passing the third story. "I thought *this* San Diego location *is* corporate headquarters."

Mira laughed a bit. "Oh my no. Corporate is located in Georgia, but someone high up in the ladder told me to give this to you as part of Steve's presentation."

When Rae Anne saw the black iPhone that looked brand new, she asked, "What do I do with this?"

The iPhone tune jingled and turned on.

"Link the iPhone to your laptop *after* you sit down at the desk they give you," Mira ordered.

Instead of an application initializing on the iPhone, Rae Anne saw instructions: "When you get to your seat, beneath it you will find a flash drive taped at the bottom edge. When the north-east corner camera light blinks twice - then stops - then blinks twice again, put the flash drive into your laptop's USB port and type the password, comet tail. The lights will extinguish throughout the building. The power to the wafer fab will continue as well as the IT server farm, allowing Georgia's mainframe to interface with San Diego's servers and download some information to Accounting that Steve Lerrefeiht has kept secret. In ten minutes, the download will be over."

"Understand?" Mira asked, in a secretive voice.

"Perfectly," Rae Anne replied, closing the program and jamming the iPhone into her purse. She would have ten

Corporate Revenge

minutes of dark time. Mira would have ten minutes to do what *she* needed to do, while Rae Anne could access that seventh floor, chip-fab lab and grab and go what *she* needed.

The ticking countdown on her mission would soon start, and the pace of her mission of discovery was accelerating. She was aiding a group of employees she had never met, including people from a corporate office she hadn't realized even existed. Her anxiety was increasing exponentially. She didn't know which would be worse, the thought of Tim possibly divorcing her, or being accused of participating in some type of corporate corruption. Who were all these people with whom Mira was secretly conversing? She wanted to expose RTI, but not be part of some fraud scheme! *What the hell am I getting myself into?*

When she turned to Mira to tell her that, Mira touched her arm and smiled. "Someone *big* is coming from the corporate office in Georgia. I know you're feeling confused."

"Sure am!"

"But trust me…I want to get Ginnie her job back," Mira said.

Rae Anne had more planned that just that. "Okay, go on."

Mira gestured at Rae Anne's large handbag, now the seat of her plan as well. "Those instructions came directly from RTI's highest executive level," she whispered.

"When's corporate arriving?" Rae Anne asked.

"I'm not sure," Mira replied, "but in any event, since you're the one in that meeting who is in charge of facilitating the presentation, I'm going to be holding down the fort back on my floor.

"Okay," Rae Anne said.

"At least through me, and anonymously, corporate has picked *you* to initiate the program that's linked to RTI's San Diego servers."

Rae Anne was now more puzzled than ever, completely caught off guard. Something big was going on. She sensed something great was on the verge of happening, and she had only just begun working at RTI. Were they trying to make her a hero? Or was she to be the next scape goat?

Glancing around as if she had been suddenly dropped at a haunted house, Rae Anne took a step back. The elevator appeared to stall on the fourth floor! So many questions were flashing through her brain, and so many things could go wrong—right smack dab at the center of all of RTI's corporate executives. Another thought occurred to her. Maybe the requisition to hire her didn't originate in Steve Lerrefeiht's office, but at the corporate office in Georgia. She could easily see how her skills at being a hacker would help secure her position as Assistant Director of System Architecture. Perhaps they wanted someone from the outside, and her job was more secure than she originally thought.

The elevator stopped on the fifth floor, and as some employees shuffled out, Mira whispered: "When you feel stuck, look up to the corner camera. I have that corner camera patched through to my computer. I'll be with you each and every step of the way."

Turning quickly to Mira's ear, layered over with gray strands of hair, Rae Anne whispered, "How?"

Their conversation still muffled by all the elevator noise, Mira said askance at her: "When you see the red eye of the camera flash twice, insert the flash drive. The lights should go our right after you tap, *enter*."

"Flash drive, then *enter*, then lights out, right," Rae Anne said, nodding and enunciating each word.

"Comet tail!" Mira's line-of-vision was darting everywhere. "Don't forget, *comettail*, the words together without a space between them, is the password!"

"Got it…comet tail is the password," Rae Anne repeated.

Then Mira turned to face the door. Obviously, the solution she had used to block the lens had evaporated or deteriorated. Now Security could see them and as well as read their lips.

The door was beginning to close on the fifth floor. "But who from corporate is coming, Mira? What's going to happen when that person arrives?"

Surrounded by warm elevator bodies, Mira said, "The

Corporate Revenge

original founder of the company. That's all I can tell you right now." Gazing at the beige elevator tile, she went silent, and motioned for Rae Anne to maintain silence as well. That's all Mira could say, without the cameras catching her.

Rae Anne remembered what Tim had told her: No RTI employee had ever seen or heard of Justin Phillips. He was a ghost, with only a blank plaque for a name at the end of RTI's Walk of Fame at the entrance. That rumor wasn't true. Mira must know Justin Phillips, and Rae Anne might meet Justin Phillips soon. Would he arrest her, or shake her hand? She had to act quickly when the light extinguished to fulfill her plan and have proof of corruption or other criminal acts before the lights re-illuminated after that ten-minute darkness.

When they reached the tenth floor, Mira brushed her out into the corridor. "Go straight down to the right until you reach the carved oak double doors. Claude Filmer will tell you what to do next." Glancing up into the camera, she said, "I have all the programs we worked on yesterday up and running." As the door closed, she winked at Rae Anne and smiled. "I'll call you during the break to see how things are going."

As the elevator closed with a thud, Rae Anne felt dizzy, as if someone had spun her around with a blindfold over her eyes. What kind of game have I gotten myself into? Where is this presentation supposed to take place? Here, or on another floor?

More than ever she was puzzled about who might be showing up from RTI's corporate headquarters in Georgia. Hearing the noise of rollers on a dolly, she looked down the long white corridor and noticed men in uniforms rolling out huge boxes from another chip-fab lab at the end of the corridor. She saw the words, *Fl-10 to H. T. & C.*, on the sides of those boxes. Most likely, those huge boxes contained the faulty sensor chips RTI was shipping to Hermes Trading & Cie. The men were making round trips from the chip-fab lab on the seventh floor to another room down the hall.

Taking out her camera phone, she held it behind her purse.

J.P. Osterman

As she was about to snap a picture, a woman dressed in a white lab coat came up to her from behind. "May I help you, Ma'am? You look lost."

Startled, Rae Anne turned and shook the technician's hand. "I'm Mary Hershel, a new assistant to…to Mira Padeson." Ginnie was gone, so she had to be reporting directly to Mira.

"By all means proceed then, Ms. Hershel…'cause I believe I read the memo about you since we'll be collaborating in testing chips together sometime in the future," the woman said; "but to get any closer to the delivery going down to the seventh floor, you'll need Mr. Filmer's personal signature on the shipment's roster."

Rae Anne stepped back but slid slowly toward the large room that appeared overwhelming. She had to get a solid view of it and a snapshot; furthermore, if she could capture Claude Filmer in the room next to some of those boxes, that would be an added piece of evidence. "Thanks, I'm heading to Mr. Filmer's office right now."

"See you at the presentation later," the woman said. "I'm part of the Testing team here at RTI, so a few of my team will hear Mr. Lerrefeiht's presentation." The woman proceeded to tell Rae Anne more about her job…

Suddenly, Rae Anne heard a group of technicians talking behind her. One mentioned H. T. & C., and she began eavesdropping on their conversation while trying to stay focused on this woman's description of her job and her schedule. She overheard one vital piece of information: Several boxes would be opened at the chip-fab lab on the seventh floor. All the chips hadn't yet been processed! Their next point in the Architectural Design process would be at that site she had visited yesterday with Mira, on the seventh floor. She could nab one of the faulty chips there! However, she remembered the cameras—monitors in that white corridor were strategically positioned everywhere in the chip-fab lab. She then contrived a plan: *I'll make it a contest, see if I can do it 'cause I know I can find a way to infiltrate that place!*

After she said goodbye to the lab tech, she slowly passed

Corporate Revenge

the sliding doors to the large room, and snapped several pictures. Thus far, she hadn't seen Claude Filmer. Too bad, because if she had, she could implicate him in criminal activity. The room was as a small warehouse with opaque windows. It had rows of large boxes with the H. T. & C. symbols ready for shipping. At the back of the room stood a fork lift, with workers preparing to start their jobs for the day. Obviously, this room had a private elevator leading straight to the first floor. While finding a parking space, she remembered seeing a large docking bay at the south end of the building. That's where they were quickly transitioning the boxes to trucks, and then to RTI's corporate airplane. She had to grab one of the contents from one of those boxes on the seventh floor *after* they left this warehouse or she'd never have a chance of getting any proof of faulty chips. From what Tim had told her and what she had been able to glean in her short time at RTI, those boxes had to contain the false sensor chips RTI was sending to Hermes Trading & Cie. They were coming from the chip-fab lab straight down the hall. If she could just nab one chip out of the box, she could quickly test its validity; and if fake, then high-tail it out of RTI and never look back.

To do that, she would have to create some sort of huge diversion to get inside the lab on the seventh floor. She had learned from the lab tech that Steve's presentation was at the opposite end of the tenth floor. *Tenth floor to the seventh floor…that's three floors, and about a five minute ride on the elevator.* She'd have to make a quick escape from the seventh floor, use her disguises in her handbag, and dodge buff security guards and lots of cameras. She wondered how she could ever accomplish all of that before the boxes of chips were shipped! Everything felt so overwhelming, each task insurmountable. With lightning-flash quickness, she shoved her mini-camera into the side pocket of her handbag.

When she reached the end of the hallway, a door on the right flew open, and a man rushed in front of her. She jumped back as if facing dinosaur teeth. It was Claude Filmer, the V.P. of Contracts whom she had met yesterday. Only his initials were on the door: C. F., V.P. of C., the title hard to understand, unless he meant for his office to be difficult to locate. Or he could have many suspicious offices!

Filmer squinted to read her name on her tag. "Oh, good morning, Ms. Hershel."

"Good morning, Sir," she said, following him to the Executive Conference Room. "Mira sent me to meet you before the presentation. She thought you might have more instructions for me prior to the presentation." She took out a flash drive from her purse, making sure she'd nabbed the blue-tipped one with Steve's presentation, and then she gave it to him. "Ms. Padeson and I worked yesterday to make this Power Point for Mr. Lerrefeiht. This copy's for you, Mr. Filmer."

"Thanks!" He began rubbing it nervously between his fingers as he continued to ramble on about the presentation. He had a crooked smile and duck tail haircut, the tail of which was curled over his back collar. He began telling her today's schedule of events and the various presenters. When he turned to talk to her, she noticed dark wrinkles under his eyes and cadaverous skin. He had to have been drinking heavily into the wee hours of the morning, he looked so malnourished.

When they approached a private elevator in the middle of the north-facing wall, he suddenly stopped. "This isn't supposed to be shut!" He walked inside, checking the elevator's status.

This was another time she could use to her advantage as she took out her iPhone and told him she was receiving an incoming message from Mira. She wasn't, and instead tapped the camera app that turned on, ready for a video recording. After attaching her phone strategically to her handbag, she pushed the record icon. Her hands were free. He couldn't suspect anything.

Obviously satisfied that no one had interrupted the elevator's automatic schedule, he quickly imprinted his code to close it: 23872. The elevator paused with its doors fully open. "There, only executives can take this one because of the

Corporate Revenge

overcrowding that tends to happen in all the *staff* elevators."

"Sure, of course, Mr. Filmer." She quickly stopped the recording and shoved her phone into her large handbag.

They were now at the north section of the tenth floor and had arrived at the Executive Conference Room. The entryway was lined with grand double doors and ornate trim. Peering past the Reception Area, she noticed a theater type interior with a large IMAX screen. The sign above one of the doors read, *500 Maximum Capacity.* Definitely the room could accommodate executives, departmental heads, and any select clients. This was also the place new customers could come if they needed confidential information on any of RTI's special products.

"We have about forty-five minutes before *the staff* enters the conference area, so help yourself to some breakfast," he said, motioning at a breakfast bar.

She realized what Claude Filmer meant when he said the words, "the staff." Everyone below RTI's top-fifty executives were condescendingly considered *staff* in their hierarchical corporate ladder. Filmer was now constantly glancing at his Rolex. His body language turned dismissive as his iPhone began jingling with an incoming call. As he began whispering into his phone, she spotted Steve Lerrefeiht enter the Reception area with a few more high-level executives walking behind him. They had to be heads of more departments and customers. Their ID badges were all different.

As she poured herself a glass of water, she inspected Claude Filmer from head to toe. She began seething with anger. She remembered how she first felt about him after Tim had told her he was fired. She wanted so badly to retaliate against him. He was the V.P. of *all* Contracts, the one who had to be responsible for the fraudulent packaging of the sensor chips, or who was one of its money-grubbing masterminds. With complete indifference, he had cheated Tim out of his commission. As she ate a few bites of breakfast, chewing hard, she noticed Filmer standing in the corner, talking slyly to some executives. He had his hands by his sides and his body was tipping forward in a goofy posture whenever he was emphasizing an opinion. Indeed, with his three-piece suit of shiny, pin-striped, 160-thread-count Italian wool suit, he looked like a comedy-club comedian.

With the smells of cherry jelly, coffee, and white frosting circling through the room, Rae Anne pulled her blazer tight around her chest and shoved her handbag snugly under her arm. She felt as if she were concealing a pistol, not a camera and disguises prepped and ready for spy work. She kept itemizing them in her mind, including all the places where she had hidden them inside her purse.

A line of starch-groomed employees walked through the grand wooden doors. They began helping themselves to pastries. The reception area was bright with large recessed lights in the ceiling. She wondered if they were also cameras, or if spider-ware drones were attached somewhere along the inside edges. One thing the employees had in common was their secretive whispers. She hated that, and from eavesdropping on their conversations, she gleaned they weren't supportive of one another, but terrified of losing their jobs, and always on the lookout for competitive advantages.

A Hispanic man said with his lips covered in apple strudel sauce, "I think Harvey Wallace is making us work overtime and overheating our cubicles just so we'll quit."

Talking into her glass of orange juice, another employee replied, "If RTI keeps pressuring us to work under all these hostile conditions, I wouldn't be surprised if someone commits suicide right inside this place!"

That scared Rae Anne; and just as she was about to say something to help the person, she spotted a small stack of special executive badges at the corner of the table. Claude Filmer must have accidentally set them there while waiting to give them to a high-level employee. *That badge can give me access to any room, Smart-card reader, or key-pad-protected facility at RTI!* Furthermore, she had Filmer's passcode if she'd need it. She'd only need to tap open the video she had taken of Filmer at the private elevator.

Corporate Revenge

The badges were now like *shining* diamonds! This was her chance to act. *But do I have time?*

She checked her watch: 9:14 a.m. She had about forty-five minutes before she had to enter the big conference room, help run Lerrefeiht's presentation, and work Mira's covert plan. She needed just *one* of those chips. And taking one of Filmer's special badges to access special places would surely send of a massive hunt if he'd discover it missing. Feeling discouraged, she suddenly perked up when she saw a batch of RTI coasters. Their red edges appeared to blend it with Filmer's special executive badges. Grabbing a few, she began smoothing the paper coasters together into one flat pancake. Walking in front of Filmer's badges, she reached for the sugar, but instead lifted them off the table, and then set her coaster invention at the bottom. She stuffed the one she had stolen up her sleeve as a magician would a card. Unless Filmer would flip through those badges, he'd never know that the one she placed on the bottom was fake. Still, she didn't have much time, and she also had to cover herself.

"Where's the restroom?" she asked the Hispanic man.

He pointed in the direction of the elevator. "Down the corridor, before the private elevator."

From the logo on his badge, the man was part of Testing. "If Mr. Filmer asks about my whereabouts, can you please tell him I have a change to the presentation and am quickly running to my officer?"

He appeared reluctant, "I—well—"

"I'll text him as well," she shrugged, "but leaving right now isn't a big deal, and we still have quite a bit of time before ten."

He sighed. "Okay...Mary," he said, his eyesight homing in on her badge.

"Thanks!" Before leaving, she took off her little "bugged" RTI pin and stuck it behind a tiered platter filled with pastries. With her hands in her pockets and maintaining a calm disposition, she slid out of the reception area and began walking toward the private elevator. Passing employees along the way, she smiled, greeting them; all the while, she kept her eyes focused on the long white walls and checker-board tile. She didn't want to attract suspicion by glancing into any cameras.

In the restroom, she quickly doffed her suit and put on her new dress and black wig. She took off her earrings and ring, but didn't change her blazer. She had to wear it to maintain a professional appearance. On it, she affixed the special RTI badge she stole from Claude Filmer, and then she buttoned up her dress to her neck to disguise herself as much as possible. Rolling up her skirt and blouse neatly so as to avoid wrinkles, she put them and her accessories inside a double-plastic bag and tucked the bag behind the large toilet tank so she could access them quickly later.

After putting on a pair of reading glasses, she wiped off her maroon lipstick, dabbed on peach-colored lipstick, and then dashed out of the stall, briefly grooming herself in front of a long mirror. Taking in a relieving breath of air, she began inspecting herself. She had to make sure she had concealed each and every strand of her hair beneath her black wig. She noticed how ridiculous she looked, more like an older woman trying to pass as a college student. Her eyes were the size of green buttons under her fake reading glasses, and her long-haired wig looked a bit frizzy like a hippie's hairdo after a long night of partying. And besides, the wig kept rolling off her head. She forgot hair pins, so she'd have to keep adjusting it while on her covert mission to the seventh floor chip-fab lab. "I look like a mannequin," she said to her reflection. "God— can I succeed at pulling this off?"

She glanced at the time: 9:19 a.m. She started her stop watch. The bobbing second hand boomed like an exploding bomb in her brain.

"Time's running out," she whispered to her reflection. *Who will win…Filmer or me? I'm gonna win!* "Go!"

With her handbag tight under her arm, she retrieved Filmer's code from her iPhone. Arriving at the elevator, she quickly entered, 23872. The doors opened, and she pushed the button to the seventh floor. The elevator stopped on the ninth

Corporate Revenge

floor. Another high-level executive at RTI had to have remotely admitted the employee. Exchanging a quick nod of greeting with her, he entered, but didn't press the button. If no one would press that button after her, she'd have to figure out a way to wipe off her prints to cover her trail. On the eighth floor, two more people entered, but they weren't RTI employees. From their dialogue, she determined they were customers because they conversing about which R & D ideas might best help their companies. Someone high up in the echelon must have admitted them into the private elevator as well.

Afraid to address them because they might be forced to pick her out later, or a monitor might be taping voices, she just nodded at them as well, greeting them. They gave her a questioning glance. She was portraying herself as a high-level executive, but didn't say anything to them, the customer. Before the door closed, three hurried employees begged admittance into the elevator. The customers peeked outside and then looked to her for approve. Rae Anne waved the three inside.

"Morning, Ma'am," they said. The doors thudded closed, and one of them pressed the button to the third floor. They quickly turned away from her, giving her a cold shoulder.

She wanted to say: Hey, why are you treating me like I have a disease?

Happy that one of them had punched the button and covered her fingerprint, she also realized why they might have negative feelings and attitudes toward her. *My badge*! She had just donned a special executive insignia that vaulted her to a position of instant glory at RTI. Everyone else was *staff*, and in their eyes, she embodied success and power. She wanted to laugh as she pondered the idea that a piece of fabric could insight such fear and wield such power over everyone who wasn't wearing it. There was also the unseen side of the badge, the side closest to her skin that felt heating up, burning her. Because of her *special insignia*, she was now embroiled in a class war and silent struggle. Of course employees below her level wouldn't smile at her! After what Tim had been though—and having to endure the terrible working conditions and knowing about Ginnie Reidel's sudden firing for no apparent reason—she would hate her too if she were to come face-to-face with herself as an executive in the elevator!

Taking out a Kleenex and sneezing into it, she moved in front of the elevator buttons. When the door opened to the seventh floor, she quickly dashed out onto the secure floor; and prior to the elevator door closing, she stopped it, thrust her face inside, and said, "Have a nice day!" The door closed, almost catching strands of her wig, but she quickly straightened it and backed up into the white hallway.

She quickly adjusted her special badge toward her shoulder as much as possible. Cameras were high up and monitoring her. Now, she had to walk and work fast while maintaining confidence and composure so as to not give off bad vibrations to Security. Remembering Claude Filmer's code, she input it on the keypad, and then quickly bumped up against it so as to cover her fingerprint. Thus far, she hadn't heard any alarms, and only two technicians were in the background, the rest most likely in another area or up on the tenth floor.

Upon entering the chip-fab lab, she saw machine arms whirring and heard electronics zapping from behind Plexiglas windows. She smelled the ozone-air, and listened to the squeaking of her soft-soled shoes on the shiny white tile floor. Then she spotted the sign: Shipping and Receiving. It had a red-blaring logo beneath it, a symbol of the room's Confidential status: S&R, Special Clearance Required. The S&R logo was also on her badge. She remembered the bar code on the opposite side and underneath the Velcro fastener. At the door, she would need to take off her badge and use that code to enter the room. *That's where the boxes of faulty chips from the tenth floor must be!*

Keeping her back to the cameras while maneuvering around machines, she felt like a fast-paced mall walker. After arriving at the door, she swept off her badge and swiped it through the Smart-card reader. The light turned green; the

Corporate Revenge

clasp on the security door clicked; and with a Kleenex in her hand, she opened the door and entered S&R.

Scanning the walls lined with boxes, she saw the opening to the assembly room. At the far-end of the room, packers were busy forklifting giant boxes toward a large loading elevator. The kiosk entryway was temporarily vacant. Through another window, she could see a red emergency light flaring. A machine had broken down and the kiosk checker and several technicians were hurriedly fixing it. Again, she didn't have much time, but this easy access felt like a blessing since she wasn't forced to confront anyone as to her identity or reason for being in R&D.

She quickly pressed her badge against another Smart-scanner, and the door opened when the light blinked green. Upon entering, she saw shelves of boxes, software, and chips from several RTI departments. *This is the place where special techs test Top-Secret chips and select designs*. Machines were thudding, chopping, punching, and hissing everywhere like robots about to mount an assault on the company. Mechanical arms were rising and falling, lights flashing yellow and blaring green. The sounds were drowning out the squeaking of her shoes and her breathing. Sidling between a row of mechanical arms passing chips, and barely escaping a printing press imprinting codes on tiny sensor packages, Rae Anne ducked beneath a robotic forklift and crawled to the opposite end of the room where employees had just closed the elevator door to offload a shipment onto the first floor.

In an unsealed sealed box being packed by a mechanical system, there they were…*Fl-10 to H. T. & C. This is the shipment from the tenth floor*! Timing her movement so as to reach through a hammering computer arm, she grabbed a small box containing one sensor chip. She couldn't conduct an in-depth analysis of it right then and there; but if the chip were faulty, she'd have proof of illegal money laundering *and* criminal activity. Furthermore, the Hermes Trading scheme was someone's method to distribute illegally to foreign countries. Such a venture would be raking in billions for the corrupt people responsible for its inception and promulgation! She didn't know for sure the breadth and scope of the corruption, but at least now she was holding solid proof. Now, she could go to someone important and take down RTI once she tested those chips.

An alarm sounded. Trouble!

Quickly she stashed the small box deep in her handbag and back tracked her movements until she exited Shipping and Receiving. But before she could leave the giant chip-fab lab, she heard voices outside the door, and a card sliding into the Smart-card reader. Feeling like an animal about to be snagged, she spotted a dark recessed space in between two bookcases stacked with software boxes. She hid between the bookcases, hoping their combined shadow would hide her from the burly guards. With her spine against the wall and holding her breath, she peered at the guards through slits in software until the men disappeared into the Shipping and Receiving room. Obviously, they were now focusing on the special chips. As the S&R door clicked shut, she made a mad dash out of the chip-fab lab. Racing down the corridor, she heard guards yelling from the behind the Plexiglas windows.

"There! Who is she?" one shouted.

She walked faster as they headed toward the chip-fab door. From the corner of her eyes, she saw the other guard snap a picture of her on his device. She was almost at the end of the hall, but couldn't take the private elevator. They'd nab her there for sure. She remembered four other elevators around the corner and down the hallway. That's the way Mira and she had entered this place yesterday because after they had finished their brief tour, and after Mira showed her the writing on her arm, they went to IT to check out portable devices. They took those employee elevators down to her office.

As she walked quickly toward that elevator exit, she began encountering more employees. Quickly, she shoved her special badge into her pocket.

Coming after her now, she could hear the guard. "She has clearance though. We saw it."

Corporate Revenge

The other replied: "Still, I don't see anyone with her description having been issued that Executive badge. We need to question her."

She checked her stopwatch: 9:40 a.m. She was running out of time. Guards or others along the way back could apprehend her. She had twenty minutes to travel up three stories, change, and return her executive badge to its rightful place. *How am I going to manage to accomplish all that without getting caught?*

J.P. Osterman

Chapter 11 – Unexpected Help

Nearly out of breath, she leaped into the elevator. She hadn't checked the directional arrow; and once inside she noticed the arrow pointing down, then the red indicator light: 5. The elevator was descending to the fifth floor! *How am I gonna make a U-turn and head back up to the tenth?* Breathless, she slid between several employees while whipping off her executive badge. She felt overwhelming dejection, and numbness. She felt as if her feet were melting into the elevator floor that was going down, down, down…and everything around her appeared set in the shadow. Her risky adventure to expose RTI's corruption was over. She wanted to cry, and put her hands over her face to hide her tears. Now, all she could hope for was to escape with her life!

"I'm in *big* trouble." People looked at her in shock as she backed into an employee who reeled away from her. She saw her name tag: Flora Henderson.

Flora Henderson was a young black woman whom Tim had mentioned and Rae Anne met in the cafeteria. Mira had introduced Flora and a few of her friends to Rae Anne when they noticed she was the new hire to their Department of Systems Architecture. Flora looked like a young Whoopi

Corporate Revenge

Goldberg, in addition to having the actor's bubbly personality. She had an eager team always at her side. They were the rare easy-going crowd at RTI, always exuding innovation and creativity. Ginnie had sent out emails and had asked Flora and her team to greet Rae Anne. By now, they had to have known about Ginnie's sudden demise as well.

"You okay, Mary?" Flora asked Rae Anne. She gently touching Rae Anne's shoulder but immediately pulled away. Her tender response was one of caution mixed with compassion.

Still, Flora's expression of empathy warmed Rae Anne's fearful disposition. She hadn't experienced such compassion in a long time. She gasped, trying hard to hold back her tears. The elevator jolted. It was about to stop on the sixth floor. Through sobs, she said, "No, I'm not okay at all, Flora." She thrust the emblem into her pocket and covered her face with until she felt the bones of her eye sockets.

Another employee turned to her and said, "What's wrong?"

There were so many employees in the elevator, the cameras appeared obscured; but given the information Rae Anne had discovered on RTI's spider drones and tracking pins, appearance didn't reflect reality even fifty percent.

Rae Anne had no choice but to entrust Flora and her team with her situation. "I'll tell ya what's wrong!" Before she could expound on everything that had happened, she grabbed a Kleenex out of her handbag, folded it, and then covered the camera. She checked in each corner.

Obviously gleaning what Rae Anne was doing, a woman took out hair gel, removed the Kleenex, and dabbed a glob of gel on the camera lens. "Now, we're safe. That stuff make hair stand up for hours!" she laughed.

"No spider-ware or insect-flying drones in here," Rae Anne said, and Flora and her team jumped, afraid something might be flying around and might sting them. Rae Anne remembered that the employee pins had GPS tracking, but not necessarily full-on monitoring capability. The pins couldn't transmit audio.

J.P. Osterman

Flora and her team appeared shocked by her investigative actions of the elevator, but Rae Anne motioned for them to remain quiet while she continued to clear the room. Sighing when she realized they were alone, she began telling them everything: from Steve firing Tim, to RTI employee pins that were monitoring employees, even after hours.

"Damn!" Flora yelled.

"Holy—"

"Sons-a—"

"I know," Rae Anne began, "but being angry right now is not going to bring them down."

"I wanna take this piece 'o…" She was trying to pull off her company pin.

"No, not yet," Rae Anne began, "don't do that just yet. If you can discover documentation and find designs of the spyware and spider-ware drones, you can prove Invasion of Privacy."

"And have the responsible person arrested," Flora added.

Rae Anne told them that by that point, she'd most likely be in jail. Still, they could continue their hunt for corruption and illegal activities. She talked so fast, she couldn't feel her lips. She also feared they might think she was delusional and might turn her into Security. But the more proof she gave them, the more accepting of her they were becoming, and not at all judging her as being crazy, but listening as if their lives were in jeopardy. Anger, hurt, and betrayal were mounting by the second, playing in all sorts of expressions emanating from their eyes and body language.

When the elevator stopped on the sixth floor, Flora motioned for people to move away and catch another elevator. She then pressed the upward arrow. "Go on, Mary, tell us more, 'cause by golly, I'm sure ticked off!"

Now the elevator was moving upward…

Meanwhile, Rae Anne continued to tell them some details behind Steve firing time, and most likely the same conspiracies at play in the firing of Ginnie Reidel as well. Finally, she said: "Please help me. I just need a little more time. I have one

Corporate Revenge

chip as proof." She tapped the bottom of her handbag. "But I need more proof, and I'm almost ready to show criminal activity here!" She felt drained as if she had been through a week of working nonstop, 24-7 without a break and no sleep. "Jail," she kept saying, "that's what they're gonna do to me." She put her head on Flora's strong shoulder.

"I believe you." Flora yanked a Kleenex out of her purse and said through kind eyes, "You're not going to jail, Mary, 'cause we're not gonna letchya."

"You bet you're not," another woman said, "'cause we're all gonna help ya, Mary."

Flora pointed to her name on her badge. "Flora Henderson's gonna see to that 'cause this is my team you're confiding in, and we're the best!" She and her four-woman team had a proud gleam of fight in their eyes as the elevator passed the eighth floor.

"Listen up, everybody," Flora began, "we need to search for evidence in between all our work duties, and ask our friends in other departments to help us."

"But keep *everything* we're doing secret," her colleague said.

"Yep…but we can do this," Flora added. "We can pool evidence and add to what Mary's found."

"*If* we can," one friend said, doubtingly.

"Not if, when," Flora corrected, "then we can make some changes here at RTI."

They began whispering about their current projects, and what type of proof of illegal activities they could acquire from visiting various departments.

"See?" Flora said excitedly. "We *can* do this!" She had her hands clenched into fists as she bounced on the balls of her feet. Then her face suddenly changed. "Oh…I remember! Someone really high up is coming from Georgia."

"When?" Rae Anne asked. "I heard that too, from Mira."

"Don't know," Flora replied, "either today or tomorrow. Steve's presentation is supposed to go on for two whole days…*whew!*"

"We can hand over everything we find when that big shot

gets here!" another woman exclaimed.

Rae Anne could hear their cell phones ignite into action, and they began texting. An entire corporate revolt was ensuing within minutes, in secret.

The elevator stopped on the ninth floor.

"I have an idea," Flora said, "follow my lead, everybody."

She gestured for everyone to encircled Rae Anne, and huddle over her.

Buried under their protective care, Rae Anne realized they were hiding her from other people in the hallways and cameras. A guard peeked into the elevator, obviously looking for her.

"We're getting ya to the stairwell, Mary. Just follow our lead," Flora instructed.

Exiting the elevator, they began walking toward the stairway, Rae Anne completely hidden from sight like a tree in a forest.

"The tenth floor is probably a two-minute climb," Flora began. "I'll find a way to get someone to that bathroom to help you. I'm not attending the presentation, but two from our department are, and should be there right now."

"I'm texting some right now too," a team member said.

Flora opened the door and gently guided Rae Anne into the stairwell. She had received a text message. "Jessica is in the Conference room now. She's getting your suit from the bathroom."

"Yep, behind the toilet in the third stall," Rae Anne said.

"I'll tell her to bring it to you on the stairwell. The hallway's gonna be crawling with Security. They're lookin' for ya." Then she stepped back into the center of her team. From her enthusiastic expression, Flora appeared to be enjoying the chance to be a part of a whistleblower opportunity. "When you get up to the landing, your clothes should be there and people talking in front of the door to buy ya more time." She checked her watch. "Ya have ten minutes before that presentation begins!"

"Thanks, Flora...thanks, everybody," Rae Anne whispered,

Corporate Revenge

deep relief permeating her body.

Flora asked quickly, "What else can we do to?"

Rae Anne replied: "We need to gain access to the executive accounts. See where they're funneling money off-shore to private banks."

Flora's expression turned pensive. "I know people in that department. Accounting is on the sixth floor."

"And someone can check RTI's patent office. See if you can locate any patent violations." Rae Anne turned to bound up the stairs as the team began texting into their Smart phones.

An Asian woman standing next to Flora suddenly perked up: "I just typed up the paperwork for a malicious lawsuit RTI is filing against Vibrato Industries." She had on a starch-perfect blouse and skirt, suggesting she was heading to court. "Vibrato developed a sensor chip a fourth of the size of one of ours with ten times the resolution." She was a paralegal, and also assigned to Mira and Flora's team on an as-needed basis.

"Wow," another woman exclaimed, "I bet that didn't go over too well with Kent Smith, the big V.P. Engineer." She sounded terrified of Smith. "He has a bad case of N.I.H."

"What's that?" Rae Anne asked.

Chuckling, she replied, "If it's Not-Invented-Here, it's no good." Her logo indicated the woman was from Systems Architecture, but relegated to engineering specs. She was an engineer.

"Huh," Rae Anne began, "that sounds like an ego trip just so someone can monopolize the technology."

"Sure is," the paralegal said, "and I bet Kent Smith was ticked off to hear about Vibrato's invention!"

Another woman on Flora's team said: "Yeah, that's why our engineering department didn't want to form a strategic alliance, so Vibrato went to one of our competitors. But Kent Smith instructed one of our lawyers to sue Vibrato just to stop their deal."

The engineer huffed. "Well, that lawsuit will *definitely* put Vibrato out of business."

The paralegal scowled. "Sure will! Our legal department

will tie Vibrato up in court so long and drain all their cash reserves."

Rae Anne shuttered at the reality. With billions of dollars in assets, and in a blinking of an eye, RTI can squash the creative inventions of startup companies. "Well, if you have proof, can't you do something to stop the malicious lawsuit? Think of all the families…and children!"

The paralegal appeared downcast. "And lose my job? I don't know," she reeled. "I'm already up against a pile of obstacles. You think I want to make life harder on me and my family?" She glanced at the exit sign straight above Rae Anne's head, obviously motioning for her to get going. Then she resumed texting, her hands shaking and her shoulders hunching. Every now and then she glanced at the engineer who had stopped her texting. The two of them were caught in a dilemma. They had guilty expressions on their faces.

"I don't like what I do," the paralegal said, "but I don't have any choice."

The engineer said, "Heck, there are a lot of things I *have* to do for this darn company, things I hate doing!" Her eyes looked watery.

"I have children," the paralegal said.

"I understand," Rae Anne said, "and I do to. That's why I'm doing what I'm doing. I'm trying to make a difference and exonerate my husband of wrongdoing. I need your help, along with Flora's help."

The engineered walked over to the paralegal, and they began whispering as they showed each other some attachments on their iPhone emails. Flora joined them.

When the paralegal peered up, smiled, and gave Rae Anne the A-Okay signal, Rae Anne believed they too had discovered some type of corruption that when added to her own evidence would help build a solid case against RTI.

"I have some files you can use when you present your case of fraud to the police," the paralegal said. She had an expression of anger on her face.

"No! We'll *all* take what we find and present our

Corporate Revenge

information to the big corporate honcho who's coming either today or tomorrow," Flora said. "We're all in this venture together...and later on, Mary, I know we'll have some *real* evidence bombshells to add to your collection." She looked happy, and gave an invigorating bounce on the balls of her feet.

"Thank you." Rae Anne inhaled a breath of relieving air. Suddenly, she heard a noise. Someone was whispering to her from the landing above. "I gotta go!" When the door boomed shut behind her, she felt energized. Then she heard loud tapping way below her. Her shoes would give her away if she'd climb the stairs with them on. Doffing them quickly, she began racing barefoot up the stairs toward the tenth floor. She had four flights of stairs. Panting as she rounded a 90° turn, she stopped. Below, she could hear foot soldiers—Security guards shouting and giving orders. Sirens began blaring on all the floors. She could hear echoes of doors opening and locking beneath her. Racing upward, she still had another flight of stairs left before reaching her helper waiting for her on the landing.

"We're on lock down!" a man called to someone in the stairwell. Obviously, he had stopped and was listening for proof of life in the long ten-story stairway.

At the landing, she saw a hand extending out the door. It was holding the plastic bag she had left in the restroom. *Whew*! Flora had helped her! Without it, guards would definitely apprehend her and haul her off to jail. Now, more than ever, she had a good chance of succeeding in her plan; but still, she had a ways to go. She grabbed the package containing her work clothes and dumped the contents, making sure to catch her ring and earrings. She shoved them in a side pocket of her handbag. She'd have to make to put them on quickly soon because she had them on prior to changing into her disguise! Then she noticed a dismantled camera high in the corner. Someone had given it a disabling blow. Peeking through the crack in the door, she noticed a large crowd gathered there. The congregation was helping her, gesturing her to hurry.

J.P. Osterman

Doffing her wig, she threw it in the plastic bag she'd set in the corner; then she quickly changed clothes. When she heard the door knob jiggle, she gasped.

"Give me the bag when you're through!" a man called.

She handed her thrift-shop disguises to the man who was propping open the door. As a last measure, she brushed down her suit, straightening out the wrinkles.

Guards were approaching fast! She could hear loud thuds and clicks on the stairs below her. Someone had closed down the eighth floor entrance to the stairwell. If not for that bought time from her helpers, she would have surely been caught, and she wasn't in the clearing yet. She guessed she had thirty seconds before guards would spot her. She opened the door, took out the executive badge, and attached it to her blazer. People parted to let her through, while talking, laughing and guiding her toward the Executive Conference room. She smoothed back her hair and dabbed off her old lipstick. She saw her disguises float right past her as if they were object in a mosh pit. Then she quickly put on her ring and earrings. Armed guards raced past her, into the stairwell. They had their guns drawn, and were blaring orders into their microphones.

Rae Anne looked at her watch: 9:54 a.m., the second hand pounding out the dregs of time to the start of Steve's presentation. *Will Claude Filmer have missed me and begin interrogating me? Did he believe my text message and believe I was retrieving a last-minute addition to the presentation from my office?* She was afraid.

Quickly, she charged the middle of a small line leading into the Reception area. A woman with a lace apron was motioning for her to hurry up and get in line behind another woman waiting in line. Then she grabbed Rae Anne's arm, positioning her behind the woman.

Giving out a deep sigh, Rae Anne said, "Thanks, thanks for helping me."

The woman smiled and said something Rae Anne couldn't understand because she was speaking Spanish. Once next to

Corporate Revenge

the place where she had stolen the executive badges, Rae Anne grabbed her pin from behind the pastry dish, pulled out the badge, wiped off her prints and threw the badge on the floor. Claude Filmer's was standing at the center of the reception area his head turning in search of someone. It had to be Rae Anne. Now, the reception area was filling with guards and other high-level executives scurrying around like disturbed ants.

Pretending as if she had just seen the executive RTI emblem, Rae Anne picked the badge up off the floor and whipped it into the air, waving the emblem like a banner. "Mr. Filmer, look what I found!"

Jerking his head in her direction, Claude Filmer dashed over to the table and grabbed the emblem. "How did *that* get down there?" He marveled at it as if the badge were priceless. "We've been searching for this for the last fifteen minutes!" He smoothed back his hair into a duck tail.

Shrugging Rae Anne said, "I'm not sure, Sir. But I'm glad *you* found it."

"Call off the alarm," he commanded, running his fingers over his sweaty forehead. After he calmed down the employees who were recovering from the sound of the blaring alarms, he said: "Okay everyone, let's all get started on this presentation. We're running just a bit behind schedule."

Rae Anne noticed the time as she held her handbag tight against her waist: 9:58 a.m.

"Ms. Hershel," he said, nodding at her and brushing down his collar, "please follow me."

"Yes Sir," she replied, listening to muffled voices in the Executive Conference room, and the clicking of a *PowerPoint* remote. She still had no idea what she was supposed to do, really, except for what Mira had instructed. She had everything ready for Steve…and gave Filmer the addendum she had rushed to her office to retrieve. She had purposely made the addendum last night, really an itemized list of employees Steve had unjustly fired. But until that point in the presentation, either today or tomorrow, Filmer instructed her to sit in a

J.P. Osterman

specific location, and display *PowerPoint* slides at Steve Lerrefeiht's directions. She continued following Filmer through the Reception area and to her designated seat. At its underbelly, she spotted Mira's flash drive camouflaged in piece of masking tape to make the seat appear recently fixed. Soon, she'd get her hands on it, and anticipate Mira's plan!

Corporate Revenge

Chapter 12 – Anticipation

"This way, Miss Herschel." Claude Filmer began escorting her down several aisles to her first-row seat. She marveled at the top-floor plush accommodations.

The Executive Conference room provided for Wi-Fi connectivity, coupled with the elegance of a movie theater. The tables were various sizes and built on steel-rod platforms. The cushioned chairs were high-back, and could swirl so the occupant could easily collaborate with others. The walls contained exceptional acoustics, and speakers; and the ceilings were smooth, glossy and cream-colored. All tables provided internet connectivity, with power supplies and ornate outlets. At the front of the room, executives were seated at a long U-shape table and talking to one another. Their conversations were gently echoing off the walls, sounding like chirpings.

When they reached the front row, Filmer stopped a pointed to a seat. It was special, with a laptop on a white wooden desk. It had several portals and even a small transparent monitor. She could see through it as Steve, or another facilitator, would be giving his presentation. "This is your set up, Ms. Hershel. Just use this *PowerPoint* remote to change the slides when Mr. Lerrefeiht instructs you." He walked away.

"Yes, Sir." Rae Anne slid into her cushioned chair as he

walked away. The back was so high, she couldn't see behind her. But within her line of sight in the upper corner of the ceiling, as Mira had said, she saw the camera flashing one red bleep. Underneath her seat, she touched the flash drive that Mira had taped there. Now, she had to wait for the corner camera to flash red twice. Then, she would make her next move.

Taking out the RTI iPhone that Mira had given her from out of her handbag, she linked the iPhone to the laptop. Now she had to sit tight and wait.

Suddenly, Barbara Winston leaned into her. "What are you doing?" As RTI's Main Receptionist, she was carrying two laptops, flash drives on strings, computer mice dangling over her arm, and name tags. Obviously she was heading to the front to offer them to the executives.

Rae Anne gasped. "This iPhone has an app I can interface with Mr. Lerrefeiht's Adobe Reader." She turned the iPhone to show her the screen.

Barbara Winston took a half-step back. "Oh, that sounds okay." She moved on.

Whew, Rae Anne sighed, feeling relieved that Barbara hadn't pushed her for more information.

At the front of the conference room, Claude Filmer sat down at a long table next to an older man who could have passed as a Beethoven look-a-like. With a long pointy noise and powerful jutting cheekbones, the man shone the intensity of a hard-working scientist, a genius. He moved testing instruments and the oscilloscope to the side. He synched them with his Galaxy S4, iPhone, iPad, and laptop. Behind him, in a picture-within-a-picture, his blank presentation areas appeared on the IMAX screen. He was preparing something big…something he would be weaving in with Steve's ideas. From the look in his deep-set eyes and strong chin, Rae Anne surmised he was a powerful person, and no one at RTI should dare cross him. She noticed the name on a long gold plate: Dr. Thornton Manning, Vice President, Technology. His name appeared on screen. *Thornton is the brains behind RTI's*

Corporate Revenge

innovative technology!

Not everyone was present yet for the presentation, for there were several name plates with empty seats behind them. The conference table arrangement was akin to the one she had seen in her high school physics lab, with beige counter tops, except on one had a large unique Bunsen burner. That one was in front of Thornton Manning. Situated in several locations were transparent touch screens. Powerful CPUs were directly under them. Behind the tables and high on the wall was a curved IMAX screen, now illuminating more visuals, obviously more executives were adding their spaces among the entire scene. Claude Filmer and Thornton Manning began whispering. They stopped when three more executives seated themselves at the long table. One was Steve Lerrefeiht.

Glancing at Rae Anne, Steve nodded at her and then began staring at her as if discerning her appearance.

She ducked behind her laptop, hoping to hide her face, hoping he'd become distracted with something else and stop inspecting her. She couldn't hide herself, however, behind the transparent monitor. She couldn't continue to sit there like a mole!

Suddenly, in walked another man who began standing in front of his name plaque. He talked with Steve for a few seconds, and then stood stoic, obviously waiting for someone to wait on him. He was Kent Smith, the V.P. of Research and Development, the executive Tim described as one who rarely appears in public. She recognized him from yesterday in the cafeteria! He had a habit of watching people from a distance—a real voyeur—walking around the room and stopping now-and-then, sneaking up on people from behind, and then offering them salt and paper shakers if they noticed him.

Kent Smith looked like Omar Sharif, except his face was thinner, and his lips had the broadcast power of real pucker energy. Three female employees rushed over to him and began handing him notes and flash drives. He began speaking to each one enthusiastically like a juggler while intermittently scanning the room for women. When he spotted someone

159

appealing, he'd stare at her with his intense dark brown eyes, and gesture at her with desire. He reminded Rae Anne of her ex, Gene Mure.

Now, he had his back to room and laughing with three young women. He was holding them spellbound with a joke while waving his hands during the punch lines. Together, they looked like kindergarteners, except Kent Smith, who never appeared engaged with the women during his long-winded joke. He couldn't keep his back to the audience for long. Turning around so the women had *their* backs to the room, he began noticing other women enter through the doors. When he spotted someone appealing, his eyes grew into romantic black pools, beckoning the woman to attend to him. When their eyes met his, Rae Anne discerned his beacon of enticement pining on his face: *Notice me...I long for you!* Most women turned away and grimaced behind his back.

What a sicko! Rae Anne remembered when his eyes caught her attention yesterday. Of course, when anyone stares at someone, at some point, the object of that person's unwanted attention is bound to notice! She was *the new girl*, and his face lit up like a child ogling candy, and then he flashed her his pearly whites. Red-faced, Rae Anne turned quickly back to eating lunch and adjusting silverware on her tray. She kept ignoring him while conversing with Mira. Most likely, he didn't like that rejection, but he should! Kent Smith was a married man! He had children.

His poor wife! Rae Anne had learned a powerful lesson about men like Kent Smith and her ex, Gene. Behind their perfect faces and sweet talk lurked the personality of a narcissist. Now, in the conference room, the more she looked at Kent Smith, the more her stomach churned and her flight reflexes kicked in, prodding her to scat right out of RTI; however, she had to remain in her seat. So many people were now helping her, and they needed her. Perhaps when the day was through, they'd have RTI cut down to its bare bones! Grounding her was Mira's red-light camera, still flashing one continuous stream of data. The time wasn't yet ripe for their plan.

Corporate Revenge

"Ms. Hershel?" Steve suddenly bellowed.

His words made her jump. "Yes, Sir?" After nodding at him, she peeked at the camera. It was still flashing only one red beam, but her *go* signal could occur at any moment.

"Begin the *PowerPoint*, Ms. Hershel," Steve ordered.

The lights dimmed as Rae Anne picked up the *PowerPoint* remote and began clicking through sections. Each executive had his-and-her brief sections. She was now monitoring that change of venue with each succeeding presenter. This entire slide show was the Introduction.

On the giant screen, she then saw Thornton Manning's name. She checked the time: 10:45 a.m. All the introductions had ended, and he stood, motioning for Rae Anne to change the slide to project his prototype of a new generation chip. The chip's description materialized on-screen as a monolithic, hyper-spectral, imaging chip, destined to be the key system sensor on the next planned shuttle to Mars. For his second invention, he directed Kent Smith to display his latest engineering project. He had created a subatomic carbon-based string that could manipulate DNA.

Thornton began showing pictures of intelligent organic atoms that would naturally interact with the human brain. "And because of the remarkable cortical plasticity of the brain," he began, "signals from implanted prostheses will, after adaptation, be handled by the brain like natural sensor or effector channels." He was beaming with pride as he continued to proclaim his new organic chip as *the* giant leap in neurological technology: brain-computer interface. Then he concluded his presentation by wiping sweat off his brow. He stood suddenly vulnerable, like a conductor after his orchestra's performance, waiting for the executives' reactions.

J.P. Osterman

Chapter 13 – Flash Drive

Steve Lerrefeiht was the first to stand, and he clapped. Rae Anne kept wondering when Mira would signal for her to hack into the presentation which would shut down all the lights in the entire RTI building. She remembered seeing generators in several of the labs and facilities. That power couldn't extinguish in those locations, otherwise the company could lose vital technology costing millions by the minute!

As the hour continued to drag on into a well-needed lunch break, Rae Anne felt her blood pressure lurch from her chest into her stiff shoulders. Repeatedly, out of the corner of her eye, she had glanced at Mira's red-light camera, waiting for it to blink two flashes. They were like flaming SOS signals on a deserted island, and she, marooned, praying for quick rescue.

After a Thornton showed a summary of how his new technology would interface with that of NASA and several of NASA's subcontractors, people clapped loudly.

"You always impress me, Thornton," Steve Lerrefeiht said, walking up to him and patting him on the shoulder.

The executives then applauded. Their clapping was a boon to the ears of Thornton who then politely gestured for them to sit down. "You didn't think I'd introduce only *two* designs, did you?" His cheeks turned peach colored. Silence ensued.

Corporate Revenge

Facing the audience, and standing in front of an experimental stage, he was postured like an orchestra conductor in front of his little inventions as if he were about to infuse them with life. Out from under a little podium, he lifted a covered plate and then smiled at it proudly. "This is the most advanced sensor in existence. It's taken me the *entire* year and *millions* of corporate dollars to produce this prototype." Gently, he set the covered brass plate on the table.

"Millions of dollars that *I* procured for you," Steve interjected, laughing, and a little wave of laughs bounded through the audience. Then again, pin-dropping silence.

Thornton's hair was jet black waves of curls, his lab coat pristine white. He emitted such a velvety enthusiasm and vibrant energy to all his mechanical devices, technical inventions, and instruments on the table. He enjoyed living an undisturbed laboratory life.

Then, he breathed deeply, his focusing hard on the brass plate in front of him. Steadying himself, he gipped the edge of his experimental table. He was on the fringe of announcing and igniting a new era in technology. "This will make today's hardware computer obsolete, like the personal computer killed the typewriter."

Oohs and aahs reverberated, followed by silent anticipation.

Holding the brass plate in the air, he began moving it from side-to-side like a magician showing off a covered birdcage. When he whipped off the brass cover, the plate appeared bare. A special light began beating down on the center of the plate, and the center began glowing as if on fire. Thornton's black eyes reflected the beams intensity but lack of heat.

The audience inhaled and began murmuring questions. "What is it? I can't see anything though!"

The executives jumped out their seats and raced to him. Thornton handed Steve a special magnifying glass. He took the plate out of its special light beam and allowed Steve to look at the center of the plate through the magnifying glass.

Immediately, Steve backed away in amazement. "You did it! My God, you did it, Doctor!" He appeared to be on the verge of crying.

People were breathless, standing, and leaning forward. "I still can't see anything though," someone said.

Nothing was on the plate, although something profound had to be there because two people had seen it.

"Back away, Steve," Thornton ordered. After Steve stumbled to his seat, Thornton stepped up on a tiny platform and lifted the shining brass plate up into the special light beam. The fixture on the ceiling was bulbous like the inside of a sunflower, the shimmering yellow seeds projecting intense light onto the brass plate. "Ladies and Gentlemen, and RTI employees, let me introduce you to RTI's newest chip design, the *Ultimate Information Interfacer!*"

A bright blue gelatinous substance appeared and began bubbling in the center of the plate. The quantum-light directly over the new technology was interacting with it, growing it. The chip began glowing. Thornton then nodded to Rae Anne to show the next *PowerPoint* slide. A brief description of the chip appeared on the IMAX screen. Thornton Manning had managed to separate particles from waves to achieve the impossible.

"The Ultimate Information Interfacer is half-technology and half living entity, Ladies and Gentlemen. It is nano-organic combined with amphibian DNA." The substance began emitting hissing sounds under the quantum-driven ceiling fixture. The object stopped growing, its shape now a flat blue-glowing chip. "In seconds, I will be able to pick it up and attach it to any portable device." The blue chip was taking on solid form. "The Ultimate Information Interfacer, or as I call it, the UII is now linking with Wi-Fi. At my command, it will download information into my CPUs." Gesturing at the computers under the table, he then said into his transparent monitor, "Begin downloading the UII Introduction." As people marveled, he glanced at each executive, and smiled proudly. "Now, the UII will display its brilliance!"

The chip began growing strings of appendages, taking on the form of a living bioluminescent creature, feeding on the air.

Corporate Revenge

The electronics surrounding it began downloading data into Thornton's *humming* CPU. The new chip technology was a powerful conduit, expanding Wi-Fi and uniting all frequencies. Peoples' laptops and all portable devices began displaying the RTI logo and emitting New Age music, followed by pictures of various employees and scenes from their workplaces. Those images then transferred onto the IMAX screen. The entire ensemble resounding through the conference room resembled an orchestra of technology playing harmoniously!

Suddenly, *poof*! Another *poof* and *sizzle*. Smoke swirled on the brass plate over the glowing chip. *Crackling* and *hissing* resounded from the quantum-driven light fixture. The chip exploded. The light fixture blew up in a popping frenzy.

The explosions threw Thornton against the wall under the IMAX screen. With frightened expressions, people reeled, screamed, and began stampeding the aisles toward the doors. Guards charged the executive table as a fire alarm sounded. They began extinguishing popping flames and crackling LED glass that had fallen to the floor from the light fixture.

Lying on the floor, Thornton coughed while struggling to sit up. When he saw the hissing plate and smoke, he covered his face with his hands. "All gone! My God, I don't see how that chip could have failed! I duplicated the results! This failure is impossible! My experiment!" He began to expound on the long hard hours it took him to develop the technology, the dollars, all the man power. What he had worked so diligently to invent was curls of smoke on a plate and bubbling ash on the ceiling.

Guards lifted him up, and executives circled him as they checked his condition. Thornton pushed them away. "I'm okay. I'm all right. I gotta get back to work...now!" He kept glancing at the hardened chip on its brass crucible and the smoking quantum-driven ceiling fixture, saying: "I don't understand what happened...what went wrong!" He was bent over it and distraught, a parent crying over the death of his child.

Steve Lerrefeiht turned away, giving Thornton a view of his

back as he walked toward the guards who were busily escorting people safely out the conference room. Other executives plopped down in their chairs, glancing at one another in pouts and scowls of disappointment.

Rae Anne felt sorry for Thornton Manning, who finally managed to stand up. His shoulders shone a sagging disappointment, his face was red with shame and anger. She predicted Steve would fire him the minute he could get him alone. She also realized that probably no one had documented what had happened and the events occurring around her.

She had an idea…

Corporate Revenge

Chapter 14 – Call for Help

Taking out her iPhone, she snapped a picture of the smoking plate. Then she noticed that Kent Smith had a tiny vial concealed in his hand. *Click, click.* She took a picture of him, and several others. Then Kent Smith walked up to Claude Filmer, began whispering in his ear, and huddled into him. *Click.* They were snickering and laughing. *Click.* And then they went their separate ways. Filmer whipped out his cell phone and placed a call. *Click.* Shortly thereafter, in walked Susan Gurkle, RTI's Chief Financial Officer. *Click.* They all formed a circle, began gesturing in Thornton's direction, and then laughing as if applauding the success of their espionage. *Click, click.* Rae Anne snapped more pictures and was about to take another of the four of them congregating when her cell phone lit up and jingled.

The instant message read: "You go girl! We found two patent infringements on the fifth floor where Susan Gurkle keeps all her records. They just flat-out stole the inventions of two small companies. Look for the company transfer data. We're scouting the internet for attachments! *F.H.*"

It was Flora Henderson! She had gathered another circle of support and was hunting for all the corruption she could find.

Rae Anne sank low into her cushioned chair and sighed in

relief. At least if she were caught and exposed, others would rally behind her, backing her up—employees who could expose RTI's fraudulent overseas company, and now patent theft.

Glancing back at the group of laughing executives who had betrayed Thornton, she believed they had definitely set up his experiment to fail. Again, she lacked proof, but perhaps she might discover the evidence as she continued on her mission to glean everything illegal to expose RTI illegal activities. Again she snapped pictures of the executives who seemed to be poking fun at and gossiping about him. Every now and then, she glanced up at the camera, but still did not see Mira's two, flashing red-light signal that would give her the go-head to insert the flash drive into her laptop's USB port, which Mira said would initiate a company-wide blackout. A half-an-hour transpired since the accident. People were taking lunch breaks. Eating a bag lunch that a delivery man had given her, she realized that nothing from Mira would appear until after lunch. She just had to sit tight, wait for employees to return, and remain vigilant for two, red-light camera flashes. *Maybe that will happen right after lunch*!

She then experienced a revelation. Thornton Manning had to be innocent of fraud. At first, she had suspected him. He was on her list of RTI criminals; but now, she eliminated him. Through his technical advances, he was helping the company, not destroying it. He was completely dejected over the failure of his experiment he believed would change the world. His motivations were pure—his intentions were to help people, not destroy and hurt families and children. Furthermore, inventing technological innovations motivated him, not amassing money.

To her amazement, Steve Lerrefeiht *appeared* to be innocent too, at least of sabotaging Thornton's brilliant experiment. Because of the failure, other executives appeared to shun him, and Steve had stomped out of the conference room, obviously angry that the experiment had failed. Rae Anne believed that if she could narrow down the suspects, she could discover who

Corporate Revenge

killed Thornton Manning's experiment, and the motive behind the devastating sabotage. A half-an-hour later, at 12:45 p.m., everyone had settled back into their chairs, anticipating Steve returning to the conference room and announcing Thornton Manning's condition.

Then, two lights began flashing on the camera, high in the corner! Mira was signaling her!

Rae grabbed the flash drive from under her chair and wiggled it into her USB port. A prompt came up on her laptop, and she typed in "comet tail".

The lights extinguished. The conference room went dark. A huge *hummmm* resounded, generators activating in the labs and facilities on other floors to keep those places at stasis temperatures.

The room echoed with screams, gasps, and shouts of "What's going on?"

Rae Anne realized Mira's plan was succeeding; however, she had her own plan to finish besides acquiring the faulty chip: find and retrieve documentation of corruption, and proof that some executives were monitoring employees after hours and breaking privacy laws by illegally terminating people. Acquiring evidence of destroying Thornton Manning's experiment would be a perk. Perhaps the culprit was about to steal the technology and sell it to the highest bidder. She remembered several executives huddling around Claude Filmer after the experiment failed. He appeared to be the corrupt executive, and perhaps Kent Smith as well. During Thornton's experiment, the two kept whispering to each other. She would target one and search his office, and then the other. Making her mission easier, Claude Filmer's room was minutes away, at the opposite side of the tenth floor. Kent Smith's office couldn't be too far away.

Leaving the room as if maneuvering on night vision, Rae Anne squirmed through a throng of people, pushed through people scattering out of the reception area, and dashed down a dark corridor. Flashlights began illuminating on portable devices, but most people were still screaming, panicking, and racing toward the elevators and four sets of staircases. The stampede and wild voices reminded her of insects flying out of a hive. While they were vying to leave, she was fighting traffic in the opposite direction, heading toward Claude Filmer's office. She remembered its exact location at the opposite end of the tenth floor. She had just squirmed past a set of elevators. The air was hot and stale with hot breaths all around her. Using her iPhone to guide her and counting the doors, she felt along the walls until she came to that special name plate with the unusual ornate design. Putting her fingers inside the lettering like a blind person reading braille, and briefly shining her iPhone light onto the lettering, she felt the large letters: C. F., V.P. of C. *This is his office*! She typed in his code: CFVPC. The letters didn't work! Until her app rearranged the letters into their corresponding numbers: 23872. The door clicked as the green light illuminated.

Once inside, she gently shut the door, turned on her iPhone light and peered around. The room was neat, with shelved books arranged in order of height. Organizers were stacked neatly under a giant picture window, but not one picture was on a wall. The office appeared to have no safe. In the center of his office set three large transparent screens with icons ready for touch-activation. Beneath his redwood desk set three revving computers. There were no chairs in his office and no benches. Filmer was keeping everything covering like a pianist protecting a gilded piano. Outside, she hurt a rushing sound of feet tapping on the tile. The halls appeared to be clearing, and she kept peeking at the door. She didn't have much time. If she were to discover anything, the information would have to be in his computer.

Touching prompts on the monitor, she saw two RTI icons.

Double clicking them, she noticed two company folders. Clicking one open, she saw a business plan written in code. Inserting her flash drive, she dragged over the file and waited for the green light to display "download complete."

As her anxiety rose, she couldn't feel her fingers. The words, "jail," "hospitalization," and "federal prison" flashed

Corporate Revenge

through her mind, compelling her to hurry and make a fast getaway. She felt glued to the foreign file. That file had to contain the evidence she'd need to prove the fraudulent company. Both it and the business plan would surely show not only Filmer's ultimate purpose, but also his past actions leading up to his illegal designs.

The word, "Translate," flashed on the large touch screen.

"How do I translate?" she asked, stretching her fingers in frustration.

A voice-activated system lit up the screen to yellow as an English translation of the document flooded the screen. At the bottom flashed the name of a foreign owned company: Hermes Trading & Cie. Her heart raced into her throat and her body numbed. This would take some time! Inhaling, she still couldn't catch her breath as she kept repeating: "I've worked so hard! I can't quit now!" She continued dragging documents to her flash drive as the *translate* task continued.

More voices resounded from outside the office. They were guards heading to the conference room and ordering an emergency connection to another generator. Their tapping sounds quickly subsided right outside the door. She extinguished her cell phone light. When another guard said he could hear no noises inside Filmer's office, they resumed walking to the conference room.

Whew, that was close!

Suddenly, another document popped up on the screen. It was a list of foreign-based companies along with contact names and phone numbers. Again she began dragging information to her flash drive, and began snapping pictures.

Then, she discovered fraud.

"Here," she whispered, opening a file with a zoo icon. It was completely out of place in a list of corporate files. The zoo icon had to open something vital. She tapped it open. Five American companies appeared. She began speed reading their information, and what products they had ordered and bought:

Claude Filmer had incorporated five companies in several

different names and had collected electronic payments of over five billion dollars. He was absconding with the corporate accounts and funneling money to foreign banks. She also saw pages of chip designs and patents that were signed by Kent Smith. Then there where images of patents signed by Thornton Manning.

"Claude Filmer did all this!" She closed out that icon, and opening another file.

"He's been selling Thornton Manning's patents! What a jerk!"

The door knob rattled.

She could hear Claude Filmer's voice growing louder.

Quickly, she ejected her flash drive.

His voice grew louder. She could see light under the door. The keypad entry device began bleeping his coded numbers. He and someone else were on their way into the office. Any moment, she'd be caught! *What do I do*?!

Hiding the flash drive and iPhone up her sleeve or in her handbag would be a complete waste of everything she had done. They'd search her and find them for sure. Trying to see through the darkness, she scanned the office for a place she could hide the flash drive, her iPhone, and her handbag. Hiding them in separate places, she could hope for safety in numbers. If she could explain her way out of this predicament, later on she could come back and retrieve them, or tell someone she could trust where to find them.

Dashing over to the window sill, she stuffed the flash drive and her phone behind the blind and hid her handbag between two CPUs under Claude Filmer's desk. Whatever would happen next, she couldn't predict, other than she was definitely about to be caught. Spying a shadowy niche between two bookcases, she sucked in her breath, slipped inside it, pressed her chin against the wood, and began breathing lightly, and praying.

Corporate Revenge

Chapter 15 - Apprehended

Swoosh, the door flew open.

"What's this?" Claude Filmer rushed into the room and punched the light switch. "That monitor's active!"

All the lighting suddenly restored on the tenth floor. The droning sounds of generators subsided. Now, it was blindingly bright.

No way am I gonna stay hidden long!

"The files!" Kent Smith screamed, racing to the large touch-screen monitors. He shut them off.

They hadn't yet seen her, most likely their eyes still adjusting the influx of light. Slowly sliding out of her small crevice between the bookshelves, she glanced at the door and began sliding toward it. If they failed to see her, she still had time to escape, to save herself.

They spotted her.

"Grab her!" Kent Smith cried, racing after her.

Claude Filmer snatched her by her collar. He flung her around and planted himself in front of her face. Together their eyes shone the madness of hate and the anger of red-faced revenge.

"Who ordered you to do this?" Smith asked, his steely pupils shining murderously as he pointed at the mainframe computers still humming in activity.

"Never mind who gave the order, I just want to know what she's taken," Filmer said. He began searching the books for everything out of place.

Just then she heard the sound of helicopter blades swirling outside. *I'm really in big trouble! The FBI and police and maybe even the CIA will all have me in handcuffs!*

She imagined the look on her children's faces as U.S. marshals carted her off to jail. She imagined facing a judge and Tim in divorce court.

I've lost everything now. It's hopeless. She choked back tears through her feelings of terror.

"I haven't done anything," she told them, her heart racing. "I just got lost in the wrong room when the lights went out. That's all. I remembered seeing you input your code at the private elevator, Mr. Filmer. I was only trying not to be trampled in the hallway." She saw skepticism in their eyes. Perhaps they believed her lies. "You know how bad that hallway was…and smoke was still in the air…and people panicking. I had no other choice but to run in here, Mr. Filmer, really!" The only option she believed she had was to play innocent. Then she smile.

Claude Filmer grabbed her wrists and held her against the wall. He began searching her, running his boney fingers over her sides and then patting her pockets.

She felt violated, and retaliation surged through her as she tried hard to kick him. "Get your *stinking* hands off me! You have no right touching me!"

He ordered Kent Smith, "Search her purse."

"I can't find it yet," Smith said, pushing books out of the bookcase.

Rae Anne inspected them for weaknesses, and her best chance for a quick escape. Filmer's body was rigidly tall, like a funeral director. She had kicked him with no results, not even a moan! Kent Smith was Mr. Casanova. Filmer had to be the sociopath and Smith the narcissist. Out of the two, Filmer would have no qualms about murdering her, but Kent Smith

Corporate Revenge

was too fixated on his appearance to get his hands dirty. Then again, maybe she was wrong. When it comes to getting caught and going to jail, either one could kill her and cover up her murder easily as they had already succeeded in hiding so many other criminal activities.

She wiggled away from Filmer's tight grip and raced for the door, her only gateway to freedom.

Kent Smith seized her by the wrist and yanked her into his face. Eyeball-to-eyeball, and through clenched teeth, he said, "I know you took something from this office." He shoved her toward a transparent monitor and showed it to her. The time of access to a file was displaying 2:22 p.m. A strand of black hair fell onto his forehead. His jaw was tight, his eyes brutally vindictive. "What did you download? Give me the device!"

"You're hurting me! Let me go!" She tried jerking away.

"Give me what you took," Smith said softly, "that's all we want. Then we'll let you go." He pushed her back against the bookcase and then covered her mouth. "I can sap every bit of breath out of you...so talk, *now*."

The back of her head stung. She saw spots in front of her eyes. She began gasping for breath. "I—"

"Talk!" Filmer said from across the office. He was rapidly opening file cabinets, inspecting their contents to discern if any files had been jostled or taken.

Smith's eyes looked twice their size as he pressed closed her. She could see her reflection in them. "Just hand whatever you stole back to us," he said. "That's all I want. I'm not gonna say it anymore...not gonna give ya anymore chances to fork everything over to us." He stopped suffocating her, lifting his hands in the air as if surrendering. "I'll give ya thirty seconds." He glanced at his watch. "After that...Ms. Hershel, I'm gonna kill ya."

"I told you, *ah ah*, I don't, *ah ah*, have anything."

"I found it!" Kent Smith pulled her handbag out from under the desk. He tossed it to Filmer and then raced to his side.

Claude Filmer dumped it out and began searching through

the contents. Rae Anne continued to search for an escape route. She wanted to scream, but when she opened her mouth to try, she could only exhale. She never believed her plan would lead her to the point of needing to scream, and no one ever taught her to shout *fire* in case someone might try to abduct her.

"I can't find anything in her purse," Filmer said, glancing askance at Smith.

She sighed in relief, remembering that she had dumped out all her disguises.

"Check around here some more for anything out of place," Filmer commanded him. "She must have hidden a flash drive or camera. Oh…I know I saw an iPhone flash when we were together in the conference room."

"So it was *her* taking pictures!" Smith exclaimed as he searched a corner and then began looking on shelves and through metal file holders.

She had to keep him away from the window sill! Panic pulsing through her, she said, "You sabotaged Dr. Manning's experiment, didn't you?" She knew she was treading on dangerous territory, but she had to divert their attention away from her flash drive and iPhone.

"What makes you think that?" Filmer asked, taking out a small gun from the inside of his blazer. Smith was now dumping out pencil and paperclip holders, tearing apart the office.

"I saw all of you talking after the special chip exploded, that's all," she said. "I want to know why."

"Hah," Filmer huffed, "*why* would *we* tell you?"

She looked askance at the door, hoping they might believe she had seen someone glancing in at them. Then she had an idea: If she could get them to turn on each other, they might become distracted, and she could make a run for it. "If you don't tell me why, I won't deactivate the file I discovered when I hacked into your PC. The file is now in another code as well. I rewrote it…and you'll never find it…without me." She nodded at the CPU system under his desk. She felt superior

Corporate Revenge

now, and having the upper hand as they both paused, their breaths stuck on their tongue.

"What?" Filmer asked.

"I downloaded a timer app that will automatically send the new file to an email address at the FBI." She grimaced at him. "Thanks to someone's file I discovered—" She remembered Kent Smith's office being on the sixth floor. "On the sixth floor in Engineering, I was able to link my new re-written file with the FBI."

"She's FBI?!" Smith's face turned white, and he began scowling at Filmer.

Then she realized her plan could backfire! The two of them engaging in a struggle for power might lead to her death as well as her withholding the whereabouts of the flash drive and iPhone.

Claude Filmer shot her a murderous stare through his deep-set eyes. "Let's take this witch down!"

Kent Smith dropped two piles of software through which he had been searching. "You really think *she* could be capable of developing a *Time* app and can re-write code?" He laughed and sneered at her. "She's just a System's Assistant!" A condescending glare shone in his eyes. "I saw your references, Ms. Hershel. You don't have any kind of advanced experience in Chip Architecture."

Someone had dabbled with her resume! Someone had changed it!

"I saw absolutely no experience in that engineering field whatsoever." He waved her off as if she were scum.

"I'm a hacker," she snapped, "of course I did that. You're just too stupid to read! You're too stupid to realize that someone high up in the corporate ladder might be helping me find evidence to put you away for good!" She was breathed wildly, and hunting to see a camera, anything she believed might call out for someone's attention. "I guess you were just *too* stupid to check out my references." She knew she was really pushing his anger buttons when he came at her with a closed fist ready to punch her. As he was about to strike her, she said: "You have to let me go, or everything will send in fifteen minutes."

There was a second where they both exhaled and retreated. Obviously giving into her threat, Filmer said, "We killed the experiment because we sold the technology to the Chinese."

She remembered one of the files she had seen on Claude Filmer's computer. The file icon had Manning's R&D insignia on it, with a skull and cross bones alongside it. *That must be the design Filmer stole*, she told herself; *and if I can't persuade them that I'm hold a royal flush, this is probably one of the last thoughts I'll ever gonna have.* She was too afraid to prepare for death.

Filmer was now angry. "Why did *you* tell do something to our files in your office, Kent?" he asked. "I almost shot her, and then we woulda had serious trouble after those files sent!" He moved his gun to his waist as if deciding whether to holster it or shoot it. He was waiting for Smith to finish searching the rest of the office. "Hurry! If we can discover where she hid her iPhone, all this stops, and I kill her."

Smith dashed over to another spot hidden from view and peeked into a corner shadow. "She needs to stop that file from sending, that's all." He sneered at her as he walked back over to Filmer. "I think she's bluffing. I don't think she needs anything to stop the sequence of events, just her own deactivation code.

Filmer suddenly laughed. "I think we've just been duped!"

"What?" Smith asked.

"I just shoot her. Then I get Susan Gurkle down here to hunt for whatever Hershel hid in the email," Claude Filmer replied. "She knows several people in engineering who can hack and stop with Hershel started." With a serious jaw and rounded shoulders, he began texting them. They were using all their reserves to win and silence her.

Rae Anne imagined her dead body curled up into a ball in a giant trunk, or dumped in Mission Bay, or rolled up in a carpet and left in a dumpster. Her arms numbed, her mind cleared.

Kent Smith rushed at Claude Filmer and grabbed his arm. "You're not going to kill her right in here are you?"

Corporate Revenge

Filmer flashed him an evil glance. "Do you have any other ideas?"

"Well—"

"You know she probably has more than just a cell phone hidden in here," Filmer began. "The only way to succeed with our new start up is to get rid of her and sweep the entire room."

"Those lights were out for quite some time," Kent Smith said. "That was enough time for her to steal more files from our computers. Ya think she might have people helping her?"

"I doubt it." Again Filmer began searching her, but this time her legs. Then he pulled off her slip-on shoes, tossed them to Kent Smith, who tipped them over in search of evidence.

She tried to push free of Claude Filmer, but he shoved her against the bookcase. "Ouch!" she yelled, and Kent Smith pinched her cheeks, squelching her scream.

Satisfied that she was free of bugs and devices, Smith shuffled a few steps back. "Nothing's on her, so I guess you're right. Killing her is the only way to keep every secret in this office."

Claude Filmer took off the safety to his gun and grabbed a book to silence the sound of gunfire. "Kent, go get two plastic sheets out of the closet. When I looked this morning, they were still there from when the painters had repaired the ceiling when the air failed last week."

"Just let me set up some of this stuff I knocked over," Smith said, picking up pencils and kicking aside paperclips. "Leaving a mess will surely tip someone off if someone comes in here between the time we pack her up and take her out...to bury her." He said those last words hatefully at her.

"No!" Rae Anne said. "Please!" She had to continue to fight for her life. She thought of her children, but she didn't want to mention them just yet for fear Filmer and his band might target them as well. Besides, they still believed she was Mary Hershel. "I'm telling you...that program will activate. You *will* be caught! I might not be here to see you pay for what you're doing, but you *will* go down for corruption and murder!"

Filmer shoved his hand over her mouth. "We'll wrap her up and come back tonight to get rid of her."

Kent Smith opened the closet and began opening boxes in search of the plastic painter sheets.

When Filmer let go of her cheeks, she yelled, "You're crazy!" Her lips were so close to his wrinkled throat that her spit hit it.

Watching him wipe it off, she realized she had gained a few more seconds of life. She had to try and stall him for time. Surely, people would be missing them soon. She had an idea. Her best-kept secret could now save her life. "You destroyed my husband. That's why I came in here." She was fighting to catch her breath, and nearly fell against Filmer's chest.

"What?" he asked with surprise in his sickly eyes.

"Who's her husband?" Smith asked, pausing with the plastic sheets in his hands.

"Just what I said. You destroyed my husband." She kept gasping for breath, glancing from the gun to the Filmer's evil-set eyes. "I'm not Mary Hershel. My name is Rae Anne Westman."

"Westman?" they both repeated.

Kent Smith began rolling up the sheets that sounded like crackling Cellophane. "I fired Tim Westman last week."

"Yeah, I know," Kent Smith said. "I was the one who emailed you, telling you that the guy had intercepted a few emails from Hermes Trading & Cie."

"I knew it!" Rae Anne said. "You're both corrupt pigs!" She craned her neck and spat in Claude Filmer's face. He grabbed her by the throat as he wiped the spit off on his shirt. All Rae Anne could see was the wet blotch on his black suit jacket. At least it would be DNA evidence, that's if a detective would find her body, question him for murder, and notice the spit stain. All her thoughts now were on images of life after her death. Whipping off his jacket, Filmer threw it on the floor. Beads of sweat appeared over his upper lip and on his

Corporate Revenge

forehead. As Kent Smith lay the plastic in front of her, Filmer aligned the gun barrel right between her eyes until she could see the little circle enlarge like the inside of a rod. Closing her eyes, she held her breath. The noises in the room faded into a ringing sound in her ears.

Death, she told herself as the faces of Joey and Carolyn popped into her mind. She'd never see them again, never touch Tim, never see the sunshine. She had never really considered the importance of each and every moment: The bad as well as the good, the failures as well as the successes. She was *really* going to die!

Suddenly, voices in the hallway intensified.

"Who's that?" Filmer asked.

Smith ran and put his ear against the door.

She could hear the sounds of boots and shoes thudding in the hallway. The floor was lightly vibrating like a platoon of soldiers about ready to break down the door. No, she wasn't going to die like this, right here and now, not with a gun in her face, not with scum criminals disposing of her body in the Pacific. Noticing that Kent Smith and Claude Filmer were momentarily distracted, she energized for a real fight.

"Help!" she screamed, and then kneed Filmer in the crotch. Kent Smith reached for the gun, the book fell out of Filmer's left hand, and the gun fired, *pop*.

The bullet missed her, and hit the spine of a book in the case behind her. She dropped to the door, but Filmer tried grabbing her. He even appeared ready to bite one of her ears as Kent Smith reached out to nab her by her hair or collar.

As she stretched her arms toward the door handle, the door swooshed open. She fell face-forward to the ground. She heard the words, "You're under arrest," several times, believing the police were about to lift her up off her feet and take her to jail. When she finally stood up, gasping for air, she came face-to-face with Mira and Ginnie Reidel. Then she fainted.

J.P. Osterman

Chapter 16 - The Boss

When she woke up on the floor, she noticed the entire office had turned into a throng of mad technicians working on Claude Filmer's CPUs and portable devices. They were analyzing monitors and confiscating keyboards as Steve Lerrefeiht stood by, watching them closely and ordering them not to leave one paperclip unturned. Next to him was Mira calling an ambulance, while Ginnie was kneeling next to Rae Anne and dabbing Rae Anne's face with a wet towel.

"She's coming to!" Ginnie Reidel drew close to her face. She looked concerned beyond belief.

The first thing Rae Anne noticed was Ginnie's unique blue-brown eye which reminded her of her mother's eyes. The appearance helped her regain consciousness, and quickly she sat up. Seeing security guards darting in and out of the office, along with FBI agents not far behind them, she fell back in relief onto a few books covered by her blazer. Someone had put it there as a pillowcase. "Ouch," she exhaled, feeling dizzy, her neck sore and a spot at the back of her head aching. At least they hadn't arrested her, yet; and she began crying. She grabbed Ginnie by her arm. "You wouldn't believe...you can't *possibly* believe what's been going on here, Ginnie!" Then she saw Steve glance at her.

Corporate Revenge

"Just rest, Rae Anne," she whispered, "just stay put for a little while longer until a medic can check you out."

Nodding, she closed her eyes. When she opened them, she saw Steve staring at her with inquisitive eyes. Could she trust him, and say more about everything she had discovered in front of him? Was he one of Filmer's accomplices? He was standing there, so obviously Claude Filmer and Kent Smith hadn't implicated him, at least just yet. Right now, until he was out of sight, she decided to remain secretive with the facts she had discovered and not divulge where she had hidden the flash drive and her iPhone. Together with the chip in her purse, they would be abundant evidence to incriminate everyone involved with illegal activities, corruption, theft of intellectual property, and invasion of privacy.

"Finally you're awake!" Mira Padeson said. "Get the paramedics up here to check her out!"

"No, take her to the hospital," Ginnie ordered.

Rae Anne saw Flora Henderson appear in her peripheral vision, and she signaled to her that she was okay. "Really, I'm all right." She dried her eyes on her sleeves.

"She's really shaken up," Ginnie said, followed by short statements of what Rae Anne must have enduring, being cooped up so long with Filmer and Kent in his secret office. "Poor girl!" She gave her a glass of water and began making Rae Anne take little sips.

"Really," she sipped some more. "I don't need a medical bill right now at this early point in my career, so please, no doctors." She sat up. "Besides I can't leave right now. I just need a little time, and then I'll tell you everything I found."

"Wow, the lady's makin' a joke?" Flora marveled. "I'm gettin' our group together! We can add to what she found and hand everything over to you, from emails to attachments." They backed away, inspecting Rae Anne from head to toe, patting her arms, and making her take sips of water.

"Really, I'm fine." Rae Anne breathed as if for the first time as Ginnie thrust a wad of Kleenex into her hands. She dabbed away her tears and blew her nose.

J.P. Osterman

Police officers rushed into the office, and several people with special RTI badges began directing them toward more evidence. They were corporate executives, but Rae Anne had never remembered seeing them. The she began telling Mira, Ginnie, and Flora that Claude Filmer and Kent Smith had tried to kill her. She remembered the items she had hidden. Steve was gone out of the office, so now she could reveal what she had discovered. "Oh, over there, on the window sill, you'll find a flash drive and my iPhone. I downloaded evidence of corruption, stolen intellectual properties, and proof of illegal monitoring."

"Invasion of privacy," Ginnie said as Mira retrieved Rae Anne's flash drive and iPhone. "I knew it. I knew those spider-ware drones were eavesdropping on conversations."

Looking as if she were dressed in a diving suit, Flora moved as if in slow motion to add flash drives and documents to the pool of evidence. "Here ya go, and people in several departments risked their jobs to get us this evidence." Flora handed presented them proudly into Mira's hands. Then she stood straight up, checking the time. "I have to get back down to accounting to let them know that everything we've done worked." She hugged Rae Anne, and Rae Anne returned her kind gesture.

"Bye, Flora, and thanks. I think I'd be in jail now if not for you." Rae Anne sat back down against the bookcase and watched Flora walk away in excitement with her team of special RTI investigators. She'd see them again soon, at least she hoped so; and it wouldn't take too long before the entire corporation would hear about the arrests of Kent Smith, Claude Filmer, and Susan Gurkle.

"I took lots of pictures and downloaded files that will prove Claude Filmer, Kent Smith, and Susan Gurkle were participating in illegal activities, perhaps even in military weapons systems," Rae Anne said, sipping water. Her lips and throat no longer parched, and her breathing felt near normal. She grabbed her handbag, rifled through it, and handed Mira the faulty sensor-chip. "Here, I found this before the lights

Corporate Revenge

went out. It was in the chip-fab lab. You better stop the next chip shipment from exporting to several fake companies, or RTI could be permanently out of business." Then she handed them a document she had quickly printed prior to them catching her. "And this print out shows millions of diverted dollars, and the names of employees Filmer blamed to cover up his tracks. He made *them* take the fall." She had tears in her eyes. "Families suffered. Filmer and his collaborators lied to employees when they hired them."

Mira suddenly gasped. "A big shipment of sensor chips was supposed to ship an hour ago to several of these companies on the list, but I don't recognize this foreign company as being one of our customers!"

Rae Anne heard the worst news ever. "That shipment better not fly 'cause we all lose our jobs!" She inserted her flash drive into Mira's laptop. A list of foreign addresses appeared on screen.

Ginnie Reidel bent her head low to read the addresses. "I've never heard of this company...Hermes Trading & Cie. It's definitely foreign." She had a look of anger in her eyes. Filmer had lied to her, but she believed his deceptions, and they fired her to look back, so they could make money and start a new company. She began mumbling every cuss word at them under her breath.

"Oh, now I see!" Mira said, in complete understanding. "This is the name of the company you left for me to find on my desk. I had an assistant working on discovering the background information Hermes Trading for the past two hours."

Rae Anne said, "Hermes Trading & Cie is part of Filmer, Smith and Gurkle's money laundering scheme."

Ginnie and Mira gasped and glanced around the room.

"Those three were selling sensor chips illegally to foreign companies," Rae Anne began, "but what I want to know..."

"What?!" Mira and Ginnie asked.

"Is if the three of them are working alone," Rae Anne said. Mira and Ginnie appeared flabbergast. "Yes, we think we've apprehended the people responsible…but have we, or are there more involved in the scheme to steal and sell designs, launder money, and illegally invade peoples' privacy?"

Feeling the little square chip if it contained an invaluable gold coin, Mira said, "This could be the thing that really hangs those executives. I don't know who else might be involved," she whispered, "but an investigation is just beginning, and big shots from corporate are incoming, and soon we'll discover who *exactly* exploited the people here and the technology."

Ginnie's face suddenly whitened with fright as her iPad returned a wait-mode answer on the Swiss company shipping and receiving order. "Did that shipment go out? I can't get an answer!"

The expressions on Mira's face contorted: "My gosh! I hope not!" She stood up and called out a number her cell phone. "I need to give this chip package *personally* to the corporate boss who's on the way here right now!"

Then, an FBI manager approached them with an evidence box. "Ma'am, I have a special team incoming to guard this evidence." The box was rectangular and metal with a key pad and a Smart-lock device. "We can't gain access to it."

"Of course not," Mira said, "it has precautionary protective measures like missile launch codes." She gestured for everyone to back away, input her code into the key pad, and then slid her special badge through the Smart-card reader. Slowly, she opened the box and peered inside. Sifting secretly and quickly though a collection of chips, she suddenly had a shocked expression on her face. "These chips can't go anywhere!" She slammed the box shut.

"What's wrong?" the agent asked, jumping back a little.

Mira appeared about ready to cry and also go into a rage. "I can't let this box leave this building. RTI technology is compromised, and so might be the United States government!"

Rae Anne inhaled air into the bottom of her ribs. "Did something I do, or designs I found make things worse?" She could hear light tapping sounds emanating from the box. Something had ignited, sparked, or caused something inside

Corporate Revenge

the box to activate. She looked up. The ceiling lights in Claude Filmer's office were not florescent, but a special LED light. Perhaps he had in his office a variation of that light fixture that Dr. Thornton Manning had invented so he could conduct a few experiments privately.

"No, the opposite, Ms. Hershel. You might have saved the United States of America!" Mira handed the box to four RTI *Floor 6* technicians. She then whispered into Rae Anne's ear: "What's in here is for the DOD, completely new! Its contents are Top-Secret, so *shhh*." The contents had to be part of RTI's Testing Department since the techs' badges had the imprint of the sixth floor. "Put these immediately into cold storage," she ordered them. After they accepted the box, signed for it, and left, she addressed the agent: "Call the Secretary of State. Send him information I'm about to transfer to you over your secure line." The agent whipped out a Samsung phone—obviously a prototype, because when it activated, a light illuminated. It had to have holographic potential! Tapping the screen, he input a jingling sequence of numbers, and then held it out for Mira to accept her data. She continued: "The Secretary of State will know what designs I'm referring to after he receives this file. He *knows* me. I'll send him my *new* contact information and call him later." She tapped an icon on her special phone, and then touched her phone to the agent's device, transferring the data.

"Okay, ma'am," the agent said.

Then Mira handed him the chip Rae Anne had stolen from the chip-fab lab. "Please make sure you log this faulty chip in with all the other evidence you're collecting against the ring of criminals." The agent walked over to another small secure evidence box and inserted the chip. "There's an executive on the way here from RTI's corporate office in Georgia. He needs to see this faulty sensor package immediately, so don't haul everything away just yet."

"Yes Ma'am, we won't, and besides, we're still holding Filmer, Smith, and Gurkle in the bottom-floor cage for continued interrogation," he said, and then he dashed away when more agents summoned him from down the hallway.

Rae turned to Ginnie Reidel and said, "I'm so glad you're back, Ginnie."

Patting her arm, Ginnie had tears in her eyes. "Yeah, me too, thanks."

"What happened? Did you get your job back?" Rae Anne asked.

Shrugging, she replied: "I'm pretty sure I will now. I told Mira that I had accidentally accessed a file that could possibly get Steve Lerrefeiht fired."

Rae Anne gasped. "Really?" she whispered, feeling victorious. "Yes! I just know the guy's a criminal...I can see suspicion and fear written all over his face."

The little brown splash in Ginnie's right eye changed to near purple through her tears. "I guess only time will tell if I was right about the information I discovered though."

"I'm sure you are! You did great!" Rae Anne said, patting her shoulder.

"Claude Filmer *appears* to be the ringleader of what's been happening around here." Ginnie began wiping her eyes as a human traffic jam blocked the entryway for a more secure escort of computer devices. Filmer's office had transformed into an evidence room. "We just don't know for how long all this illegal activity has been going on, if more employees are involved, and even if outside contractors are involved."

Rae Anne sat down in a chair that an agent had set in front of the bookcase, and Ginnie sat alongside her. Rae Anne felt stronger now, but still shaken, on edge, and hyper-vigilant. "At least Steve won't be firing anyone else for a *looong* time."

Ginnie gave a hard nod in Mira's direction. "She's going to make sure of that!"

Mira turned back to them. Her body appeared relaxed now, the tenth floor having been cleared of the enemy. "That shipment didn't go out, thank goodness." Then she gave Rae Anne a skeptical glance.

"What's wrong?" Rae Anne asked. Mira appeared not to recognize her!

Corporate Revenge

"An FBI agent downstairs told me that the fingerprints they found on Claude Filmer's computer don't match your name."

"What?" Ginnie said, reeling.

Closing her eyes and sighing, Rae Anne said, "Oh, I can explain."

"Are you in some kind of trouble, Mary?" Ginnie asked, whispering. "If you are, after everything you've done here for us, I wanna help you."

Rae Anne gave her an expression of innocents. "I can explain...really!"

Their eyes shone keen interest and their breaths seemed to rise in anticipation.

Rae Anne began to tell them her story: "Mira, remember when you talked about the man whom Steve Lerrefeiht fired?"

"Yes..."

"The man who sold over a hundred million dollars in sensor chips?"

"Yes…"

"You talked about him during lunch yesterday."

Mira and Ginnie glanced at each other askance, a look of puzzlement showing in their faces.

"You mean, Tim Westman," Mira said, "I remember that conversation."

Ginnie said, "I helped Tim Westman fill out his employment contract." Then her face lowered. "I also got his office after he, well, left."

There was a momentary silence.

Mira finally squelched it by asking, "What about Tim Westman, Mary?"

When Rae Anne heard that name—her alias—she felt her face heat up. She rolled her shoulders. She couldn't contain her big secret any longer. "Tim Westman is my husband." She breathed deeply, waiting for their response.

"What?" Mira's lips dropped.

"Your husband?" Ginnie repeated.

"Yep," Rae Anne exhaled, "my husband is Tim Westman."

"Oh my gosh!" Mira exclaimed as if he were in the room

with them, happy to see him.

"But you're name's Mary Hershel," Ginnie said.

Mira nodded no. "The FBI said her fingerprints don't match the name of Mary Hershel." Her expression turned somber. "They want to talk you. Now I understand why, but I'm sure you have a good explanation, especially considering that you—you alone—brought down an *entire* network of corruption." She tapped her cell phone screen, and a picture of Flora and her team of helpers appeared. They were smiling in the picture, with more RTI employees rallying behind them. She closed the picture, and tapped on another that was making headlines in the news: *FBI closing in on a Major Corporate Scandal!* "This will be all over the networks tonight." Mira had a pensive expression on her face. She might have to address the media blitz.

Seeing those letters, FBI, Rae Anne felt her stomach lurch. Looking Mira and Ginnie straight in their eyes, she continued, "While I was home paying bills, Tim called me after Steve fired him."

Ginnie's eyes lit up, "I remember Tim talking on the phone to someone when I was waiting to give him his severance package."

"Me," Rae Anne said, "Tim was talking to me."

"I'm still confused," Mira said. "The whole name change thing."

Huffing, Rae Anne said, "It's a long story."

Ginnie said, "We have a little time to hear it though." She rubbed her arms in a show of support.

Rae Anne folded her hands until she felt her knuckles. "Well, I was so upset after Steve fired Tim."

"That makes sense, 'because I was upset when he fired me!" Ginnie exclaimed.

Rae Anne sat up. Finally, some could empathize what it's like being fired!

"Go on, Mary," Ginnie encouraged.

Mira motioned for her to stop when she received an incoming jingle. She opened the message. "Rae Anne

Corporate Revenge

Westman is her real name." Mira squinted in a self-chastising manner for so suddenly forgetting the names of Tim's family members.

Rae Anne continued, "Tim told me that he'd never be receiving his commission...then I, well—"

"Decided to do something about all the unfairness, right?" Ginnie asked, giving her a giant nod and folding her arms.

"Yes!" Rae Anne replied, trying to defend. "I was so mad! I'd have to uproot my family again...possibly lose everything again!" She choked back tears as Mira touched her shoulder softly. "I didn't know if Tim was lying to me by blaming Steve, or if RTI employees were the real scoundrels he was making them out to be." She felt her heart race in anger. "You said yourself, Mira, that Tim had sold over a hundred million dollars in sensors."

"He did!" Mira said.

"And Steve fired Tim for no reason other than for over booking sales," Rae Anne said.

"*Hmm*, of course Steve would never admit that though," Mira began, "because he told me that Susan Gurkle had miscalculated manufacturing costs."

"Obviously, from the evidence Flora discovered, that was wrong," Ginnie said. "Gurkle, Filmer and Smith were siphoning off profits to that fake company, Hermes Trading & Cie."

"And paying Tim's commission would subtract from *their* funds," Rae Anne said angrily. "But now, we have proof of that." She felt victorious. "I can vindicate Tim, who can now hire an attorney to get what RTI owes him." She saw frightened expressions on their faces. "Not you...now sue you!" She laughed.

After they sighed in relief, Mira said: "He *should* get that commission, so before you seek a lawyer, let's wait for the corporate big shot to arrive. We'll talk out everything that happened, with you along with Ginnie and me."

"I wanted to get proof, right in my hands, that someone purposely cheated Tim by getting a job at RTI," Rae Anne said. "Now, I believe him. I feel horrible about ever doubting him, but now I know he was telling me the truth, and has been truthful with me from the very start." She wiped more tears from her eyes while also watching more technicians add to the pile of evidence. "I guess V.P. of Sales and Marketing sure has its perks when sales are up, but boy when sales are in a lull, or production is off, the job can be like a pressure cooker...and the executives in charge can fire them at will, and use any excuse, even if the excuses aren't fair."

"But Tim's dismissal wasn't fair in this situation," Mira began, "and I'll back him up...and maybe even be able to get him re-instated here at RTI."

Ginnie gestured like a fighter about to throw a punch. "What a *great* idea you had, Mary...I mean Rae Anne!" she said that as if wishing she could pull off such a smart but covert plot.

"I knew no one would hire me as Rae Anne Westman." Her body sagged in a bit of hopelessness. "I had to do an awful lot to become Mary Hershel." She also knew she was probably going to face a gauntlet of FBI interrogators. She felt the future was beginning to look a bit grim in spite of all the good she had accomplished and the people behind her, supporting her.

"Completely cool," Ginnie exclaimed with a smile beaming on her face.

Mira heaved in a deep breath, and then exhaled hard. "What a stunt, Mary...I mean Rae Anne...what a—a—"

"Adventure," Ginnie interrupted, thrusting her hands into the air. "One giant ride!" She tapped Rae Anne playfully on her shoulder. "Wait until this gets around RTI. Your name will be in print on the cafeteria wall!"

They laughed, and Rae Anne felt her eyes water with tears. "I don't know about that," she began, feeling humble, "but at least we don't have to move now. Or at least I hope we don't. I hope I still might have a job..."

There was a long paused filled with sighs of relief.

"What are you going to do?" Ginnie asked Mira.

Corporate Revenge

Mira leaned in hard. "Tell the corporate boss when he arrives, that's what I'm going to do. We can be with you if you want us to, when you have to meet with the FBI, Rae Anne. Right, Ginnie?"

"My gosh, yes!" Ginnie said without hesitating.

Rae Anne felt relief beyond measure. "Thanks, I'd like that."

Mira added: "I'll vouch for you. With your skills, I know I can procure a position for you here at RTI."

"I hope so," Rae Anne said, drying her eyes. "I hope the corporate executive from Georgia will understand me after hearing me out. Tim doesn't have a job, and right now, I'm not sure if I'll have one, and our new home is in jeopardy." She swallowed hard, stopping her tears. "I hate to move again. I really do." She fell short of telling them just how many moves she had been though during the past seven years.

Suddenly, Flora rushed back into the room where agents were still bustling to sift through evidence. "Do you feel well enough to do a little more work, Mary?" she asked Rae Anne.

Standing, she still felt a little dizzy. "Just a second." She steadied herself as Mira and Ginnie began questioning Flora. They wanted to know what could be so urged as to need Rae Anne's immediate attention. Walking around the chairs and stretching, Rae Anne said: "I'm fine now, really." Holding onto her balance, she noticed Flora's frazzled appearance. She had her blouse out of her skirt, her light-blue eye shadow was blotchy under her eyebrows, and the whites of her eyes were pink-tinged. "You look worn out, Flora, like you've run fifteen times around a track."

"What's going on?" Ginnie asked.

"After I left the clothes for you in the stairway," Flora began, "I went down to our legal section. A few of us accessed the attorneys' computers and discovered that someone had turned the legal department into a profit center." *Ha-huh,* she gasped, glancing wildly at each of them and around the office.

"What?" Mira asked.

"Whoever did all the criminal finagling created a

palindrome of blame on us innocent people!" she exclaimed.

"Flora, calm down! It's gonna be all right!" Mira said, grabbing her hands and holding them gently. After Flora's breathing returned to near normal and Ginnie made her sit down, Mira said, "Now, tell us more, Flora." She activated a cell-phone recording app. "Go."

Flora said, "We found an attachment!"

"What kind of attachment?" Mira asked.

"Susan Gurkle, the CFO, has been using RTI's legal department as a profit center instead of as a cost center. Then she covered up her tracks by using employees' emails and linking them with private employee information. Now we look responsible...and the FBI wants to interrogate us!"

"Oh my gosh," Ginnie exclaimed, "our legal department is no more!"

Mira gestured for them both to calm down, and Rae Anne handed them cups of steaming coffee she had asked techs to bring into the office as refreshments.

Flora began sipping hers as she continued to speak to Mira, and into Mira's cell phone, recording every word: "They've been stealing, Filmer and his band. They've been using the intellectual property of startup companies."

Mira asked a sixth floor tech for his iPad, and she launched several Top-Secret and Confidential files.

Rae Anne realized they were company secrets that other clients and subcontractors had entrusted to RTI, because Mira lifted the iPad in front of her face, totally obstructing its perusal.

"I see some of those designs," Mira said, closing the apps and giving the iPad back to the sixth floor technician. "Take those to Mr. Lerrefeiht and Dr. Manning. Have them wall off the technology for complete review for when the corporate boss arrives, and we can discuss these files and intellectual properties." After they left, she told Flora, "See, I'm taking care of this to make sure, that in no way, will you and your team be blamed for anything."

Flora sat back in relief. "Thank you, Ma'am."

Corporate Revenge

"Now, go on. Tell us more," Mira ordered.

Flora sipped more coffee. "Claude Filmer knew full-well that those smaller companies can't fight back in court." Cold-hearted anger welled in her every gesture. "If I can get my hands on that—"

"I know," Mira said, gently. "We're all pretty ticked off right now, but let's stay level."

"Yes, Ma'am."

"The more we remain calm and present evidence, the better we'll be able to resolve all our problems and re-open RTI for business."

"Yes, Ma'am...you're right, Ma'am."

As Ginnie poured her more coffee, Flora continued: "RTI's legal department's been launching preemptive patent infringement lawsuits against the companies they steal technology from. That forces these tiny companies to spend all their money in legal fees, and then forces them to sign over their inventions to RTI before they allow the little company off the hook and settle. In the end, these little companies have no choice but to pay the exorbitant legal fees if they want to get RTI off their back and stop the financial bleeding."

Mira made sure her cell phone was still recording and sending Flora's statement to a secure FBI cloud site. "I'm launching a review of all our lawyers right now."

Ginnie pulled up RTI legalese on her iPad. "What they did is *completely* unethical, and a *totally* illegal method of profiting from their theft of small company IP." She had a chastising tone of voice as she folded her arms over her flowered blouse and peered at Rae Anne, Flora, and Mira from under the rim of her white cat-eye glasses. "Good companies we *could* work with will go out of business if we don't make what happened right with them."

The police and FBI had almost amassed all their evidence, and Claude Filmer's office was now a pterodactyl's nest of orderly white file boxes. Agents and Steve Lerrefeiht were questioning heads of departments in the offices next to Claude's and across the hallway.

J.P. Osterman

"It's only a matter of time before Filmer, Smith, and Gurkle head to federal prison," Mira said.

An agent interrupted. "They might sing like canaries and incriminate more people to avoid life sentences. We're working on gettin' 'em to talk right now!" Then he dashed out the office.

Sighing in relief, Rae Anne said: "Well, I also hope that the information on the flash drive I stole from their computers will help the FBI build a strong case against them, along with pictures I took that prove that Filmer and Smith sabotaged Dr. Manning's experiment."

After Mira closed the Record app on her cell phone, they began walking toward the Executive Conference room. Rae noticed a profound change in the atmosphere. Ginnie and Flora agreed with her. Prior to the company closure just hours ago, people appeared sullen and guarded. Now, they had energetic and enthusiastic bounces to their steps. Their company badges were off their pockets, jackets and sweaters. They were ripe to receive a new direction and new bosses.

Thus far, Mira said no one had been fired or laid off, only put on administrative leave until the corporate boss from Georgia could make a presentation, make a statement to the FBI, instigate some major changes, and then re-open RTI for business. *Big changes are coming* were the buzz words circling through the company—an entire revamping of policies and procedures. As they were about to enter the Executive Conference room, a refined woman in her late forties walked in front of them, quickly opened the door, ordered her security guards to keep all the doors open, and walked into the conference room. Mira began helping the guards adjust the door jams.

Rae Anne watched the distinguished woman walk down the long aisle toward the center of the room. Dressed in the nicest light-blue suit Rae Anne had ever seen, she looked like royalty. She held her head high, and scowled at portable devices FBI agents were confiscating from employees who were lined up at the opposite side of the room. They were turning in their

Corporate Revenge

devices for perusal. Mira walked down to the woman who had planted herself at the site where Thornton Manning's experiment had failed. She appeared lost because of the light fixture's still-smoky appearance. She began talking to Mira.

Rae Anne said, "Who is—"

"She must be the executive from Georgia!" Ginnie proclaimed.

Chapter 17 – Corporate Arrives

As the blue-suited woman began directing agents where to search for information, Rae Anne surmised the woman had to be a powerful executive, yet she hadn't seen a picture of any corporate leader anywhere. "Who is she?" she asked Ginnie.

Leaning into Rae Anne, Ginnie replied, "I don't know, but she looks like she's a real estate agent, not a business woman."

"*Hmm*, maybe," Rae Anne said.

"Maybe she's here to assessing the company…but then again, she doesn't appear to be appraising assets." Ginnie squinted at her, and then gasped. "No, she looks like that star of that old TV show in the late eighties…Oh, what was that called," she said, snapping her fingers. "Oh, I know, *Murphy Brown*. She looks like Candice Bergen!"

"Huh? But what would *she* be doing here, unless a Hollywood writer had heard about our problems, decided to write screen play about corporate scandal, and was here to beat other writers to make a deal with a producer."

"Ha!" Ginnie giggled.

"Yeah, that's pretty crazy, 'cause it's too soon for that," Rae Anne said, craning her neck to get a better look at the elegant woman assessing damages from earlier in the day.

Ginnie then waved her hand as if correcting a terrible error

Corporate Revenge

in perception. "Oh, she's much younger than Candice Bergen, but she looks like she visits a salon every day. She's so regal looking. That's the only way I can describe her, striking and rich!"

"I agree." Rae Anne noticed the woman's brightly polished nails and smooth skin.

"She sure does look like Candice Bergen," Ginnie said, puffing up her bouffant and then smoothing down her 1950s style skirt.

Giving a slight shoulder nod, Rae Anne said: "I'm more interested in your *first* guess at who she is."

"Oh, real-estate agent you mean?" Ginnie asked. A long pause ensued as they watched the commanding woman engage in a heated discussion with two FBI agents. She was pointing at several locations around the building as if intimately connected to each room and concerned about each employee.

"Do you think that corporate will be selling RTI?" Rae Anne asked.

Shrugging, Ginnie said, "I don't know, but I can sure understand why corporate would want to change names." Her face shone a sign of urgency. "RTI better do something, 'cause if not, the company will have a terrible reputation and go bankrupt!" She frowned. "What a scandal, and too bad, because most everyone here has a family."

"I have two children," Rae Anne said, remembering she had told Ginnie she was childless. She had lied, but only to secure her position. Now, she wanted to tell her the complete truth and clear the air.

With downcast eyes, Ginnie said, "I saw the pictures Tim had on his desk." She had a glint of shame in her eyes. "I'm sorry I was so—well—negative before, when I asked you if you had children."

"It's okay," Rae Anne said, seeing her so vulnerable.

An expression of fatigue rolled over Ginnie's body. She said she really enjoyed the day off after being fired, and then she added: "All the overtime some of our employees have to work really puts unbearable stress on them. Two men had to be carted out of here because of chest pains last week. One woman broke down in the bathroom crying because she couldn't attend her daughter's championship soccer game, and a man Steve fired a month ago returned and threatened someone with a gun in the parking lot." She looked near crying, her face red, her head shaking in obvious self-blaming.

"That's terrible." Rae Anne patted her arm, trying to support her through her tears, and then she handed her a Kleenex. "Look, now I understand why you were so negative about my having kids. You were just trying to warn me about Steve's policies, and that I'd have to work a lot of overtime if you'd hire me."

Ginnie smiled. "We're okay then, as co-workers, maybe friends, right?" She had a pleading expression in her eyes.

"Of course," Rae Anne replied. They were still in the aisle, far up in the Executive Conference room and waiting for Mira to summon them, and introduce them to the sophisticated female visitor who was asking maintenance workers to retrieve everything from Dr. Thornton Manning's experiment.

Steve walked up to Mira and the visitor. He was straightening his collar and his hands were shaking. The elegant woman had angry eyes and gave him an order the second he approached her. Steve nodded almost in a salute, turned, and walked up the aisle toward the exit while mumbling. He had a sarcastic expression on his face, and appeared angry enough to retaliate at her chastisement, but he hadn't. The female visitor was definitely someone high up in the corporate ladder, and intimidating.

"Wow, did she just lay into him!" Rae Anne whispered to Ginnie.

"She sure did!" Ginnie agreed, gesturing in fear.

"I bet *he* won't be outside RTI anymore in the morning, with his little notebook and pencil in hand, jotting down names of people who don't arrive fifteen minutes early for work," Rae Anne laughed. He was getting at least a bit of what he deserved: someone scolding him. "I wonder how long he's going to last here at RTI...I wonder if he was a part of

Corporate Revenge

everything bad that happened." Her gut told her yes, but she hadn't discovered proof.

Ginnie laughed. "She's definitely someone important!" She nodded at the blue-suited woman still talking to Mira and directing agents. "She *really* knows what she's doing."

"Let's walk up and see," Rae Anne said, "I'm not waiting in the shadows any longer." She had taken great risks already, so approaching an important stranger who appeared to have a movie star persona, seemed to pale in comparison. Ginnie and she slowly joined a little crowd now congregating around the area where Dr. Manning's experiment had failed.

Standing in front of a lead FBI investigator, the elegant woman handed him a folder. "In here you'll find all the commands to access the main RTI server. I had passwords to open our iCloud accounts. We have a private company that handles most of our cloud computing, so call me when they need proof of my identity." Her voice sounded soft and pleasant, and she was wearing a faint light perfume.

Two FBI agents approached her and handed her Claude Filmer's name plate. They told her they changed the access codes to the office, now a formal evidence room. *No one* could gain admittance there until an entire team—involving several official departments—from D.C. would arrive to categorize the evidence.

Handing the agents her business card, the elegant woman said: "I intend to cooperate fully in all areas of your investigation. I am relocating here at this moment to be available for questioning." She breathed, spotted Rae Anne, and began glancing at her intermittently, with inquisitive eyes. Obviously, she had recognized her, and Rae Anne believed the woman would soon be approaching her. Now she felt a bit nervous. The woman continued: "This company also intends to make full restitution to all the companies that Mr. Filmer, Mr. Smith, and Ms. Gurkle harmed. Hopefully, we can revitalize or salvage some of those lost deals and strike up a new partnership with them."

Taking notes, one agent said, "We've read them their rights

already, and have advised them to seek legal counsel."

The refined executive asked him, "What are you charging them with exactly?"

Standing like a referee announcing a winner, the agent replied: "A whole string of things!" He flipped to a page in his black notebook and tapped his pencil on the first charge. "We have 'em on fraud for shipping the fake sensor chips, absconding with RTI funds, money laundering, the malicious patent infringement law suits, stock manipulation, and insider trading on several foreign accounts." He stretched the notebook out in front of his eyes, taking a second glance. "That's just for starters!"

Whew, the sharply-dressed business woman sighed, lowering her face in obvious shame.

Rae Anne believed that if she were in her position, she'd feel completely overwhelmed, and she was shocked the woman wasn't collapsing with all the bad news hitting her from every direction.

The woman's long fingers glided down her forehead to her cheeks. She exhaled and said: "What a deluge of illegal activities! What a mess for the new lawyers." After she told Mira to begin the process of hiring a new legal team, she asked the agent, "How long will you be tying up all the company funds?"

Appearing powerless over time, the investigator replied: "Well, maybe we can cut a deal with these crooks. If their stories line up, your funds should release with the court's approval."

"What kind of deal though?" she asked, looking at him askance, "I hate to see the offenders get off lightly for all the hell they've unleashed here at RTI."

He closed his black book. "In exchange for handing over all their hidden accounts and returning the stolen funds, we can place them in a better prison facility, but that's about the extent to which we're gonna cut these bozos a deal!"

"That's good enough for me," she said firmly. "I just hope their jail terms will help save our reputation. Our investors, and the public, are going to bury us after learning about all this corruption."

"Well," the agent began in an accusatory tone, "people sure will be asking questions, like, why didn't someone notice all the rampant criminal activity from the outset?" He had blaming eyes aiming at the blue-suited executive.

Anyone else might have cried, or launched a longwinded self-defense, or lashed out in a narcissistic explosion. Not the blue-suited executive. Her facial expressions and body language remained calm and pensive. She could think under intense pressure, obviously always considering the consequences of her actions, and not impulse driven.

Then the FBI agent left with a band of police officers who were hailing him at the top of the stairs. However, she still had things to say to him; so she motioned for Mira, Ginnie, and Rae Anne to accompany her up the aisle toward the exit. After they exited the conference room into the long white corridor, the woman said goodbye to the agent. The hallway was chaotic. People were rushing everywhere as if dashing for trains. They were carrying everything from files to portable devices, from wheeling cards to rolling cases of equipment. She heard one woman call to another, "Hey—we gotta be down to the first floor conference room at three o'clock! Save me a seat!"

Something big was on the verge of happening at RTI.

Turning to Mira, the woman suddenly stopped at the side of the hallway. "I'm calling a meeting for 3 p.m. It's for all our employees."

"All?" Mira asked, peering at her iPhone.

"You got it," the woman said.

"Yes, I see the announcement here," Mira said.

Rae Anne checked her phone as did Ginnie. "I see mine," she said.

"I sent out massive texts and emails," the woman said. "I'm taking back *my* company."

Rae Anne felt stunned, until all the pieces of the past few hours began assembling into one solid picture of the regal woman. From her words, the conversations she had had with the FBI agent and Steve, the immaculately dressed woman had to be the founder of RTI!

The woman shook hands with Ginnie and introduced herself. When she extended her hand to Rae Anne, Rae Anne said, "Hi, I'm Rae Anne Westman." Then she looked down, afraid she might be in trouble for using a fake identity.

"I'm Doctor Justina Phillips," the woman smiled, "and the founder of RTI." She shook her hand. Her grip was strong and affirming.

The warmth in Justina's eyes and the realization that a big corporate icon had managed to disguise her identity for quite some time made Rae Anne's fears of being prosecuted and thrown into jail fade. She gave sighed in relief and held her hand over her heart. She wanted to know more about Justina Phillips. "I'm so pleased to meet you, Ma'am...but I thought your name was Justin Phillips. That's what my husband Tim told me, although he never saw a picture of you in the Executive gallery."

Justina appeared taken off guard, but paused in obviously reflective thought, perusing Rae Anne. "Yes, I made a terrible mistake doing that, but now I'm in the process of correcting it."

"I'll set up a photo shoot for you, Dr. Phillips, for after this afternoon's meeting," Mira said. She had three assistants now. Justina had to have given her a new temporary position until RTI's Engineering department could return to work.

After accepting Mira's offer, Justina continued: "I founded Riata Technology. I created and patented several pixel designs and image sensor architectures that were the foundation of this business." Her blue eyes watered with tears and she swallowed hard as anger shone in her every gesture. Criminals had invaded her company. "RTI was *my* startup, my creation. But several years ago, investors advised me to create a pseudonym. They said the corporate world was a man's world. They told me that I'd never survive on Wall Street or any other street with the name Justina."

Corporate Revenge

Anyone else would have broken out in a pout, or ranted and raved about being victimized. Not Justina Phillips. She lifted her head high, obviously occupied with fixing her mistakes and taking action. She was a real solution generator.

"*Hah*—I call what happened to you a misuse of power," Rae Anne said angrily, continuing to walk down the hallways with her.

"Power has its strengths and its misuses," she said to Rae Anne and Ginnie. Her walk around the tenth floor had to be part of Justina's plan. Every now and then, employees would notice her, stop, and greet her. Justina would introduce herself, shake their hands, thank them for their services, and pay each person a compliment.

Rae Anne realized she was standing with a woman who had allowed people to dictate her identity, who had fallen into the trap of believing that in spite of her advanced education, she needed to let others run her corporation. No more. Justina Phillips was back for good at RTI, and strong, and determined.

"Well, you're taking RTI back now, Dr. Phillips," Ginnie said.

"Completely," Justina said, her chin high, "and I will press charges against every corrupt employee in this company."

Rae Anne wondered how Justina would ever be able to accomplish that feat, considering only three employees thus far had been discovered.

Chapter 18 – Steve, a Changed Man

When they reached the first floor, someone held the door open for her into the auditorium that had the capacity to seat five thousand people. The maintenance crew had already replaced name tags at the center stage from where Justina would be making her presentation. Workers were busy bees, counting seats, corroborating with departments, and bringing in more chairs. Electricians were adding plugs and wiring to tables as a catering crew was setting up a row of tables on both sides of the auditorium where they would be serving refreshments. Rae Anne, Ginnie, and Mira walked down aisles to the center of the auditorium with Justina.

Before Justina could talk to Mira, Steve walked up to her with his head bent low, exuding contrition. He didn't speak a work. He was a difference man. He should have caught on to all the criminal transactions and activities happening right under his nose; and if he had been a part in the corruption, Justina would surely fire him immediately. On the long table at Justina's waist level, set Dr. Manning's failed experiment.

Suddenly, Thornton Manning bounded into the auditorium like a conductor. "Dr. Phillips! I have another!" Carrying a brass-covered crucible in his hands, he had a second prototype ready for display. He was smiling as if starting a new career.

Corporate Revenge

He had been vindicated from any wrongdoing. "I have a new light fixture in manufacturing, ready to produce more prototypes, and Testing has already set aside time for me and my team. So in a week, if RTI re-opens, I can complete my new chip, and in two weeks give another demonstration."

"Great Dr. Manning," Justina encouraged.

"I know the next time I take center stage, there will be no interference, and my new design will be successful and will change the world." He put the brass plate in front of her, but did not lift off the lid.

"Yes, Dr. Manning," Justina said, tapping the shiny brass-covered crucible, "and RTI will be privileged to be a part of this change. Now, I have only an hour until the company presentation. I have some details I have to iron out to rally support and fire up employees so they'll want to stay and be a part of a new company."

Rae Anne began helping Mira and Ginnie message all their company contacts, set up departmental meetings, and call clients whom Claude Filmer had alienated.

Still, Rae Anne remained fearful and tried to keep her distance from Justina even though she or another executive hadn't dismissed her for interrogation with the FBI. But that moment was coming, and all Rae Anne could do in the few minutes she had left of being an RTI employee was to work hard to impress Justina, and show her she could accomplish big things in a timely manner. At some point, Justina would want to talk to her privately, or with the police, or the FBI, but hopefully, not at the San Diego County jail!

Chapter 19 – The New R.T.I.

After all the employees seated themselves comfortably in the auditorium, the noise lowered as Justina walked in front of the long table at the center of the auditorium. The lights dimmed softly, and a low beam shone gently on Justina from above. With the mid-afternoon sunlight streaming in through long windows along the baseboards, and the employees gossiping excitedly about experiencing changes, RTI appeared a newly erected building.

Glancing at faces around the room as if acknowledging each person, the founder of RTI said, "I'm Dr. Justina Phillips."

All the employees began listening to her words through pin-dropping silence. With hope in their eyes, many looked eager, but some also appeared skeptical about pledging their loyalty to her. Justina would have to win them over—win them back—with action, not words.

Clearing her throat, Justina said, "I want to apologize for not being more active in my company." Her blue-green eyes appeared to meet the gaze of each employee.

"I want to tell you why," she began, "not as an excuse, but as a way for us to start over." Tears were in her eyes, and she began dabbing them away, after which time she clicked on the

Corporate Revenge

giant IMAX screen and began presenting her history, and a case for renewal and change to her employees.

From articles in various magazines and newspapers, the public believed that the multi-billion dollar business tycoon was a man. However, as the news media was now breaking all the corruption at RTI to TV and radio stations, RTI employees began learning the truth, not only about Justina Phillips, but also about all the corruption that Rae Anne, Mira, Ginnie and Flora had uncovered. Justin was *not* a recluse whose life was on the verge of decline as in the story of Howard Hughes' later years. She was a woman who had retreated to New York's Upper-Eastside where most of the upper-class families, like the Rockefellers, Roosevelts, Whitneys, Dukes and Kennedys had lived for decades. There, Justina took on the false identity of Justin Phillips, Chairman of Riata Technology, and became what her powerful investors and board members demanded her to be: silent and secluded in their shadows.

"Now, I am throwing off that image," she said, her shoulders straight in pride and her chin high. "I will no longer run RTI from my Upper-Eastside home office in New York, but from right here in San Diego."

Employees stood and applauded. Some people cried in the realization that they had just been saved.

"Things will be different at this company as we move forward," Justina said, "and I intend to repay all the damages incurred by a few *former* corrupt executives."

Looking down into the parking lot from a small window along the baseboard, Rae Anne spotted TV vans and lines of cameras waiting to interview Justina. She felt proud and teary-eyed at the realization that she had participant in so many discoveries throughout the day, and had been a part of something big in the corporate history of America.

After an hour's worth of presentation in which Justina voiced her vision and plan for RTI's future, she dismissed all the employees for the day. As people began leaving, she asked Rae Anne, "Ms. Westman, will you please stay so you can debrief?"

"Yes, Ma'am," Rae Anne replied.

"Mira," Justina added, "can you stay as well and record the meeting?"

Maybe Justina had cut a deal with the FBI...or perhaps Justina had agreed to question her and then send the discussion for perusal to the FBI or other government organization. Whatever the case, Rae Anne felt a bit more at ease, but not yet cleared of criminal activity. In reality, she had procured a fake ID. She had agreed to use the assets of Witness Protection, and that act had to have consequences, for Gene her ex, and her. Now, she felt afraid.

When they were alone in the theater room, Justina faced Rae Anne with frankness. "Ms. Westman, it took a lot of courage to do what you did." She had an expression of awe written everywhere on her face.

"Please call me Rae Anne."

Mira agreed with Justina. "If not for Rae Anne, corruption might have continued on for some time, and RTI would crumble into ashes at some point."

Justina exhaled in amazement. "Yes for sure! So thank you, Rae Anne."

"You're welcome," Rae Anne said, folding her hands and setting them elegantly on her lap. Justina Phillips was becoming her model. "I know I lied to get hired here," she choked back tears. "I'm sorry."

Justina listened compassionately as Mira touched Rae Anne's shoulder and handed her a Kleenex.

"And from what you just said, that I was courageous, well, you must know that I used the name Mary Hershel. My name *is* Rae Anne Westman." She looked up from her hands to peer into Justina's light blue eyes.

Justina nodded, "Yes, I know. I do have all that information." She opened a file on her iPhone and Rae Anne's resume appeared. "It's been modified though. You're much brighter...and much more experienced that this resumes portrays you to be...an Engineer."

"Oh, Flora modified her resume a little after she helped her

Corporate Revenge

in the stairwell," Ginnie interrupted. "Flora had to cover Rae Anne's trail, because we didn't know who was responsible for the criminal activity, but someone had discovered Rae Anne—I mean Mary—and Flora and her team were helping her."

"Whoow," Rae Anne gasped, "so that's why they said I was only an assistant. Thanks! I owe Flora one heck of a party!" They all laughed.

With Mira at her side, Justina sat tall and said to Rae Anne: "You helped this company, *my* company, and for that, I'm grateful, and I will do everything to help you and be at your side during any type of questioning." She really meant it! She'd drop any meeting and be there for Rae Anne...the certainty was in her eyes. "I have friends."

"Really? Thanks!" Rae Anne said, sitting up straight and sighing in relief.

"If not for what you did, I don't think I would have discovered all the corruption and fraud for months—"

"Or until we had the FBI storming RTI's doors!" Mira added.

Justina gave her a hard nod of agreement. "That's right, especially if those fake sensor chips had shipped. We'd be in worse trouble!"

"What I did was a good thing," Rae Anne said, energetically. Then she turned her gaze to the white floor. "Even though what I did was a bit fraudulent."

Justina slapped her lap. "That's the past, and I won't bring up your alias anymore if you'll forget her too."

"Sure," Rae Anne said adamantly, "so Mary Hershel is no more."

Justina laughed. "And Justin Phillips is gone too."

They laughed again, but this time through an atmosphere of hope.

"Here's what I'm going to do." Justina pushed aside Thornton Manning's failed experiment that he had given her for evidence and reached for a folder. She set the folder on her lap, folding her hands over it firmly. "I'm offering you a position as Assistant Director with Ginnie Reidel in our

System Architecture department. As before, Ginnie works for Mira, so the three of you will be collaborating often." She opened the folder. Inside there was a contract, and she pushed it right under Rae Anne's eyes.

"Wow, great!" Rae Anne said, marveling at the contract as if it were an invaluable scroll. Skimming over the first page, she noticed no double wording or tiny print needing a magnifying glass.

"I'm glad you feel so excited about the position," Justina said, tapping the contract. "Read it over tonight, and take it to a lawyer if you'd like...take your time."

"Oh, tonight's fine," Rae Anne said.

"Then please come in tomorrow morning so we can negotiate the terms and talk about any concerns you may have," Justina said.

"I don't know what to say," Rae Anne sighed, "but yes, I'll read it over and be in at nine!"

"At first when you return, you'll be interfacing with Engineering."

"They've got serious problems," Ginnie said, "so we have to instigate big changes in software protocol, disclosure policy, and micro-architecture. We all need to get on the same page with collaborating, chip design, and testing."

"Yes! As soon as the court releases all our files," Justina said adamantly. Then she directed Ginnie to gather all of those policies before she left for the evening and send them to her company email.

"I'll need to leave now though, Justina, 'cause this is gonna take some time," Ginnie said.

"Good, go, and then go home," Justina order, "'cause it's been a long day, and I need you fresh and ready for action on Monday."

After Ginnie said goodbye and left, Justina received an email that had to contain more bad consequences. "*Rrrr*...that I let several moneygrubbing investors run *my* company! I just learned several of them recommended Claude Filmer!" She was smoldering over her entire experiences since founding

Corporate Revenge

RTI. "Mira, please get Mr. Westman on the speaker phone."

"Tim?" Rae Anne asked.

"Yes," Justina replied.

"Yes, Justina," Mira said, and she brought the phone to the long table on which Dr. Manning's experiment still set.

As Mira tapped in his number, Justina continued to address Rae Anne. "If you're willing, I would like you to start tomorrow, Tuesday, with a salary of $155,000 a year, plus all the usual benefits and 401K. That is, after we make any modifications to your contract."

Rae Anne thrust her fingers to her lips. "Yes! I don't know what to say!"

"You deserve this," Justina said, wide-eyed and leaning into her. "You are qualified."

Mira pulled out a brochure from the back of the folder containing Rae Anne's contract. "Dr. Phillips has another opportunity for you as well."

"I have a fund that contributes to our employees pursuing their continuing education," Justina said. "You could use it."

"I'd like that," Rae Anne said.

"Did you ever consider studying to be an attorney?" Justina asked.

Rae Anne never believed she was smart enough, but now she had someone affirming her abilities. "I could check into it," she said when Justina put another form in front of her.

"I think you'd make a great attorney," Justina said.

Rae Anne believed RTI would need a whole new slew of lawyers to get them out of what would obviously become a long, drawn out excruciating process. "Yes, Dr. Phillips—"

"Please call me Justina," she said, leaning into her and touching Rae Anne's hand.

Tim answered the phone. "Hello, this is Tim Westman."

Rae Anne felt her heart race in excitement but also fear. Where was he? She hadn't talked to him in a while. Who was he with? The last person he had talked to was her ex, Gene! Tim had agreed to her scheme, but only for a few days. Still, he was pissed at her! Their marriage was in jeopardy, and she had no idea what Justina was about to tell him.

"Hi, Mr. Westman, my name is Dr. Justina Phillips, and I am the founder of Riata Technology." She had a soft and apologetic tone.

"Yes?" he asked, his voice lilting in suspicion.

Justina began recounting everything Rae Anne had done to expose RTI's former corruption, after which Tim said: "I warned her not to do it, Dr. Phillips, but I guess she did do a great thing! Is she okay? Has anything happened to her?" He had told her she could be thrown in jail!

Rae Anne felt relieved and whispered to Mira, "Well, when he comes home, we're really going to celebrate!" They laughed.

After picking up another folder off the table, Justina had concern in her eyes. "I hope you haven't taken another position yet, Mr. Westman."

"No, Ma'am, I haven't," Tim said.

"Then I'd like to offer you your previous position," she began, "with all your previous benefits, including that $250,000 commission the person who hired you promised you. In fact, because of the trouble Claude Filmer and his band of criminals caused you, I intend to *Gross-Up* your commission to $360,000. That should cover all your taxes." Then she shook her head in disgust. "I'm so sorry Susan Gurkle didn't honor your commission and failed to acknowledge all the hard work you accomplished for the benefit of RTI. In fact, I have asked accounting to cut the check today, so Rae Anne can bring your commission home with her tonight."

"Tim, that's enough for us to pay off half our new house!" Rae Anne exclaimed, right into Justina's phone.

They continued to speak as Tim gasped in amazement at what Justina was offering him, including RTI's continued financial support in paying for their rent and storage, something Steve Lerrefeiht had promised but reneged on.

"Mr. Westman? Can you start as RTI's V.P. of Sales and Marketing on Monday?" Justina asked. "That will give you time to arrive back to Carlsbad and recover from your long

Corporate Revenge

trip." Mira was taking notes, and now-and-then glanced up at Rae Anne, giving her the thumbs up signal, and smiling.

Tim said, "Yes, of course." His tone of voice was sheer shock and amazement.

"I want to turn over a new leaf here at RTI, and make sure our employees are encouraged to disclose any wrongdoing internally," Justina began. "It will now be the company's policy from this moment forward that we reward employees for having the courage to do so. By rewarding internal whistleblowers here at RTI, I want to make sure all of our employees know that it is safe and desirable to disclose wrongdoings they see internally. It's important to me that everyone sees that I have noticed and care about doing the 'right thing' every time." Justina then said with a stern face: "I want you to know that if I find proof of fraud directly stemming from Steve Lerrefeiht, I'll fire him as I did the others." She pursed her lips, implying she hated firing people, but couldn't tolerate dishonesty either. "In that case, I intend to make you my President." She put the folder on her lap and began leafing through its contents. "You're just as qualified as Mr. Lerrefeiht for that position. And you will have it—that is, if I do find that Mr. Lerrefeiht was involved in any fraud."

Tim said, "I'll be happy to meet with you on Monday, Dr. Phillips to sign all the contracts."

"Mira Padeson and I will see you at 9:00 a.m. then on Monday. Have a nice rest of the week, Mr. Westman," Justina said.

Tim replied in an excited voice: "I'll take the next flight home. See you tonight, Rae Anne!"

"Bye Tim!" Rae Anne heard a giant, "Yippee," as he hung up the phone, and she gasped in relief. No divorce court, no separation, no anger. They would be all right.

She suspected Steve Lerrefeiht might be involved in the fraud. The evidence could be in one of Tim's emails she copied from computers and sent to her computer. Justina needed to know.

When she told her about sending several RTI files home so

she could weed through them, Justina said: "I want every iota of corruption and fraud exposed in my corporation. Send those files to the FBI as well." She handed her the agent's business card. "I want nothing held back. If my company is going to be successful from this point forward, every bad seed has to go." Her words were direct and authoritative. "Their lives will never be the same after we're through with the criminals. I want them prosecuted to the fullest extent of the law!" Mira handed her a draft of a future policy, one that many new corporations were implementing to protect their employees and instigate improvements to stay in business. "I want to make a difference in how and if employees make disclosures in the future. One of the great trust destroyers in any company is a policy that is not uniformly and consistently carried out. Affirming a culture of trust requires that all our policies be upheld and enforced consistently. This means that RTI's policies will be applied consistently every time and uniformly to all employees regardless of status from our line supervisors to me, the CEO."

Rae Anne felt a shot of shame flow through her. She understood Justina's need for justice, and she believed the criminals needed to make restitution. However, what if Filmer, Smith, and Gurkle had children? She had never considered that! Definitely, their children would suffer alongside their parents. They'd always be known and labeled as children of crooks and scoundrels. Feeling sorry for them, she confided in Justina. "I might hurt children. I don't know how I'm going to live with myself!"

"You're right...I never considered the children, and how their parents' consequences will damage them," Justina began, her hands over her heart. "Showing mercy distinguishes us from the animals." Her voice was soft but vibrating with tender compassion. Deep in thought, she glanced at Mira who had her iPhone *Reminder* app in anticipation of an order. "I know you want the best for people, Rae Anne, and I'll discuss the matter concerning children and spouses with the district attorney, or whoever will be prosecuting the criminals." Mira

Corporate Revenge

wrote her words in her *Reminder* notebook. "I used to be money oriented and driven…and there was a time when I would do anything to see my chip designs in new designs and changing the world and cementing my name in history—"

"Like Bill Gates or Warren Buffet," Mira said.

Justina laughed sarcastically, "Well…they're giving away billions to improve the world, not hog their fortunes even though they earned it. So RTI needs to implement a policy to focus on one need in the world, ask our employees to rally around that need, and we all work to solve the problem and help people—be it in America or Africa," she said, "but that's only after we set up some type of fund to help those children."

Mira *googled* an old story on Mark Madoff, Bernie Madoff's son and then showed Justina and Rae Anne his picture. "He hung himself in 2010. He couldn't live with his father's reputation and change in financial status."

After a pause of silence, Justina said, "So there…those will be RTI's new projects when my company re-opens." She stood up. "Ladies, we can't do anything more today. I'm sticking around, but it's time you two leave and get some rest."

"Tomorrow will be here before we know it," Mira began, "so after I finish uploading more reminders, I'll leave too."

Just as Rae Anne stood to leave the auditorium to go home, the door opened and shut with a thud. That loud noise echoed off the auditorium walls like coffin lids closing!

Chapter 20 – Shaking in My Shoes

"Good afternoon, Ladies." A new FBI investigator stood at the door. "Are you Dr. Justina Phillips?" He had a bushy eyebrows and scraggly hair.

"Yes, I am, Sir."

"And who are you, Ladies?" he pointed at Mira and then Rae Anne.

"I'm Rae Anne Westman."

"I'm Mira Padeson, V.P. of Systems Architecture."

"Where is…Ginnie Reidel?" he squinted.

"She's gathering company policies at Human Resources," Justina said.

"Okay, I'll send someone there to talk to her." He smiled and showed them his iPad. "Great that I have you three together here though. I've been lookin' for ya…especially you, Ms. Westman. I got a couple 'o questions for ya."

"Sure, yes, Sir," Rae Anne said, breathing hard and then plopping down in her seat.

"It's okay," Justina whispered to her as Mira typed in message on her iPhone.

Rae Anne was hoping the person on the other end might be a lawyer, because she might soon need one!

The man walked down the aisle toward the center of the

Corporate Revenge

auditorium. His face appeared pale, his tie crooked, and the lapel of his suit coat was rolled over as if Detective Colombo had left him his famous raincoat. With each step, his feet dragged on the carpet. He had his eyes fixed on Rae Anne. When he approached them, they could read his visitor's badge: Devan Ronald, FBI (SAC). Justina, Rae Anne, and Mira stood to greet him, but he said, "No, please stay seated." He whipped up a chair and sat between Justina and Mira who scooted their chairs back to accommodate his strong presence.

Justina said: "Agent Ronald, may I help you?"

"Yes, Ladies, I'm the Special Agent in Charge of investigating San Diego corporate espionage. I have a few questions for ya." He handed each of them his business card.

Justina put her right hand over her cheek in a gesture of *what else could go wrong?* She stood up, waiting for him to ask more questions. He told her to sit back down, and then she quickly said, "Get lawyers down here, Mira."

"I message them already, Dr. Phillips."

Agent Ronald stood up, walked away, and began working to open an app on his iPad. "Just a minute, Ladies, I gotta download something…but this thing is buffering again!" He began whispering curse words at it as he stood yards away from them, tapping the device and telling his agents to bring him another.

Justina was tapping messages on her cell phone. The two of them appeared engaged in some type of race against time!

Meanwhile, Rae Anne whispered to Mira, "I see trouble. I wonder if he's going to arrest Justina, or me."

Mira shrugged and glanced from the agent to Justina to the exit. "I hope not…I don't think so. The FBI needs her, and she's been cooperating with them."

"I know that, but cooperating doesn't mean freedom from jail tonight," Rae Anne said, remembering how Justina had handed several flash drives, portable devices, and even confidential passwords and codes over to FBI investigators.

Mira pulled up a link with Justina's schedule and then sighed in relief. "Justina just sent an email to Agent Ronald.

Smart move! She's meeting with him for the entire afternoon tomorrow. She welcomes his team too."

Rae felt her insides sicken. "I'd hate to be Justina and have to undergo *that* intense line of questioning."

"You mean interrogation." Mira's body shook a bit in a display of fear.

Agent Ronald returned to their small circle and took his seat. "Ms. Phillips, I spoke with an agent at the CIA." Now, his iPad was working, and he had it positioned just right where he could hold command over it, and them.

Justina's head reeled back a little. "CIA? The CIA isn't interested in RTI is it? We're not involved with any foreign businesses." She motioned for him to take a seat.

"Well," he chuckled, "yes ya are, Ma'am." He gave Rae Anne and Mira a questioning gaze as Justina gasped.

Mira suddenly said: "May I record this discussion?"

After he tapped her request into his iPad, he returned with a skeptical look on his face. "Well, okay, but your cell phone will have to be logged in for a special confidential line. I'll need it after we leave the auditorium." Mira nodded in acknowledgement, and then began recording the conversation.

Agent Ronald turned to Justina. "Is there somewhere we can talk for just a moment, Dr. Phillips?" Their conversation would be sensitive.

Waving her hand and implying that there was nothing to hide, she replied: "It's fine to talk while Ms. Westman and Ms. Padeson are here. They pretty much know everything that's been happening at RTI. Ms. Westman was the one who found out all the corruption. She—"

"Yeah…right," he said, gesturing for her to stop while bringing up more information on his iPad, information only he could see, and he kept moving his line of sight from it to Rae Anne. Another agent walked into the auditorium, pulled up a seat, and sat down behind him. He had silver cuffs on his belt. Then Agent Ronald ran his tan fingers over the back of his neck. "Yes, Ms. Hershel—I mean Ms. Westman. You've been pretty productive the last two days." He chuckled a little,

Corporate Revenge

coughed, and added more notes to his iPad.

Is he helping me, or sizing me up for an orange jail suit? Rae Anne felt herself shaking in her shoes! Then she felt suddenly annoyed. He didn't even acknowledge all *her* hard work in *her* covert operation. He would most likely get a promotion for his hard work. She felt proud of what she had accomplished, but still a little embarrassed at being an amateur spy who did misuse Witness Protection resources. Still, now was the time to speak out on her strengths and accomplishments. They might save her! "Yes, Sir, I sure have been productive in exposing those criminals."

He began folding up his cuffs, a move indicating he was getting down to business. "What I'm about to talk about doesn't really have to do with all the investigating we're doing. It's more about, well, RTI's interests abroad." He said that last word with such weight that it implied a hundred connotations.

Justina's eyebrows flinched in confusion. "Okay..."

He slid over his chair to face Justina. "You asked other agents earlier about the possibility of the FBI releasing RTI funds prior to Filmer, Smith and Gurkle's court appearances," he said in a tone of voice indicating that there might be a catch to her request. "We need something first."

Justina slipped back into her chair. "Yes, I did make that request." She appeared to be negotiating a concession. "Agent Ronald, I'm not a quid pro quo person. I don't know what you're trying to position me into doing—"

"No manipulation going on here at all, Ma'am!" he exclaimed. Agent Ronald blushed a little, and glanced back at the agent behind him. He was definitely on a covert mission of some type, and on guard for eavesdroppers. "Look," he began whispering, "I need your help."

Justina breathed. "Yes...what kind of help?" That first honest move of his appeared to put Justina more at ease with him than before.

He held another business card in front of her and leaned toward her. "This guy sitting behind us is one of the highest ranking officials in the CIA, Phil Taylor." They turned around to look at the man who had on dark sunglasses with a Tom Cruise style haircut and Mission Impossible fashion design although his badge read a simple Agent Chester, FBI, an obvious lie.

He nodded at each of them, and then flipped open his business card case. He tapped the tip of the top of the card as a dealer would in Vegas, and then he handed a card to Justina, Rae Anne, and Mira. *Shhh*, he said, and they turned around quickly. "Just listen to the rest…and then call me later," he whispered.

Rae Anne didn't know whether they were being asked to make a deal with the devil, or about to be whisked away to some secret Guantanamo location! She sat still, her hands folded over her lap, all the while telling herself to stay quiet and listen.

Justina's eyes rounded in shock and her shoulders rose with deep breath. "What does Phil Taylor, CIA want with me?" Lifting the card, she put it in front of her face, and looked from the card to Agent Ronald's eyes.

Agent Ronald cleared his throat. "RTI's been reaching out to China and Taiwan, right?" he asked, whispering, glancing around the auditorium. Two agents were now at the top of the stairs, guarding the doors.

"That's correct, but I learned that RTI is just reaching out, not doing business with anyone in that country yet," Justina said, folding her arms in a protective gesture. "I have Flora Henderson setting up two meetings with one of our sales reps in Taiwan. And if my V.P. of Sales and Marketing returns next week," she glanced at Rae Anne and nodded, "I hope to send him to Taiwan to conduct some business. I trust him."

"Uh-huh," Agent Ronald said, "There's nothing suspicious about that I suppose." He glanced at the floor and then back up to her. "We've been doing some, well, digging into those foreign companies Claude Filmer and Kent Smith were using to sell technology illegally."

She sighed in frustration. "I hope what Thornton Manning developed didn't get into the wrong hands."

Corporate Revenge

Rae Anne knew that meant spies, saboteurs, and terrorists. Justina could really be in big trouble. Those vermin were experts on conducting dirty deals and succeeding in diverting blame on others to have innocent people take the fall.

"Foreign companies are out of the FBI's jurisdiction," Agent Ronald began, "but Phil Taylor here wants to meet and talk to you before you plan your next trip to Taiwan."

"Me?" Justina asked. She turned around and peered at Phil Taylor.

"You *are* looking for another sensor-chip factory in Taiwan, aren't you?" Phil asked, drawing out the last words.

"Yes, most camera manufacturers are *in* Taiwan." She seemed to infer an implication of wrong doing in the tone of his voice. "My Georgia office just set that trip up for me," she began sharply, pulling up the email, "and RTI's partners assured me that the rep in Taiwan is one hundred percent honest. I'm supposed to leave in two weeks." She showed him her iPhone, tapped on its *Passbook* app, and began scrolling down information containing her passport, confirmation, and reservations.

Phil snapped back: "A few Chinese corporations have approached you about your most recent sensor development, right?" His lips puckered when he leaned back and gestured for her to put away her iPhone.

"Are *you* accusing me of something, Mr. Taylor?" She straightened up as a defense attorney retaliating against a prosecutor.

Phil had a snobby look on his face. "You'd be surprised at the CEOs who've betrayed America…especially sub-contractors working for the military on foreign soil."

"I don't like what you're insinuating, Mr. Taylor!" Justina stood and stared him down. "I have never, nor will I ever, sell technology that the United States government has hired RTI to develop to another country without first going through the proper channels!"

Agent Ronald stood up and walked between Justina and Phil Taylor. "Everybody, just calm down," he began, and gestured for Justina to sit back down in her chair. Justina was heaving deep breaths, but then suddenly grew calm and stoic. "Dr. Phillips," Agent Ronald said, "that's his job as a CIA operative."

"Some job he's got hounding someone who is committed to helping this country, not hurt it!" Justina exclaimed.

Just talk to Phil Taylor." He pointed to Rae Anne and Mira as well. "That's all we're asking. Meet with him before your next trip abroad, you or any RTI employees." He had a calm and collected disposition, a real Colombo personality. "Our two offices want to set up an interagency coordination meeting."

"The meeting will be CIA, FBI, and NSA affiliated to ensure no Edward Snowden type conspiracies will happen here at RTI," Phil said.

"With your help in this sensitive venture, I think we can work together to release most of those confiscated funds before Filmer, Smith and Gurkle make their first court appearance, or quite possibly in the next month," Agent Ronald added.

"The collaboration appears innocent, Dr. Phillips," Mira said. She had been recording their talk in sequences, and saving them to her iPhone.

As he stood up to leave, she slipped Phil Taylor her business card. "I still don't understand what you want me to do, Mr. Taylor." Confusion appeared in the lines on her face. However, if cooperating with you means that the FBI will release my funds so my employees can resume designing and developing new technology—"

"And RTI can resume its normal business hours!" Mira added, interrupting.

"Yes, RTI re-opening and paying employees is paramount, so I'll work with your new agency," Justina said. "I'll meet with you, Agent Taylor, next week and discuss the next overseas business trip."

Agent Ronald huffed. The deal had happened to quickly for him to object, and the FBI might not like the compromise

Corporate Revenge

because he had obviously wanted to prolong the investigation of RTI.

Phil Taylor appeared happy, sitting back comfortably with his smooth Tom Cruise smile. "Well, since you're planning trips, Dr. Phillips, and I see you have a few trips scheduled to mend what Filmer, Smith, and Gurkle have done, you might want to think about—"

"What now?" she asked forcefully.

"Data collection," Phil replied with sharp-tongued precision. "Just data collection, that's all…overseas data collection."

"Oh…" In the long pause while staring into his eyes, Justina seemed to be repeating those words "data collection" in her mind; but something else was weaving through her thoughts, evincing a gleam and sparkle in her eyes. "Data collection is a powerfully packed word, Phil."

"Yes it is, Dr. Phillips," he said, giving her a sultry gleam.

"Data collection has all sorts of meanings, connotations and interpretations, especially with foreign police agencies." Agent Ronald was tapping information into his iPad. The crescendos of bleeps were data successfully sending. Justina stood up, and everyone, even busy Agent Ronald, followed her lead. "Let's talk about collecting data, Agent Taylor, as we walk out of here, and talk about it some more later on."

"Lead the way, Dr. Phillips."

"My office is at the north-end of the building. *Way* north. After hours, the view is the best! An ocean view, worthy of a wonderful dinner." She sounded enticing now, like Betty Davis in a spy movie!

Agent Phil appeared excited at the prospect of after-hour drinks. "Yeah, lead on, Dr. Phillips."

"Call me Justine, Agent Taylor."

Rae Anne knew differently. Justina wasn't thrilled at entertaining Agent Taylor at all, but attempting to pacify him by diverting his attention off RTI and bolstering his ego. After glancing at Rae Anne and Mira with an expression of control on her face, she then waved for Agent Ronald to follow Phil and her as well.

Rae Anne felt the white walls of the auditorium closing in on her. At some point, someone had to question her! *When*, kept repeating in her mind as she watched Justina round up the attention of the two agents. "*Wow*," she said, "there's a lot of corporate spying and espionage going on overseas *and* in the United States."

"It appears that way...and they're recruiting Justina to help them sniff it out, or maybe even doing a little spying," Mira said, and then she perked up in awareness. "Hear what I just said—sniff out?"

Rae Anne laughed. "I guess you ought to apply to the Department of Defense and attend Agent School."

"Maybe I will...but then again, I don't think agents lead the best of lives," Mira said. They were now almost at the top of the stairs and out the door.

"Why not?"

"You think Justina has it bad from now on, being the sole owner of RTI?" She gestured at Agents Ronald and Taylor, and the two security agents plastered at the door.

"I guess I wouldn't want that either, wondering all the time who's watching and listening in on me," Rae Anne began, "and my life would never be private." She remembered the fake company Hermes Trading & Cie. "As the owner of a company, one doesn't have many friends, but only watch dogs and villains like Filmer.

Maybe all the distracting Justina was implementing wasn't a front at all, but purposely planned. She had to be terrified of what the FBI *and* CIA might uncover in foreign accounts and businesses. Filmer and his vipers had been ruthless, and investors as well. If she could pump up those inquisitive agents and befriend them, Justina might have a good chance of creating a *real* ally in any court system if one day she'd find herself in a compromising situation with a foreign company. Justina had enemies, but now she needed to make real friends. She had to know that spy-trade configuration.

Corporate Revenge

Chapter 21 – Spy Games

Mira stopped Rae Anne and pulled her next to her ear. "You don't think Justina could be guilty of any of the criminal activities that happened here, do you?"

"I don't know." When Rae Anne noticed Justina exuding honest body language while conversing with Agent Phil Taylor, Rae Anne couldn't believe Justina had a criminal bone in her body. "But look, all afternoon, she responded sensitively and honestly to every piece of information the FBI requested of her."

"Yeah…" Mira said.

"And she was forthcoming and genuine," Rae Anne continued, "and that was reflected in her actions and speech."

Mira set her iPhone into the pocket of her handbag and then pulled her handbag tight against her side. They'd have to pull it off her to get her to surrender it. "You're right, Rae Anne, I just can't believe Justina could be a criminal. She's not the hiding type, the sneaky type, like Claude Filmer,"

"The guy had sneaky and dastardly written all over him, like Mr. Burns from *The Simpsons*." She laughed. "Since I've met her, which wasn't long before you met her, she values ethical business practices. She never once asked me to hide anything we uncovered or delete anything."

J.P. Osterman

"Yep," Rae Anne said, "and she's a listener, and a quick thinking, abhorring activities that hurt innocent people. I wish all CEOs would be like her."

"I think the world would be so different, and people happier," Mira said. "I think Justina's new program for change will become iconic, a model for other companies around the world!"

As they began walking up the last portion of the auditorium, Rae Anne said, "From everything I've seen about Justina, I'm *sure* she isn't involved in any type of criminal activity, especially spying on companies and sabotaging connections."

"Me neither," Mira exclaimed, "but *we*, I mean the United States, need to keep our eyes and ears open to the business practices in the foreign companies we visit." Mira's lips moved as if wanting Rae Anne to read them. "A lot of countries want our technology. They offer everything from bribes to illegal trading to steal it."

"Yeah, I remember all that Cold War espionage," Rae Anne began, "and I just read where some Russian spies were actually living in America."

"Infiltrating all types of businesses while holding down jobs as taxi drivers and real estate agents," Mira added, her athletic appearance looking pumped up for a drawn out fight.

"Yeah, but the FBI and CIA caught those spies and sent them packing for Russia." Rae Anne grew worried. "But for Justina to do something like that herself—like taking pictures with her iPhone or scanning the insides of foreign companies while she's there on business could get her hurt."

"Ya think that's what Agents Taylor and Ronald want her to do?" Mira inhaled in fear. "I assumed they were only interrogating her to find out how deep her affiliations were with Filmer, Smith, and Gurkle; but I guess there's more to what happened than what I picked up from their conversation."

She remembered that Tim had told her that spies wind up dead sometimes. "Justina would be putting her life on the line if she'd go alone to those foreign companies and corporations, right? She could even get thrown into a foreign prison!" She shuddered and her stomach growled.

Mira's shoulders drooped. "Well, I'll offer to accompany her on her trip to Taiwan." She tapped her lower lip—a real thinking posture. "I'll bring up the idea to her later."

Rae Anne had an idea. "I could go with you and Justina if you want."

Mira took in a deep breath. "*Hmmm.*"

Rae Anne believed it might be too time consuming to rattle off all her qualifications that could be good spy assets. However, she believed she had done a good job thus far in her amateur sleuthing. "I tell ya what," she whispered as they were now yards away from security guards who were opening the doors for Justina. "Don't delete my false identity from RTI's system."

"Huh?" Mira asked, but then suddenly gave her a sneaky look. "Yeah…whataya have in mind, Mary?" she giggled and winked.

"We could use my alias. Take her to foreign soil if Justina needs her," Rae Anne said. She began conjuring a new and exciting plot and adventure.

"All I can do is ask Justina," Mira said. Her eyes widened in excitement. "Or you could ask Justina yourself when you meet with her tomorrow."

"Yeah," Rae Anne said, "at least she'll know that she has support, and that I'm available. Heck, the three of us could be a new kind of three musketeers…call us, the Corporateers!"

The agents heard that last comment and squinted at them, their body languages signaling real eavesdropping capabilities.

After Agents Ronald and Taylor left, and after another hour's discussion with Ginnie and Mira, Rae Anne jumped into her Mustang and headed back up the I-5 freeway towards home. "Home…God thank you, I'm finally heading home and not to jail!" She began crying, tears of gratitude. "I guess someone likes me at RTI…I guess I have friends at RTI."

The ocean view along the La Jolla cliffs was a beautiful

blue. Foam was cresting on the waves stretching out as far as she could see along the shore line. Half-way home, she saw some risk-taking surfers. Near home, she spotted a tourist trying to skip stones over the ocean that swallowed his rock like shark jaws. Those were Filmer, Smith, and Gurkle. She believed Steve was part of the collusion too, and she felt determined to prove it…on Monday.

She decided to take the coast line drive to the main boulevard and pick up Joey from preschool. She past the Safeway, and later she'd return and pick up roast chicken and fixing at the deli. No longer was money a fear and concern, but only freedom in receiving soon what RTI had promised Tim: his commission, and what a great commission it would be!

Now, the butterfly pageant was gone, and only a few remained. She glanced at the golden horizon and the liquid sunshine spilling lazily over the blue shimmering ocean.

"Yes, it's great just to be alive."

###

Corporate Revenge

About the Author

J.P. Osterman was born December 21, in East Chicago, Indiana. She graduated from the University of San Diego with a BA in English (emphasis Writing) and obtained a teaching credential and an MA in Education from Azusa Pacific University. She taught English and writing for a total of ten years. Inspired by Ray Bradbury, she began to write, and in 2000, she won the prestigious Rupert Hughes Award at the seminal Maui Writer's Conference for her sci-fi novel, *The Matter Stream*. In 2001, she won First Place in the Southern California Writer's conference for her one-act play, *The Man Next to Me*. She spent a year and a half in the Licensed Professional Counseling program at Texas State University. She studied Research, and her characters reflect strong personalities of the inquisitive/driven type of individual. She writes because writing is her passion and identity.

For more information about these stories please visit Amazon.com or my website: www.jposterman.com

Other Books by J.P. Osterman

First Communication (Book I, the Neltans Series) & *Battlefield Matrix* (Book II, the Neltan Series), *Cosmic Rift, Dimension Mind, The Screaming Stone,* and *Pete's Crossroad.*

Books in the Works: *Nanobot Invasion,* Book III in the Neltan Series. Strange occurrences happen onboard spaceship *Sagan* on the voyage to Nelta! Books IV and V are in editing mode.